US

SARINA BOWEN
USA TODAY BESTSELLING AUTHOR

ELLE KENNEDY
NEW YORK TIMES BESTSELLING AUTHOR

PRAISE FOR HIM AND US

"The way that Sarina Bowen and Elle Kennedy spun the tale of these two men falling and staying in love was absolutely timeless and beautifully real." — #1 New York Times bestselling author Audrey Carlan

"I read HIM in one sitting—it's so, so good! If I had to pick two authors who I'd have team up, it would be Bowen and Kennedy" — *#1 New York Times bestselling author Colleen Hoover*

"HIM is my favorite read of 2015! Hot, sexy, romantic, funny, and full of heart. I LOVED Jamie and Wes!" — *#1 New York Times bestselling author Lauren Blakely*

ONE ·
WES

Vancouver is a beautiful city, but I can't wait to leave it.

We've just finished the longest road trip on our schedule, and I cannot fucking wait to go home. Standing in a fancy hotel room overlooking the waterfront, I shake the tissue paper out of a shirt I just bought at the boutique around the corner. Since I've been living out of my suitcase for so long, I'm out of clean laundry. But this is a great shirt, and it looked at me as I passed the storefront on my way back from signing autographs at a charity luncheon.

I unbutton it and slip it on. In the hotel mirror, I check the fit, and it looks fine. Great, even. The cotton is a fine weave, and there's a lime-green checked pattern shot through the fabric. It's very British, and the lively color reminds me that it won't always be February.

Now that my dress code includes a suit and tie three or four times a week, I've had to pay more attention to my wardrobe. In college I wore a suit maybe three times a year. But it's no hardship because I like clothes. And the hotel mirror says they like me, too.

I'm a sexy motherfucker. If only the one person I care about was here to appreciate it.

Last night we obliterated Vancouver, and it's not bragging to say that I was the reason why. Two goals and an assist—my best showing yet. I'm having the kind of rookie season that makes headlines. Though right this second I'd trade it all for a night in front of the TV with Jamie and a blowjob. I am *beat*. Whipped. Knackered.

Luckily, all that's left of this trip is one more ride on the team's jet.

I grab my phone off the desk and unlock it. With the selfie cam, I shoot a picture of my abs, the shirt parted to reveal my six-pack, my hand over my crotch. It took me a while to figure out that Jamie has a thing for my hands. I swear he likes them more than my dick.

I send the picture. No commentary needed.

The hotel room gets one last glance, but I've packed everything. I've learned in a hurry not to leave charging cords and toothbrushes behind. We're on the road so often that packing has become my new skill.

My phone vibrates with a text. *Grrrr. Just get home, would you? I don't need any pics. My poor lonely dick is so hard.*

That reminds me of old vaudeville jokes. So I reply, *How hard is it?*

Hard enough to pound nails into our bare walls, he replies. It's true that we haven't exactly decorated our apartment. We both work a lot and there's been no time.

But, as always, sex is a greater priority than home decor. *Show me*, I beg. There's a reason I keep my phone locked down. Jamie and I like to indulge in some private photography.

He doesn't answer, though. Maybe he isn't at home. It's afternoon in Vancouver, which means it's later in Toronto…

Fuck. I'm sick of doing this math all the time. I just want to go home.

I grab my suitcase and head downstairs. A few of the guys are already waiting in the lobby, just as eager to get home as I am. I wander over to where they're standing.

"Jesus," Matt Eriksson says as I approach. "My wife better be home and naked when I get there. And the kids had better be asleep. With, like, fucking earplugs in their little ears."

Eight days is a long time, I inwardly agree. But I don't say it out loud, because even though my teammates are great guys, I don't engage in these discussions. It's not my style to lie and pretend there's a girl at home waiting for me. And I'm not ready to tell them who is. So I keep my own counsel.

Except Eriksson's Nordic features have turned in my direction, and a goofy grin breaks out on his face. "Shit, my eyes! I think I'm blind."

"Why?" I ask halfheartedly. Eriksson is always joking about something.

"That shirt! Jesus."

"Seriously," the veteran Will Forsberg says, laughing as he covers his eyes with one hand. "It's so bright."

"It's so *gay*," Eriksson corrects.

This comment doesn't faze me in the least. "This shirt is Tom Ford, and it's killer," I mutter. "Bet you twenty bucks it shows up on the puck bunny blogs before the end of the week."

"Attention whore," Forsberg accuses. More than any of the other guys on the team, Forsberg eats up the media attention we get. When my mug started showing up on HockeyHotties.com, he didn't appreciate the competition.

Joke's on him, though. He can keep the entire population of puck bunnies.

"Just sayin'," Eriksson presses, "you could do well in the bars on Church Street in that shirt."

"Yeah?" I ask. "You know from personal experience?"

That shuts him up. But Blake Riley is squinting at my chest now. He's a big puppy dog of a guy with messy brown hair and no filter. "It's, like, hypnotizing almost. It says, 'Yowza. I fucking dare you to look away'."

"It says, 'Three hundred dollars, please'," I correct. "It's expensive to look this good."

Blake snorts, and Forsberg says I should ask for my money back. Then the topic moves on to another brand of smack talk and speculation that the bus won't ever show up and that we'll all die of blue balls in Vancouver.

Eventually we board, though. I take a seat alone. We're halfway to the airport when my phone buzzes with a text. I have it set so that none of my texts (especially the photos) show up on the screen unless I'm logged in. It's a pretty crucial precaution, and the text Jamie has just sent me proves why. When I authenticate my thumbprint, the screen fills with a picture that is not safe for work. It's both dirty and hysterical all at once. Jamie's very hard dick fills the shot. Only it's angled toward the wall where the full, pink head leans against a flat nail that it's presumably pounding. And Jamie has used some app to draw a happy face on his cockhead. The effect is startlingly transformative. His dick looks like…an expressive, alien creature performing some minor home repair.

I give a snort of laughter. And here they thought my *shirt* was gay. I'll show you gay…

"Wesley?"

Blake rises from the seat behind me to say something, and I press down on the menu button of my phone so hard that my knuckle cracks.

"Yeah?" I wonder what he saw.

"Remember how I asked you whether you liked living at 2200 Lake Shore?"

"Sure?"

"My stuff got moved there yesterday. I'm your new neighbor on the fifteenth floor."

Seriously?

"That's great, man," I lie. When he'd asked me if I liked the place, I should have told him all the drawbacks. *It's too far from the subway. The cold wind off the waterfront is a bitch.* Nothing against Blake, but I don't need any of the neighbors to know me. I work pretty hard to fly under the radar.

"Yeah, the view is killer, right? I've only seen it during the day, but the lights at night are probably spectacular."

"They are," I admit. As if I care. The view of my boyfriend's face is the only one I want right now. And we still have a four-hour flight until I get home to him.

"You can help me find all the best bars in the 'hood," Blake suggests. "I'll buy the first round."

"Awesome," I say.

Fuck, I'm thinking.

IT TAKES eighteen years to get back to Toronto.

By the time we've landed and gotten our luggage back, it's seven o'clock. I'm really looking forward to spending some time with Jamie, but there's a deadline. He has to leave at six o'clock tomorrow morning for an away game in Quebec with his major juniors team.

We have eleven hours, and I'm still not there yet.

Every red light on the way home makes me seethe. But

finally I'm pulling into the parking garage (a feature of the building that I'd boasted about to Blake, damn it). I wheel my giant duffel into the elevator and luckily the car climbs toward our tenth-floor apartment without any stops. I fish my keys out so they're ready in my hand.

At long last, I'm twenty paces away, then ten. Then I'm opening our door. "Hey babe!" I call out like I always do. "I made it." I drag my duffel over the threshold, then toss my suit coat on top, abandoning these things beside the door, because all I need now is a kiss.

Only then do I notice that our apartment smells amazing. Jamie has cooked dinner for me. Again. He is the perfect man, I swear to God.

"Hey!" he calls, emerging from the hallway leading to our bedroom. He's wearing jeans and nothing else except—and this is unusual—a beard. "Do I know you?" He gives me a sexy smile.

"I was going to ask the same thing." I'm staring at the sandy-blond beard. Jamie has always been clean-shaven. I mean—we've known each other since before facial hair. He looks different. Older, maybe.

And hot as blazes. Seriously, I can't wait to feel that beard against my face, and maybe my balls… *Jesus*. The blood is already rushing south, and I've been home fifteen seconds.

And yet I'm just stuck there in the middle of the room for a moment, because even though it's been eight months since Jamie and I started up together, I'm still a little stunned at my own good fortune. "Hi," I say again, stupidly.

He walks forward, his easy gait so familiar that my heart breaks a little bit. He puts his hands on my traps and squeezes the muscle there. "Don't go away for so long. If you do that again, I'm going to have to sneak into your hotel room on the road."

"Promise?" I ask, and it comes out like gravel. He's close enough now that I can smell the ocean scent of his shampoo and the beer he drank while he waited for me.

"If I ever get a winning lottery ticket and a day off, I'll do it," he says. "Hotel sex after a game? Sounds hot."

Now I'm measuring the distance to our sofa and counting the layers of clothes I'll need to remove in the next ninety seconds.

But Jamie takes his hands off my shoulders. "I ate already, but your plate is in the oven. I just put it in there a few minutes ago. Chicken enchiladas. They should take fifteen minutes to warm up."

"Thanks." My stomach grumbles and he grins. I guess I'm hungry for more than one thing.

"Want a beer?"

Do I ever. "I'll get 'em. Sit down. Cue up the next episode. We can watch it while we wait." I sound overly polite to my own ears, but coming home after a road trip usually feels a little weird. There's this brief but awkward re-entry that I hadn't known to expect.

I have little use for the domestic chatter my married teammates share. But if I were the sharing kind, it would be tempting to ask—will it always be this way? Do the guys who've been coupled up for ten years feel it, too? Or is it the newness of our relationship that makes things a little odd for an hour or two whenever I come home?

Wish I knew.

My first stop is our open-plan kitchen for two beers, which I open and then deposit on our coffee table. We've lived here almost six months, and still there isn't much furniture. We've both been too busy to really furnish the place. But we have the real necessities: a giant leather sofa, a kickass coffee table, a rug and a big TV.

Oh—and there's a wobbly armchair that I rescued off the curb and kept over Jamie's objections. He calls it the death chair. Jamie gives it wide berth, insisting that it has bad karma.

You can take the boy out of California, but you can't take the California out of the boy.

I need to change, so I take a step toward our bedroom. But then I stop to ask him a question. "Hey, what do think of this shirt? I picked it up today, because I ran out of clean stuff."

Jamie points the remote at the TV. "It's very green," he says without turning to look.

"I like it."

"Me too, then." He turns and the beard catches me off-guard again. But his smile sends me jogging toward our bedroom.

The bed is made up perfectly, so I toss my trousers, my very green shirt and my tie on the comforter, in a hurry to get back to Jamie. I throw on a pair of sweats and make it back to the living room to find Jamie propped into the corner of the couch on his side, his legs stretched out across the cushions. I don't bother pretending to play it cool. I lay down right in front of him, my head against his shoulder, my back to his front.

"Shit," I complain when I realize my error. "I left the beers out of reach."

He clamps a hand over my abs. "Go," he says.

I stretch with both hands for our bottles and he prevents me from falling on the floor. While the table is positioned perfectly for our feet when we're sitting up, this little maneuver is for beer emergencies while we're cuddling. They happen sometimes.

I pass his bottle over my head and hear him take a swig. The opening credits for *Banshee*—our current show—are rolling. "You didn't cheat on me while I was gone, did you?" I ask.

"Wouldn't dream of it. The last episode wasn't a cliffhanger, though. So you could say I haven't really been tested."

I snort into my beer and lean back into the solid warmth of his chest. Usually I'm really invested in this show, with its freaky plot and crazy fight scenes. But tonight it's just an excuse to be skin to skin on the couch with my man while my dinner reheats. His beard tickles my ear, and that's unexpected. I tilt my head back so his beard brushes my face, too. I can't see the TV at all, and I just don't care.

He dips his chin and rubs the beard against my cheek, then brushes his lips across my neck, leaving shivers in his wake. "What do you think?" he asks quietly.

I turn toward him carefully so as not to spill my beer. "You look fucktastic. Like J-Tim after he left NSYNC and got hot. But I want to feel it on my balls before I weigh in."

He tips his head back and laughs suddenly, and that's when the road-trip ice dam breaks. It's just us again and his easy laugh and the comfort I feel when he's around.

Yesss... I drop my head and lick his throat right below the border of the beard. Then I suck on his skin gently. Jamie stops laughing and relaxes his body against mine. We're skin to skin from the waist up, and the feel of his heartbeat against mine makes me want to weep with gratitude. I nuzzle my nose through his fledgling beard, taking a circuitous route toward his mouth. The hair is softer than I expected.

"Fuck. Kiss me already," he whispers.

So I do. The beard caresses my face as I fit my mouth over

his, diving in like I've been gone from him eight months, not eight days. He makes a happy sound deep in his chest. I kiss him thoroughly, reacquainting myself with his taste and the warmth of his breath on my face.

He sighs, and I slow things down, brushing my lips over his lazily.

We won't get crazy right now, but it's not out of awkwardness. Rather, we're both holding a beer bottle, my dinner is in the oven and we have all night.

This is my happy thought just as I hear an unfamiliar sound —someone knocking on the door. It's so unusual that I actually assume it's part of the TV show in the background at first. But the knock comes again. "Wesley! You crazy bastard. Open up, I have beer!"

Jamie pulls his head back, his eyebrows shooting up. "Who is that?" he mouths.

"*Fuck*," I whisper. "Just a sec!" I call. Then I drop my mouth to Jamie's ear. "My teammate. Blake Riley. He moved in upstairs."

Jamie gives me a little shove, and I get up. I have to adjust myself in my sweats to make my semi a little less obvious. I approach the front door, opening it a crack. "Hey. You found me."

Blake gives me a big, stupid grin and pushes past me into the apartment. "Yeah! I have boxes stacked up all over my new living room. Total disaster. My sisters found the sheets and made the bed for me, but otherwise it's hell up there. So I ate a burger and bought a six-pack and thought I'd come see you, eh?"

For a moment I think of throwing him out. I really do. But there's no way to do it that isn't hella rude. I mean, I'm standing here in sweats, a beer in my hand and the TV blaring behind me. I look exactly like a guy who has time to drink a beer with his teammate. And this is a guy who's asked me out for beers a handful of times already, and I always beg off unless we're on the road.

"Come on in," I say, hating the sound of it. He's already in, for one thing. That bastard. And sixty seconds ago I had Jamie's tongue in my mouth.

Fuck me.

Blake doesn't notice my discomfort. He sets the six-pack on the coffee table and sits right down on the sofa where Jamie was a minute ago. Jamie's beer is on the bar dividing our kitchen from the rest of the room, but he's vanished.

"You ready for another one?" Blake asks, grabbing a bottle.

"I'm good," I say, taking a swig of my own.

Jamie reappears from the hallway, wearing a T-shirt now, ruining the view I had of his muscular, golden chest. "Hey there," he says. "I'm Jamie."

"Ah, you're the roommate!" Blake hops to his feet and leaps over to engulf Jamie's hand in his big paw. "Nice to meet you. You're a coach, right? Defense? Teenagers?"

"Uh, yeah." Jamie's gaze lifts to mine, a question in them.

I'm just as confused, though. I've mentioned my roommate to maybe two people all season, but apparently Blake was one of them. I never talk about Jamie to my teammates, because I don't want to have to try to figure out when to stop, or how much detail is too much.

And I never want to tell a bold-faced lie about him. That's just not my style.

Blake is a big guy with a quick smile, and honestly I'd always assumed he was a little slow. That might have been inaccurate. "Want a beer?" he asks now. "Hey! I love *Banshee*! Which one is this?" He gallops back to the couch and sits.

I don't know quite what to do, so I sit down on the opposite end from him.

Jamie heads into the kitchen, and I stare at the screen for a minute, trying to figure out what's happening with this episode. Hood is trying to escape from a building where he's stolen something. His colorful trans friend is in his earpiece, trying to help him navigate out of there.

I have no idea what's happening. On the screen or in my living room.

Jamie returns a few minutes later with a plate covered with enchiladas in melted cheese. He's using a tray because the plate is hot from the oven, and I'm famous for burning myself in the kitchen. My mouth waters when I see a generous blob of sour cream and a pile of diced avocados, too. He's even thought of a napkin and silverware.

Wow.

To have your boyfriend bring you a homemade dinner is just about the best thing in the whole fucking world, except Jamie's eyes are asking if he should hand it over, or maybe this looks weird? Too domestic?

I stand up and take it from him, because goddamn it, this is my home and I can do anything I want here. "Thank you. This looks amazing."

He gives me the world's quickest wink, and I sit down on the couch to eat the dinner he brought me. It's not all I want from him, but it will have to do for now.

TWO

JAMIE

I'm not pissed. Nope, not pissed at all. I mean, what else was Wes supposed to do? Slam the door in his teammate's face? Gesture to his rock-hard dick and say "Sorry man, I'm about to bone down with my boyfriend"? The boyfriend he hasn't seen in eight days, the one who's been anxiously waiting for him in this empty condo and making sure there's dinner on the table when he got home and—

Okay. Maybe I'm a teeny, tiny bit pissed.

My mom always says I have the patience of a saint, but right now I'm not feeling too saintly. My natural state of easygoing and infinitely calm has been replaced by a deep-seated prickle of annoyance. Resentment, even.

I missed Wes. I miss him every time he's on the road, and all I wanted to do tonight was reacquaint myself with the man I love, preferably in the form of wild, sweaty sex.

The man I love. Even now, the phrase sticks in my mind with damn near wonder. I didn't freak out when I realized last summer I was bisexual, and I'm not freaked out about it now. It's not the word *man* that fascinates me in that sentence, but *love*. The way I feel about Ryan Wesley…it's something I thought existed only in the movies. He's my other half. We complement each other in more ways than I can count. When he's in the same room, I'm focused on him, and when he's gone I walk around missing him.

There's an old quote my mother once painted on a ceramic platter. *Love is friendship set on fire.* I get it now.

But that doesn't mean I'm not pissed at him.

I watch as he shovels enchiladas into his mouth. His gorgeous gray eyes are fixed on the TV screen, but I know he's not paying attention to the show. The tension in his broad shoulders would be imperceptible to anyone else, but I see it clear as day, which causes some of my irritation to dissolve.

He hates this as much as you do, my conscience whispers.

Fuck off, conscience. I'm having a pity party, here.

Blake, on the other hand, is loving life hard. Hooting at the screen when a particularly badass action sequence comes on, sucking on his beer like he has no care in the world. Of course he doesn't. He's in his third year with the team and rocking it out on the ice, according to the quick Google search I conducted when I ducked into the bedroom to find a shirt. And most importantly? He's straight. He doesn't have to hide who he's sleeping with or introduce his live-in partner as his "roommate". Lucky bastard.

A bitter taste fills my mouth as I remember that in the eyes of the world, Ryan Wesley is also straight. My boyfriend has appeared on dozens of "Hockey's Most Eligible Bachelors" lists. At every game there's no less than five women holding up signs with clever come-ons directed at him—*Dyin' for Ryan* or *Wesley is the Bestley*. Or not so clever ones—*I WANT TO HAVE YOUR BABIES, #57!!*

Wes and I laugh off all the female attention he gets, but

even though I know there's no danger of my very staunchly gay boyfriend dipping his toes in the pussy pool, all the hungry looks he gets still grate.

"Je-sus," Blake crows. "Those tits are fan-fucking-tabulous."

The lewd observation jerks me back to the present. The unwelcome present. On the screen, one of the female characters has just gotten naked—gotta love Cinemax—and I'm not going to lie, her breasts are incredible.

And since I'm supposed to be Wes's harmless, straight-as-an-arrow roomie (and already being ruder than I should to his teammate), I decide to offer my own two cents. "They're amazing," I concur. "That actress is smokin' hot."

That gets me a slight frown from Wes, and just like that, my annoyance returns. Seriously? He's letting his teammate crash our evening and he's pissy that I find an actress attractive?

Blake takes my contribution to the conversation as a sign that we're best friends and turns to me with twinkling green eyes. "You like blondes, huh? Me too, bro. You seeing anyone?"

From the corner of my eye I see Wes's shoulders stiffen again. So do mine, but that could also be because the armchair I'm sitting on is ridiculously uncomfortable. Five minutes in that thing and your whole body feels like it went through a medieval torture rack. Plus, I'm ninety-nine percent sure someone died in this chair. Wes found it on the curb and then neglected to get rid of it even though I keep asking him to.

Next week this fucker is on the *curb*.

The chair, I mean. Not Wes.

"Not really," I answer vaguely, which brings another frown to Wes's sexy lips.

"Playing the field, eh? Samesies." Blake runs a hand through his brown hair. He's really good-looking. And he's huge. At least six-three and bulky as hell. "Who has time for relationships in our world, right, Wesley? Feels like our whole life is stepping on and off a plane."

Wes grunts something unintelligible.

"I have no idea how Eriksson and the other guys do it," Blake continues. "I'm exhausted during the season, and I'm *single*." He mock shivers. "Imagine having a wife and kids. That's, like, terrifying. Do you think that's how zombies are created? Like it's not some craz-o virus, but just being so dead-ass tired that eating brains suddenly seems like a good idea?"

I can't help but snicker. I get the feeling that Blake Riley could carry on an entire conversation with himself. Which is pretty much what he's doing right now, seeing as how neither Wes nor I are saying a goddamn word.

After the current episode ends, Blake swipes the remote off the coffee table and clicks to play the next one without asking if it's cool. He also cracks open another beer.

The ball of resentment in my throat is the size of a hockey puck now. It's past nine o'clock. I need to be in bed by ten or else I'll be dead on my feet tomorrow morning. If I don't get at least seven hours of sleep, my brain goes all insomniac on me like Edward Norton's from *Fight Club*. Hell, I kind of wish my life *was Fight Club* right about now. Then I'd have a good excuse to haul Blake Riley off my couch and toss him out on his ass.

But I can't. I promised Wes I'd keep up appearances at least until the end of his rookie season. Coming out now would only hurt his career, and I'd rather take a bath in a tub full of glass shards than be the one to cost Wes his dreams.

So I sit in the death chair and pretend to care about the TV.

I feign interest in what Blake is babbling about. I even chuckle at some of his jokes. But when ten-fifteen rolls around, I no longer have the luxury of keeping up appearances.

"I need to turn in," I tell them, rising to my feet. "Gotta be at the arena at five-thirty in the morning."

Blake seems genuinely disappointed to see me go. "You sure you can't have another beer?"

"Maybe another time. 'Night, guys. Nice meeting you, Blake."

"You too, J-Bomb."

Yeah, Blake Riley gives nicknames to dudes he's just met. Why am I not surprised?

I spare a quick glance in Wes's direction as I pass the couch. His jaw is tighter than his grip around his beer bottle. His free hand is toying with the silver barbell in his eyebrow, fingers twisting the small piercing round and round. I've known this guy since I was thirteen years old. I can read him like a book, and it's obvious he's not happy at the moment.

Neither am I, but short of forcibly kicking Blake out, there's nothing either one of us can do except pretend we're just roommates who sometimes watch TV together.

Tired as I am, I make it a few paces down the hall before I realize I have a problem. I can't go to sleep in our bed. Though I haven't met Blake until tonight, I can't say with any certainty that he's never been here before. When he was checking out the building, did he see our apartment? Did Wes show him the view from the master bedroom?

Our rarely used cover story is that the guest room is mine. So I do a little u-turn in the darkened hall and walk into the guest bathroom. There's a toothbrush and toothpaste that I put in here a while ago to make the room appear lived-in.

I thought I was so fucking clever for thinking up this bit of set-dressing. But now here I stand pretending my own room isn't really mine.

Retiring to the guest room, I shut the door against the soundtrack of the TV program. Since Wes and I moved in together, this room has only been used once—when my folks flew in from California for a weekend visit. Tonight I'm the one tossing my clothes on the floor and pulling down the unfamiliar quilt to slip into the cold double bed. And I don't like it.

I roll onto my side and measure all the things wrong with this moment. The curtains are sheer rather than black-out navy. The mattress is softer than I'm used to and the pillow beneath my head is lumpier.

My boyfriend is in the living room, instead of sexing me up, like he's supposed to.

I close my eyes and try to sleep.

I'M DREAMING about a hot tub, and the jets are terrific. Only —my dick is the only part of me that fits in the hot tub. But that's okay because I'm hard and the water is incredible. Magic even.

Oh wait...

Scratch that.

There's a hot mouth around my very hard dick. And maybe I *am* still dreaming because my surroundings make no sense to me when I open my eyes. The light is all wrong, and the headboard makes a soft, unfamiliar squeak as a dark head bobs over me, a sexy mouth going to town on my cock.

Damn, that's good.

"You awake, babe?" Wes rasps.

"Kinda? Don't stop."

His chuckle massages the head of my dick. "Good. I was starting to feel like a creeper."

A strong hand grips my shaft and another husky moan slips out of me. "What time is it?" My head is still foggy from sleep. My plan had been to sneak back into our bedroom after Blake left, but I must have passed out the moment after my head hit the lumpy pillow.

"Eleven-thirty." His voice is soft. "I won't keep you awake long, promise. I just... Mmm." The noise he makes sounds like it's wrenched deep from his soul. "I missed you so fucking much."

The resentment I'd been wearing like a shield all night disintegrates to dust. I missed him too, and I'd be a real asshole if I held Blake's unwelcome interruption against Wes. It wasn't his fault that his teammate popped by. And it's not his fault he has to travel so much. We both knew going into this that as long as Wes was playing professional hockey, there would be long absences to deal with.

I weave my hands through his dark hair and yank him up. "C'mere," I say gruffly.

His warm, muscular body slides up and covers mine, and I tug his head down for a kiss. I love his lips. They're firm and hungry. They're magic. Our kisses deepen, growing more and more desperate as our bodies rock on the mattress, making it squeak uncontrollably.

Wes wrenches his mouth away with a laugh. "Dude, we are *so* lucky your parents didn't have sex when they were visiting. This bed is so loud."

"Would've traumatized me for life," I agree. Then I'm kissing him again, because damn it, it's late, I have to wake up in six hours, and I need this too much.

Wes reads my mind and thrusts his tongue through my

parted lips. I eagerly suck on it, then grunt in disappointment. "I miss the tongue ring," I tell him breathlessly. He'd taken out the piercing at the start of the season. I guess the team didn't think it was safe.

"Don't you worry," Wes teases. "I can still rock your world without it." A moment later that talented tongue is traveling down my bare chest and returning to my aching cock.

He swallows me up and my hips jerk off the bed. Jesus. We've exchanged hundreds of blowjobs since we got together, but it never fails to amaze me just how *good* this feels. Wes knows exactly what to do to get me off. His confidence is a major turn-on, and he needs absolutely no direction when it comes to pleasing me.

Of course, that doesn't stop me from muttering out orders. But that's because we both dig the dirty talk. "That's it, man. Lick the tip. Yeah, just like that." I have one hand bunched in his hair, the other clutching the sheets. It's been so long since I had his mouth on me, and the pressure in my balls is almost unbearable.

Wes's tongue licks a slow, wet circle around my head, then glides down my length, over and over again, until my dick is glistening and my patience has run out.

"I need to come," I grind out.

He chuckles softly. "Don't worry, baby. I'll get you there."

And holy shit, he does. The teasing licks turn into wet, tight pulls on my shaft that make me shudder in pleasure. His hand kneads my balls while his mouth draws me all the way to the back of his throat, sucking hard and fast until I'm ready to explode. Until I *do* explode.

Wes growls when I come in his mouth, but he doesn't stop sucking until I'm limp and mindless. As the aftershocks of the orgasm continue to flutter through my sated body, I vaguely register that he's beside me now. Kissing my neck. Stroking my abs. Nuzzling my beard with his cheek.

"Fucking love this beard," he whispers.

"Fucking love *you*," I whisper back. I somehow find the energy to lift one arm and wrap it around his big shoulders, holding him closer to me. His erection is like a hot brand against my thigh, and when I turn my head to kiss him, he moans into my mouth and rubs that hard length against me. So I run the back of my knuckles down his shaft and he hisses.

"What do you want?" I ask between kisses. "There's no lube in this room."

Wes grunts and flexes his hips against me. "We don't need lube. I want your mouth on me."

I shift a little higher on the pillow. "Get up here, then. Show the beard who's boss."

With a growl, he grabs the other pillow and shoves it behind my head. Then he swings a knee over my chest and crawls up my body.

My palm lands on his abs, and I spread my fingers wide. He feels so good under my hand—warm and solid. I'm tired of spending the night alone. I like the resistance of another body in the bed. When he's gone, I miss being able to roll over and park my ass against his sleepy warmth.

But he's not sleepy now. He spreads his big legs wide, and I grab his ass and tug him closer. His cock is rigid and leaking for me. And coming nearer. To tease him I clamp my mouth closed and he lets out an impatient noise. Grabbing his dick, I sweep the head of it across my lips, tickling the underside with the beard on my chin.

Above me, Wes gives a horny shiver. There's just enough light coming through those curtains to show me that the tats all over his arms look like shadows when he moves. The masculine scent of him is starting to drive me a little crazy. I stick out my tongue and taste him, and he gasps with anticipation.

My torture isn't quite done, though. I crane my neck forward, smash my face against his groin and nip his pubes. I swear he's practically grinding his dick against my neck now, so turned on he'd fuck any surface of my body. A desperate Wes is a fun Wes. I love forcing him to let go of some of that iron-clad control. One sportswriter called him: "Impenetrable. Unshakeable. With nerves of steel."

I know better.

Trapping his eager dick with my hand, I slowly roll my neck, rubbing every surface of his shaft with my beard.

"Fucking hell," he jabbers. "Killing me. Just suck it already."

I kiss him once on the tip and he groans. Then, all at once, I put him out of his misery. Opening wide, I swallow him down. He gives a less-than-manly cry that makes me smile around his cock. So I pull off and then give him another good, hard suck. I am merciless now. There's no rhythm, just ambition. Sucking, licking, swallowing. He thrusts haphazardly, just enjoying the ride. And it's only a couple of minutes later when he takes a deep breath and says, "Here I fucking come."

And the man isn't lying. He pumps into my mouth more times than I can count, and I swallow a week's worth of sexual tension. Then my head flops back against the pillows, and I feel the exhaustion creep in again. Above me, Wes drops his head, and I watch his chest heave as he gulps down oxygen. Lifting both hands, I spread my fingers across his ribcage. "You look thinner," I say, my thumb sweeping the smooth skin of his chest.

"I'm down fifteen pounds since the season started."

"Fifteen?" I know players sometimes lose a little weight. But fifteen?

"Yeah. It happens."

I pull him down, and he has to roll off me so we can hold each other. "That's too much to lose," I murmur in his ear. "More enchiladas for you."

"You make it, I'll eat it." He buries his face in my neck. "Jamie?"

"Mmm?"

"I think there's jizz in your beard."

"Gross."

He laughs. "Is that gonna be an issue?"

"Dunno. It's my first beard, and you're the first one to splooge in it."

His voice is muffled. "Can we get in our bed now?"

"Uh-huh." I close my eyes, though. Just for a second.

We fall asleep in the guest room, tangled up in each other.

THREE

JAMIE

Eight hours later, life isn't so grand.

I'm on a bus with two dozen teenagers. That's okay, though, because I like these kids. They work hard and they play some great hockey. I thought I'd seen a lot of amazing young players, but the Canadians grow champions in their gardens apparently. The team's season isn't going so great, but I have faith that we'll turn it around. These kids have solid instincts and terrific attitudes.

My attitude is less stellar at the moment, though.

Since Wes and I fell asleep in the wrong room, my alarm wasn't nearby. The reason I was *only* forty minutes late was that the bed was too small. I woke up when Wes clocked me in the eyebrow with his tattooed elbow. The clock on the bedside table read ten minutes to six.

I sat up like a shot, heart pounding. I took the world's shortest shower and then hopped around like an idiot, shoving socks onto wet feet and grabbing my things. The only saving grace was that I'd already packed for our tournament in Montreal. I'd been trying to save time to spend with Wes, so at least my duffel was sitting there, ready to go.

Wes came staggering out of the guest room, blinking at me. "You have to leave?"

"I'm late," I mumbled, texting the coach I'd be traveling with. *Running late. Don't leave. Sorry.*

"I'll miss you," he said.

That I'd miss him too went without saying. I gave him a quick, unsatisfying kiss and ran for the door. Somehow I managed to trip on Wes's giant suitcase when I reached for my coat on the hook. "Do me a favor and unpack this thing?"

Those were my loving words as I departed, sweating, hating myself for being *that* guy who was going to make them hold the bus. And for grumbling at my boyfriend to put his stuff away.

He never does, though. The suitcase usually sits around until he needs it for the next trip.

Now I'm drinking the dregs of a really bad cup of coffee I bought at a gas station when the bus stopped for fuel, and I'm listening to my coworker shoot off his mouth. David Danton is only a couple of years older than I am. Technically we both hold the same title—Associate Coach. But since our boys' head coach has several teams under his command, Danton steps up to act as head coach sometimes, especially on trips.

Things to know about Danton: he has a beautiful slap shot. And a hideous personality.

"This first team we're playing?" he says, moving a wad of tobacco from one cheek to the other. "They're the same pussies you beat in London last year. Their stats don't look any better these days. Keep your lines tight and score in the first period, they'll be crying into their gloves by intermission. Bunch of faggots, really."

The bad coffee turns to battery acid in my stomach. In the first place, this is substandard coaching. The other team is defensively gifted and offensively challenged, and our kids deserve more cautionary detail. They need strategy along with a good helping of bravado.

And don't even get me started on Danton's slurs. He's the kind of guy who uses "gay" to describe anything he doesn't like—from an ugly car to a disappointing turkey sandwich—and "faggot" to describe any hockey player who doesn't meet his standards.

Now, I've already asked this prick to stop with the slurs. It was after a game at our home rink. We'd won easily and I was proud of our boys. But Danton had yelled "That's showing the faggots!" as the game ended, so I took the opportunity to mention that he could get in trouble for that.

"You never know who's listening," I'd pointed out. I'd been trying to hint that someone might call him on the carpet for using derogatory terms. But my real concern was for our players. I didn't want their authority figure to validate that kind of hate. And God forbid if one of these boys was questioning his own sexuality. Nobody needs to hear that shit. Being sixteen is confusing enough.

Danton didn't listen, though. And whenever he uses the f-word, I always picture a sixteen-year-old Wes, terrified of his own sexuality. He'd told me how badly it had freaked him out to realize he was gay. He's over it now, of course. But they can't all have Wes's strength. If there's a kid on one of these teams who's struggling, I don't want him to hear any bullshit from Danton.

Working with the guy makes me feel ragey, but not because I give one single fuck what Danton thinks of me. He'd lost my respect the first time I heard him spewing his vile bullshit. He uses the n-word, too (a real piece of work, our Danton). I wanted him reprimanded. I'd even mentioned to Bill, our boss, that Danton's choice of words was often poor and rarely very inclusive.

"See if you can tone 'im down," was all Bill said, clapping me on the shoulder. "Be a shame if he had a reprimand in his file. Those are permanent."

A permanent mark on Danton's record sounds fine to me, but I haven't filed the complaint yet because I'm paranoid. In some ways, outing myself sounds like fun, because I can't wait to see the look on the asshole's face. But I can't do that to Wes. He's having a terrific rookie season, and the press needs to stay focused on his goals and assists, not his sex life. I think he's *this* close to contending for the Calder trophy. I really do.

We sit in Montreal traffic on the way to the rink, and my guts are in knots. Our first tournament game is set for one p.m., and it's past noon already.

"One more mile," Danton says, checking the map on his phone. "Boys, we're gonna have only fifteen minutes to suit up, I think. Next time maybe Coach Canning will get out of bed on time."

Fuck. I hate that I was late. And I hate him.

That's a lot of hate for a California boy. The day is not going well.

We finally pull in and hustle the guys off the bus, and I help run a bunch of equipment inside. The tourney is running behind by a half hour, thank the lord. They're suited up and ready to play with enough time that it's almost civilized.

"Let's go," I say, clapping my gloves together. "You— Barrie! Keep your chin down in the faceoff. This team was a little slow to ship the puck, remember?"

The kid nods, his face intense.

Then I turn my attention on my goalie, Dunlop. He's a highly skilled player and brilliant in practice. Unfortunately, he's developed a tendency to clench up during games. He did all right at the start of the season, but this month he's in a rut.

"How you feeling?" I ask him.

His blue eyes dart away. "You mean—do I feel like I'm gonna choke again?"

"Dunlop, look. I know what you're going through. Every goalie's had a slump. And that crap always feels permanent. But it never is. Whether your slump ends today or next month, it *will* end. They always do."

He makes an angry teenaged grunt. I haven't convinced him.

"You've got the skills. Everybody knows it, even when they're pissy with you." It hasn't helped that Dunlop's teammates are pissed off about his recent performance. "They wouldn't bother getting tetchy if they didn't believe you could do it." I cuff him on the shoulder pad. "Stay loose. You got this."

Wary eyes finally rise to meet mine. "Okay. Thanks, Coach Canning."

And there it is. The whole reason I do this. "You're welcome. Now go."

The Zamboni has finished resurfacing the ice, so our guys are allowed to circle the rink for ninety seconds, warming up. Dunlop skates out with his head held high and proceeds to scuff up the crease like a goalie does before a game. He taps the right pipe once and the left one twice—his little ritual. And I think today could even be his lucky day.

My phone has buzzed in my pocket a couple of times, and now I have a moment to check it. There's a missed call from Wes. He must be finished with his morning skate. Even as

I'm holding the phone, it buzzes with a new text. *It's hard again.*

I remember our joke from yesterday. *How hard is it?*

Hard enough to stand up and salute you.

I glance at the rink. The refs aren't out there yet, so I still have a minute. I back up against a cinderblock wall so there's no chance anyone else can see my phone. *You gonna show me or what?*

A second later the photo appears. Wes has taken the trouble to fold a small paper hat for his erection to wear. It's grinning at me from what must be our sofa. Wes has also drawn a stick arm in salute along with a smiley face. I snort with inappropriate laughter just as I hear the ref's whistle blow. *Priceless*, I text back. *Miss you.*

Back atcha babe.

Taking care to lock and stow my phone, I move up to the bench to coach the game, a few degrees lighter than I was before.

FOUR

WES

I'm not there to greet Jamie when he returns from Montreal on Sunday—I'm already boarding a flight to Chicago for yet another away game. The good thing is, after this one, we're looking at a one-week stretch of home games. One blessed week of sleeping in my own bed. One week of *Jamie*.

I can't fucking wait.

My coat goes in the overhead bin and my earbuds go into my ears, but before I sit down Forsberg yells from the seat behind me, "Guys, it's the gay shirt! He wore it again!"

I pause and give him a cheesy wink. "Wore it for you, cutie. Because you liked it so much last time."

Forsberg throws a wadded-up napkin at me, and I duck it by dropping into my seat.

Of course, the real reason I'm wearing this shirt is that I didn't do laundry, and it was lying over a chair unwrinkled. That and it's a killer shirt. Forsberg be damned.

I make myself comfortable, closing my eyes and reclining in my seat as I mentally prepare for this very important game against the league leaders. Most of my teammates are doing the same thing.

When I feel the seat next to me depress under somebody's ass, I assume it's Lemming's, because he and I often sit together on flights and the bus. Lemming, a redheaded D-man, grew up in Boston, too.

But when I open my eyes, it's Blake sitting there, grinning at me. Clearly my new neighbor has made it his mission in life to bond with me, because he yanks the buds out of my ears.

"Dude," he groans. "I'm bored. Talk to me."

I stifle a groan of my own. We haven't even begun our two-hour flight. That old Nirvana song suddenly comes to mind, and I try to remember the lyrics… *Here we are now, entertain us.* That's pretty much Blake Riley. *I'm here, and it's your duty to entertain me.*

And yet I can't bring myself to dislike the guy. He's hilarious.

Since he's obviously not going anywhere, I click off my iPod and indulge him. "You hear anything more about Hankersen? Whether or not they're putting him on IR?" Hankersen is Chicago's star forward, and so far this season he's scored at least one goal per game. He's the biggest threat to us on the ice, so if he's not playing tonight, that will definitely up our chances of beating the undefeated Hawks.

"No news yet," Blake answers. He swipes a finger over his phone and pulls up a sports app, holding the screen toward me. "I've been checking religiously."

"Well, if he's playing, hopefully our defense can find a way to shut him down." It's unlikely, but a man can dream.

"How'd your roomie do this weekend?"

The question startles me. "What?"

"J-Bomb," Blake clarifies. "His junior team had a tournament or something, eh?"

"Oh right." It still makes me incredibly uneasy discussing Jamie with my teammates. But now that Blake has actually hung out with us, it would be even more suspicious if I clam up every time Jamie's name comes up. "They won one, lost two. The team's not doing great this season," I admit. And I know that bothers Jamie. A lot. Just because he chose to coach instead of going pro doesn't mean he's not competitive. It kills him that his boys aren't seeing any success this season.

"Sucks," Blake says sympathetically. "Especially when you're the coach. All you can do is stand there on the bench and watch. If it were me, I'd be all, 'Put me in the game, Coach! Me! I can win this for us!'"

I snicker. "That's 'cause you're a glory hog." Blake even has a trademark celebration move every time he scores. It's a cross between riding his stick like it's a pony and driving a locomotive. Stupid as hell, but the crowd goes nuts for it.

"Ha. Says the guy who's got millions of puck bunnies following him wherever he goes. Like a row of baby ducks." Blake grins. "I'll bet you're getting twice the pussy I did in my rookie year."

You'd lose that bet, sucker. Time to change the subject. I point at the newspaper rolled up in his hand. "What's happening in the world?"

"The usual bullshit. Politicians being assholes. People shooting at each other."

"We shoot at each other," I point out. "And get paid well for it." It's a weird job, really.

He rolls his eyes in a move that should look stupid on a dude but somehow doesn't. "We aren't *killing people*, Wesley."

About three minutes ago we were praying for another athlete's injury, but I don't bother to point that out.

"And there's a new velociraptor they discovered in North Dakota. Get this—it was seventeen feet tall, with claws and feathers." He's nodding aggressively. "That's a *badass* raptor. Fucking scary, really. But even scarier is that new flu. Did you hear about it?" He gives an exaggerated shudder. "It comes from *sheep*. I hate sheep."

A bark of laughter escapes me. "Who hates sheep? They're, like, woolly and harmless."

"Sheep are *not* harmless, bro. The sheep down the road from my grandparents' farm?" He shakes his giant head as if recalling a crack den in his neighborhood. "Those fuckers were *mean*. And loud. When I was a kid, my parents were like, 'Oh, Blakey, look at the little lambs!' And those fuckers would come over to the fence and bleat in my face." Blake opens his mouth and makes a *MEH-EH-EH* sound so loud that heads turn all over the plane.

"That sounds like it, uh, made a deep impression on you," I say, trying hard not to laugh. "Where did your grandparents live, anyway?"

Blake makes a dismissive motion with his hand. "The West Bumfuck farmland well outside of Ottawa—"

West Bumfuck? Sounds like my kind of place.

"—Lotsa agriculture. Lotsa sheep. And now those fuckers are gonna kill us with the flu. Cheezus. I *knew* they were evil."

"Uh-huh." I give my iPod a longing glance. I could be relaxing to some tunes right now, but instead we're reliving Blake's childhood terrors. "There's always some new flu scare, and it turns out to be nothing." Though it amuses me to see a big dude like Blake wigging out. "I heard these new strains spread especially fast on airplanes."

He gives me an evil glare. "Not funny. They found a case on Prince Edward Island."

"That's not close to here, though?" My Canadian geography is a little shaky. But I'm pretty sure I can't catch the flu from someone who lives a thousand miles from Toronto.

"That shit travels, man. I mean—we could be infecting Chicago right now."

I nudge him with my elbow. "Let's tell 'em that all of Canada has been exposed. They'll cough up the puck every time on the back check."

He gives a big, bellowing laugh and slaps me on the chest with his big paw. That's when my phone lights up. Unfortunately, the name I see on the screen is my father's, so there's an instant knot of tension in my chest.

Things haven't improved much with my folks since I graduated from college. They still insist that my "gayness" is a phase. My dad still treats my success in the pros like it's something *he* made happen. My mom still forgets she gave birth to me half the time.

I spent the holidays with Jamie's family in California, and when Jamie's mom Cindy suggested we invite my parents to fly out, I responded with five minutes of hysterical laughter, until Cindy finally chided me into stopping. Then she gave me a big hug and told me she loved me, because that's the kind of mom she is.

All I got from my folks was a brief phone call wishing me a happy holiday and reminding me that if I want to come home for a visit, I need to show up alone. Yup, Jamie isn't welcome. Scratch that. Jamie doesn't *exist*. My parents don't acknowledge that I am living with a man. To them, I'm a heterosexual athlete bachelor who's crushing pussy all over the place.

"I need to check this," I tell Blake.

I unlock the phone and give the email a quick read. Quick being the operative word, because the message is all of two lines.

Ryan, your schedule indicates you'll be in Boston next month. Your mother and I expect you to join us for dinner. Hunt Club, Saturday, 9:00pm.

He doesn't sign it "Dad" or even "Roger".

"Dinner with the parentals, eh?"

I jump and find Blake peering over my shoulder. Fucking hell. It's a good thing I have a lock on my phone, because this dude probably wouldn't think twice about snooping around in it.

"Yeah," I say tightly.

"You guys aren't close?"

"Not in the slightest."

"Shit. That's no good." Blake leans back in his seat. "I'll introduce you to my folks after the next home game. They're awesome. Trust me, after ten minutes they'll be your surrogate family."

I already have a surrogate family—the Cannings. But I keep that to myself. And then I feel annoyed about keeping it to myself, because goddamn it, why does everything in my life have to be a secret? I fucking *long* for the day when I can proudly introduce Jamie Canning as my boyfriend. When I can talk to my teammates about my personal life and tell them about Jamie's amazing family, or invite them over for drinks without having to see Jamie duck into the *guest* room when he has to go to bed. Because he's not a guest in our condo, dammit. It's his home. And he's *my* home.

I'm not usually one to wallow in the injustice of it all. I understand the world I live in. I know that being gay still has a stigma attached to it. Doesn't matter how many strides are being made, there will always be people out there who won't accept that I like dick, people who will judge and spew their filth and try to make my life miserable. The fact that I'm in the spotlight now only makes it worse, because there are so many other factors to consider.

If I come out, what will it mean for my career?

For the team?

For Jamie?

For Jamie's family?

The media will swarm like a horde of bees. The bigots and assholes will crawl out of the woodwork. The spotlight will no longer be just on my game, but on the personal lives of everyone I care about.

A queasy feeling churns in my gut. I remind myself that it won't be like this forever. Next season some other hot new rookie will take the media by storm, and I'll be forgotten. And by then, I will have proved to my new team that they can't survive without me, gayness be damned.

"Ooooh ya," Blake suddenly exclaims. I look over to see him reading something on his phone. "Guess who just went on IR?"

My breath hitches. "You're shitting me."

"Nope. Right here in black and white." He holds up the phone, then twists around in his seat to address Eriksson and Forsberg. "Hankersen's out. At least five games."

A whoop sounds from behind us, and then Eriksson's loud announcement blares through the cabin. "Hankersen's out!"

There's a collective burst of excitement. Don't get me wrong—we all feel for Hankersen. An injury is the worst thing that could happen to an athlete, and I wouldn't wish it on anyone. But at the same time, hockey isn't just a game—it's a business. We're all playing toward the same goal. We all want that championship cup. A win in Chicago tonight gets us one step closer to that goal.

My phone flashes again. This time it's Jamie's name looking up at me with the text message icon next to it. But Blake is settling in his seat again, so I don't give in to the urge to unlock the screen.

My teammate, of course, sneaks another peek. "Text from your roomie," he says helpfully, as if I'm not fucking aware of it.

I grit my teeth and tuck the phone in my pocket.

"You're not gonna check it?"

"Later," I mutter. "He's probably just reminding me to grab groceries when I get back tomorrow morning. Nothing important."

Those last two words are like poison—they burn my throat and rip my stomach to shreds. I feel sick and guilty for even saying that out loud. For implying that Jamie Canning isn't important when I damn well know that he's the single most important person in the world to me.

I am such a shit.

"So," Blake says, oblivious to my pain, "I read that J-Bomb got drafted by Detroit. That's killer. Why didn't he go?"

For a second I just blink at him. "Where'd you read that?"

"Google, my friend. You heard of it? J-Bomb didn't want to move to the Motor City?"

Shit! Blake is a nosy fucker. "He wanted to coach. The dude played goalie, you know? That organization has a pretty deep bench behind the net, and he didn't think he'd ever get to play. This old coach of ours hooked him up with a job. Great opportunity." I hear myself starting to babble and clamp my jaw shut. Did I give too much detail? Do I sound like I know too much? Now I'm sitting here hating my own paranoia.

"Uh-huh," Blake says, looking distracted now. "So how do you think a guy could defeat a seventeen foot velociraptor, anyway? I mean, you'd need some serious weaponry. That fucker would be fast, too. Like Indy 500 fast."

"Um..." I lost control of this conversation a long time ago. "Taser maybe?"

"*Right*. Good idea. Be fun to taser a raptor."

Later, when Blake gets up to take a leak, I shield my screen and unlock my phone so I can see the message. The text says *MDISH*. It takes me a second, but then I understand the abbreviation. *How hard is it?* I reply.

Hard enough to operate the remote.

The picture is a carefully angled shot from our sofa toward the television. But the focus is on Jamie's cock, which appears to be aiming the remote at the television. One stick-drawn arm is pushing a button, and the other has its drawn hand on its... hip. Well, dicks don't have hips. But still.

Tell him not to watch any Banshee, I reply.

He's chosen Die Hard II.

Tell him I miss him.

He knows, was Jamie's reply.

I spend the rest of the flight with my earbuds jammed in, brainstorming dick pics that might make Jamie smile.

FIVE

JAMIE

I watch the Chicago game on the sofa alone. While live games are more exciting, there are advantages to the privacy of my own living room. I can scream at the television and nobody stares.

"Come on, baby!" I yell, clapping supportively, even if nobody can hear me. "It's gonna work one of these times!"

Wes has taken a million shots on goal tonight, but the biggest goalie in the NHL keeps swatting them away like flies, damn him. During the commercial break, I run for the fridge and grab a beer. The game is scoreless until the third period, and I'm super tense. Wes takes another shift with the second line, and I hold my breath.

When his next chance comes, I'm practically levitating with anticipation. Wes draws the goalie out of the crease with a long, risky cross to the left wing. But it works. When the wing snaps it back to Wes, he's able to slip it into the back corner of the net before the goalie can react.

Now I'm jumping on the sofa and sloshing my beer a little, but it's worth it. Another goal, another notch in Wes's belt.

He's really doing it. He's having a phenomenal rookie season, the kind that could end up in a record book. And I'm just so pumped for him.

The camera focuses on the giant goalie's sweaty face, and I imagine I can hear the guy's thoughts. *Mountain must stay in front of net.*

Snickering to myself, I sit down again and kick my feet onto the coffee table. My sister asked me the other day if I was jealous, if I regretted passing up the chance to have my own shot, and it was easy to say no. I can't lie—my poor bank account could have used the signing bonus. But if I'd gone to Detroit (where last year's goaltenders look as solid in their jobs as they always have) I would have missed being a part of this.

That's what I'd regret.

I watch the rest of the game with my heart in my mouth, wondering if Wes's lead will stand. And those last fifteen minutes of play are exciting. Good thing I don't have a heart condition, because Chicago answers with their own goal, and Toronto pulls a penalty. I nearly die of stress while Wes's team kills the penalty. In the last two minutes Eriksson scores, and they avoid an overtime situation. Toronto takes the game, 2-1.

Limp with relief, I collapse on the sofa. And now the real waiting begins. Wes will spend a solid hour or two with his teammates, his coaches and the press. Then, because it's a short trip back to Toronto, the team jet will fly back tonight.

I spend some time tidying up our apartment. The kitchen is clean already because I did that earlier, so I open our mail and cringe at our heating bill. I pay for half of the utilities and a portion of our rent, though if it were up to Wes, he'd be paying for everything. I put my foot down when he suggested it, because I can't live in this apartment and *not* contribute. Wes's name might be on the lease, but this is my home too, damn it.

Wes's giant suitcase is still beside the front door where he left it after his longer road trip. I have a little war with myself over whether to just leave it there or not. It seems petty to wash my stuff and leave his dirty. But I'm not quite sure what Wes thinks happens to his laundry when he leaves it in a suitcase or in a pile on our bedroom floor. He may actually believe there's a laundry fairy that stops by once in a while to keep him in clean underwear.

Either way, it's bugging me. So I give in and unzip the giant bag, pulling out piles of rumpled clothing. I deposit everything in the washer and start a load.

Then I go to bed, taking care to leave a light burning in the kitchen so that Wes can find his way to me.

WHEN I WAKE UP, there's light escaping around the edges of our bedroom blinds. And there's a muscled, naked man sleeping with one tattooed arm slung around my waist. I gingerly slide toward the edge of the bed, but the arm tightens its grip. "No," Wes says sleepily.

"Let me take a leak," I whisper.

"Come right back."

"Deal." On my way to the john I glance at his relaxed face. He may have been talking in his sleep just now, he looks so passed out.

After I do my thing and brush my teeth, I duck into the kitchen to grab a glass of water. I've chugged half of it when I hear soft footsteps in the hall, and I turn to find Wes in the doorway, slowly stroking an ambitious-looking erection. His gaze tracks me across the room as I set the glass in the sink.

"You didn't come right back," he rasps.

"Thirsty," I mumble. I'm distracted by the seductive motion of his hand on his dick. The blowjobs we exchanged the other night were too hurried. Satisfying, yes, but not enough. It's been too long since we've had an entire night to ourselves. An entire night to tease and explore and drive each other wild.

"Why are you still wearing those?" Wes's eyes gleam in the early morning light as he gestures to my boxers.

He's got a point. My boxers drop to the tiled floor. "Why didn't you wake me up when you got home?" I counter.

He grins. "You were deep under." His voice is gravel, and just the familiar smoky sound of it gets my blood pumping. "And we have *a whole week*." He says these last three words the way someone else might say *ten million dollars*. Wes probably already has ten million dollars. His family is rich, and he doesn't give a damn. What he wants most is *me*. And I'd be lying if I said that didn't light me up. Wes is never stingy with his affection.

In fact, he's reaching for me even now, pulling me in.

I press up against his hard body and smooth skin. As our groins make contact, my hardening dick says, *where you been?* Wes gives me a wicked grin and reaches between us to grasp my erection. "Hi," I say with a grin of my own.

"Hi."

"Nice goal last night."

"You want to chat right now?" he growls. "Because I'd rather fuck you."

"Chat later, then?"

Wes grabs the back of my head and hauls me in for a kiss.

He grunts with satisfaction as our mouths collide. His kiss is rough. Hungry.

I take over the kiss, opening him up with my tongue. Wes groans, his forehead furrowed with concentration. I thrust against him, scraping our eager dicks together, and he grabs my hips as if forbidding me to do that yet.

"Bedroom?" I manage to choke out.

He releases my mouth and gives a shake of his head. "Too far away."

The urgency on his face summons a laugh, but the sound dies in my throat when he suddenly drops to his knees and swallows my dick before I can blink.

Sweet Jesus.

My ass bumps the counter as Wes sucks me all the way to the root. His mouth is wet and hot and eager. My heart rate kicks up a million notches, pleasure gathering in my balls with each greedy suck and flick of his tongue. I love what he's doing to me, but I hate that the base of my spine is already tingling. I'm close to coming, and that just illustrates how sex starved we've become with all our time apart. Usually I have more stamina, damn it. But these days my body is so excited at the rarity of having Wes around for more than five minutes that I explode the second he touches me.

"Don't want to come yet," I tell him, tightening my fingers in his hair.

His mouth releases me. With a low chuckle, he rises to his feet and runs his fingertips over my jawline, lightly stroking my beard. A shiver goes through me. This man…fuck, this man. He does me in with one touch. One heated look.

"Turn around," he whispers. "Hands flat on the counter."

I do what he asks, and a moment later a pair of strong hands cup my ass. He squeezes and I moan, instinctively thrusting my hips forward, only to smack my still-glistening dick on the cool, hard granite. My hand slides down to grip my erection and I slowly rub my thumb around the head as Wes continues to knead my ass cheeks. When his finger slides into my crease, I push back against the teasing caress, silently begging for more.

"I've missed this ass." His breath tickles the nape of my neck, and then his tongue comes out for a taste, swirling over my feverish skin. "You don't know how many times I jerked when we were on the road. How many times I got myself off to the thought of sliding my cock into this tight ass." He rubs my opening with the tip of his finger, and the sensitive nerve endings there roar to life.

My dick leaks in my hand. Shit. I'm still close. Too close. I squeeze my cockhead hard enough to bring a sting of pain, trying to curb the release that's threatening to spill over.

"You should've hit me up on Skype," I say. "We could have jerked off together." It's something we've never tried.

That gets me a strangled moan. Oh yeah, he likes that idea. But I tuck the thought away. Right now, there's no need to think up creative ways to fuck when we're thousands of miles apart. Because we're together. We're here, in the flesh, able to fuck any way we want.

"Don't move." His rough command echoes in the dark kitchen. I hear his footsteps disappear into the hallway. I don't move. Anticipation builds inside me, and my dick pulses in my hand, begging for Wes to return.

He's not gone long. I hear a clicking noise, the unmistakable sound of a cap opening. He went to grab lube, and now his fingers are slick as he brings them back to my ass. His slippery hand torments me, sliding between my cheeks, rubbing over my balls. When he pushes one finger inside me, I simultaneously curse and sigh.

"So tight," he grinds out. He slides in deeper and my muscles clamp around his finger. "You want my cock, Canning?"

"*Yes*." I bear down harder on his finger. It's not enough. I need more. I need his thick erection filling me, pushing against that sweet spot I never knew existed until last summer, when Ryan Wesley walked back into my life and showed me a new side of myself.

He adds another finger, stroking my channel and stretching me open until I'm burning up. Until my vision wavers and my brain stops working. "More," I beg. It's all I'm capable of saying. *More. More, more, more.* I'm *begging* and Wes is still depriving me of what I want. He's grinding his erection against one of my ass cheeks as his fingers move inside me. His other hand reaches around my chest and glides downward, swatting my hand away so he can grab hold of my dick.

"Jesus," I hiss when he starts pumping.

"You like this, babe? Me jerking your cock while I finger your ass?"

I mumble something incoherent in response, which makes him laugh. The husky sound warms the side of my neck, and then I jump when his teeth sink into my flesh. Holy shit, he's driving me crazy. He soothes the sting with his tongue, licking the tendons of my neck, kissing his way down to my shoulder, biting that, too.

"You ready for me?" he whispers.

An anguished groan slips out. "So fucking ready."

With another chuckle, he withdraws his fingers and my entire body sags in disappointment, mourning the loss, craving the pressure again. Wes doesn't make me wait long—in a heartbeat, his tip prods my ass, and then his big, lubed-up cock slips through the ring of muscle and plunges inside.

We both groan. His hands clutch my hips, long fingers digging into my skin as he slowly pulls out, then slams back in again.

"Fucking hell, Canning, I fucking love you so fucking much." He sounds like he's struggling to breathe, and when half his vocabulary is reduced to F-bombs, that means Wes is barely hanging on to his control. But I love it when he loses control. I know I'm in for a wild ride and holy hell does he give it to me.

He pounds into me from behind, hips snapping, balls slapping my ass with each deep, desperate thrust. I sag forward, bent over the counter. My cock is harder than the granite beneath my palms. I want to stroke it but Wes is drilling me so hard that I need both hands to brace myself. He's attuned to my needs, though, because he drops one hand from my waist and brings it to my impossibly hard dick. Then he angles his hips in a way that has him hitting my prostate each time he drives forward.

"Come for me," he orders. "Come all over my hand, Jamie. Let me feel it."

I shoot so fast it's almost comical. All it takes is Wes's gravelly command and I come with a wild cry, soaking his hand just as he wanted. As I shudder from the release, Wes growls, his thrusts growing more and more erratic. Unskilled, utterly frantic, until finally he drops his head on my shoulder and trembles behind me. I feel his release pulse inside me, and when he pulls out several moments later, my ass and thighs are sticky and we're both quaking with laughter.

"That was...intense," Wes says dryly.

I snort. "I think you just unloaded a gallon of jizz in me."

Not that I'm complaining. I love knowing that I have the power to turn Wes into a sex-crazed maniac. Even so, I still grumble a little as we spend the next five minutes cleaning up. My own release was equally uncontrollable, leaving behind several pearly drops on the counter and cabinet beneath it. I insist on scrubbing down the entire surface, while Wes teases me about having OCD.

"We *eat* on this thing, dude," I remind him. "That's not OCD, it's basic cleanliness."

He chuckles and continues scrubbing the floor with the rag and cleanser I hand him. "So what do you want to do tonight? Should we hit up that new restaurant Eriksson told me about?"

Toronto's next home game is tomorrow, which means we actually have the entire day and night just for us. And Tuesdays happen to be half-price ticket night at all the theaters in the city. "Definitely," I answer. "But we can go there after the movie. I don't know how much longer it'll be in theaters."

"Oh shit, *The Long Pass*? Yeah, you're right. We definitely need to see it tonight." Remorse flickers in his expression, and I know he's thinking about what happened the last time he had a night off. I'd been dying to see that damn movie, but so had Wes, and he made me promise not to go without him. Except when we finally had the opportunity to see it, Wes's PR rep called him just as we were walking out the door and informed Wes that his presence was required at a last-minute press conference announcing a surprise trade in the organization. That was three weeks ago.

I don't mention it, though, because I know he already feels like shit that he had to bail on our date night. "Okay, so how about we catch the seven o'clock show and then have a late dinner after?" I suggest.

"Sounds like a plan." He grins at me. "So. Ready for round

two? And then breakfast. We have to keep our strength up for the workout I'm giving you today and tonight."

My gaze lowers to his crotch, and I raise a brow when I see the semi he's sporting. "You're a raging horndog this morning, huh?" But the sight of it has me hardening again, too, which only makes his grin widen.

"Pot, kettle, et cetera et cetera." He steps forward and kisses me, then tugs me away from the counter.

Laughing, we leave the sparkling clean and semen-free kitchen and race toward our shower. For the first time in weeks, there's a lightness in my chest. I just want to spend the entire day naked with my sex-crazed boyfriend.

But as I discover ten minutes later, you really can't always get what you want.

The loud pounding on the door can only come from one person. Nobody else in the building knows who I am, and even if they did, nobody would be rude enough to bang on the door at eight in the fucking morning. Nobody but Blake Riley, that is.

Jamie and I freeze mid-kiss in the center of our bedroom. We're both buck naked, dripping from the shower we just took and sporting raging hard-ons. He looks as annoyed as I feel.

"Maybe if we ignore him he'll go away," I murmur.

Jamie makes an annoyed sound under his breath.

"Wesley! Open up!"

Blake's muffled voice travels toward the bedroom, and Jamie's expression darkens even more.

"C'mon, bro, it's an emergency!"

My shoulders tense. Shit. For some reason, my first thought is that the truth about my sexual orientation broke out. How egotistical is that? Like the media in Toronto has nothing better to do than report on who Ryan Wesley is screwing. Still, it's my biggest fear. That the success I've been having in my first season with Toronto will be overshadowed—or worse, forgotten—because being a gay professional athlete is the far juicier story.

"This could be important," I tell Jamie, while trying to convey with my eyes just how unhappy I am with the interruption.

I throw on a pair of sweatpants and go to answer the door. Blake barrels inside wearing track pants and a gray undershirt that shows off his huge biceps.

"Thank fuck," he groans. "Do you have coffee? I'm desperate!"

I watch open-mouthed as he charges into the kitchen and starts opening cupboards like he owns the place. *Seriously*? He nearly broke down my door because he wants *coffee*? I have to bite my tongue to stop myself from pointing out that there are hundreds of Tim Hortons in Toronto, two of them within a three-block radius of our building.

"How lucky is it that we're neighbors?" Blake grabs a mug from the cupboard and heads to the other side of the counter to click on the coffee maker.

Lucky? I'm about ten seconds from committing a murder. Except I know that giant body wouldn't fit into the hallway chute that feeds our building's trash compactor.

My heart drops to the pit of my stomach when I notice the mug he's holding. It's one of a pair, with the word HIS written on it, courtesy of Cindy Canning. She gave us the mugs for the holidays, and I can honestly say it's the most thoughtful gift I've ever received. I want to snatch it out of his huge hand and say "Mine!" Maybe pee on it to mark my territory. But Blake has already filled my favorite mug with coffee and is raising it to his mouth.

He leans on the counter and sips the hot liquid, then lets out a contented sigh. "Thanks, man. I can't function without my morning vitamin C."

He's thanking me as if I graciously invited him in for a cup of joe. Which I did not.

Footsteps echo in the hall and then Jamie walks into the kitchen. He'd thrown on a pair of sweatpants too, along with a blue button-down shirt. The shirt is unbuttoned, revealing his washboard abs and smooth, golden skin.

"Morning," he mumbles without looking in my direction.

"Aw shit, did I wake you?" Blake sounds genuinely regretful. "I'm bad at knocking on doors." He holds up one massive hand. "These paws don't know how to be gentle."

"It's okay, I had to get up anyway," Jamie answers. He pours himself a cup of coffee, then glances over his shoulder at me. "Got any plans for today?"

I know he's trying to act like a polite roommate, but the pain in his eyes rips me apart. I want to open my mouth and declare, "My plan is to spend the whole day under your naked body!" and Blake be damned. I keep my mouth shut, though. Jamie and I have worked hard to keep our relationship under wraps since the start of the season. We can survive a few more months of hiding.

"Not sure yet," I say lightly.

Blake pipes up, "We have that benefit tonight, remember? Champagne and models? I feel a slutty night coming on. You?"

I shake my head. "Nope. For once I'm not on the list. The PR department only asked veteran players to make an appearance."

"Shit, they consider me a veteran? It's only my third

season," Blake protests. He takes a hasty sip. "Hope that doesn't mean they think I'm getting old."

"You're twenty-five," I say dryly. "I'm sure they still consider you a spring chicken."

He rests one forearm on the counter and I almost swallow my tongue when I realize where he's standing. The exact spot where I bent Jamie over not even ten minutes ago. My man is clearly thinking the same thing, because he offers a wry smile behind Blake's shoulder.

Blake sips his coffee and then I see a light in his eyes. "Ah! I've got the best idea. Did you know I'm brilliant?" He grabs a phone out of his pocket and starts texting. I don't ask him why, because with Blake, you're always going to get a full story of anything that pops through his big meaty head. So I enjoy the silence, choosing a second-rate mug because Blake is using mine and pouring myself a cup of coffee.

Jamie is puttering around the kitchen now, taking things out of the refrigerator. A dozen eggs. Some corn tortillas from the organic market where he likes to shop. Chorizo sausage. Salsa. He takes out a glass mixing bowl and starts cracking eggs into it. I love the care he puts into cooking. I could watch his hands all day. They'd look better on my dick right now, but this is nice, too. He puts the sausage into a heated pan and it hisses against the surface. Then he tosses the pan into the oven to cook.

"Whoa," Blake says, looking up from his phone. "Whatcha doing there, J-Bomb?"

"Breakfast," Jamie says, chucking the eggshells into the trash. "Wesley told me he has a big workout planned for later. Thought he could replenish some protein." Jamie pulls a whisk out of a drawer, giving me a meaningful glance. Then he begins to give those eggs the business.

"Holy cow! You cook?" Blake marvels, his big puppy-like face obviously impressed. "No wonder Wesley likes you."

I see Jamie bite his lip against a smile. There is a lengthy list of things I love about Jamie. His cooking isn't even in the top fifty. There's his smile, his flawless body, his easy personality, his highly skilled tongue…

Right. Now is not the time for me to think about that.

"You staying for breakfast, Blake?" Jamie asks over his shoulder.

Our neighbor yanks a counter stool out and plants his giant self onto it. "You'll never be rid of me now."

Damn. I'm going to start crying like a little girl if he says that again. I find some plates and silverware and make myself useful.

I'm only trying to help Jamie plate up the food when I reach for the handle of the sausage pan. Before I can even register the motion, Jamie's hand shoots across the kitchen space and knocks my hand away from the pan.

"Dude!" Blake bellows. "J-bomb doesn't want you touching his sausage!" Blake laughs hysterically at his own joke.

But Jamie can't even appreciate the irony of Blake's words, because he's busy glaring at me. "Again—the towel draped over the handle means…"

"It's *hot.* I forgot." I'm already famous for burning myself, and I don't even cook.

Jamie waves me out of the way and serves up the breakfast.

"Those goalie reflexes," Blake says. "They saved your mitt."

Two minutes later we're chowing down on scrambled eggs with chorizo and cheese in warmed corn tortillas with salsa.

Blake takes another bite and moans comically. "I love you, man."

"That's what all the guys say to me," Jamie deadpans. He's probably imagining the last time we ate a quiet weekend breakfast together in our bed naked.

But ultimately, it's hard to hate Blake. It really is. Especially when he collects the plates after breakfast and just starts washing them without asking. When he's done with that, he does the pans and then wipes down the countertops. Jamie pours himself another cup of coffee and plunks down on the couch while the kitchen is cleaned by someone other than him.

Even Jamie is softening toward Blake. I can tell.

Finally, Blake thanks us for breakfast and makes a move to leave. "Let me just check—ah ha!" he says, tapping on his phone. "This is awesome. I got you invited to the benefit tonight! This is a big shindig. My favorite one of the season. We're talking A-listers at this puppy—*supermodels*, dude."

"I don't think..." I start.

"Check yer email, eh? The publicist said he was pumped up to have you. Two guys bailed because their wives are flipping out at them. The team bought a table and it looks shitty if it's not full. So you're in!"

On the end of the counter, my phone starts to ring.

"TTFN, kids. And your food is da bomb, J-Bomb." Blake is still talking to himself when he leaves our apartment and closes the door.

Jamie glares at the door like it's a venomous snake, and my phone starts dancing a jig again. I walk over and squint at it. "Shit. I have to take this." I pick it up and greet the head of publicity. "Hello? Frank?"

"Morning, Ryan. Sorry to bother you on the weekend."

"No problem, sir." I'm extra polite because I'm speaking to the man who is going to have to manage my Big Gay Moment when my secret finally leaks. Whenever I speak to him, I never forget that.

"Blake Riley says you're available to go to the black-tie benefit tonight. I know it's sometimes a chore to spend yet another night away from our families, and I want you to know that I really appreciate the offer."

"Umm…" *I didn't offer* is on the tip of my tongue. "You said it's black tie?" *Christ*. I'm going to kill Blake.

"Do you have a tuxedo? I could send you the number for an emergency formalwear service…"

"I got it," I sigh. "Thanks."

"No, thank *you*. See you at eight. And Ryan…?" He hesitates.

"Yeah?"

"Do you plan to bring a date?"

"No," I say awfully quickly.

"All right," he says lightly. But he knows it's a loaded question. Frank is one of the handful of people who knows about Jamie and me. I told him last summer, because if the team was going to ax me, I wanted to know that going in. "Have fun."

As if. "I will, thanks."

Jamie is sitting on the sofa when I hang up, staring at the TV, which is not even on. I walk over there and sit beside him. I put my feet beside his on the coffee table and my head on his chest.

"Let me guess. You're going out tonight to some shindig."

I burrow my face in his neck. "I can call them back and say I'm sick."

Jamie sighs. "They might put you on the IR if they think you have that flu that's been in the news. It's starting to freak people out. You have to play Detroit tomorrow."

"Fuck. Fucking Blake." We are quiet for a minute. I reach up and stroke Jamie's beard. I'm still getting used to it. "Okay, I'll call a realtor on Monday and search for a new apartment."

"What?" Jamie laughs.

"I'm dead serious. This is... He..." I don't finish either sentence, because this is something Jamie and I don't talk about aloud. The things we do to hide our relationship—the awkward little omissions, the outright lies—it all feels terrible. I know it bothers him, too. We don't talk about it because it's embarrassing. I put him in this position because I wanted to have a rookie season judged solely on the merits of my skill. But we're only halfway through, and it's getting harder all the time.

"We can't move," Jamie says dully. "Be a pain in the ass and no guarantee of more privacy."

This is depressingly true. "I only need three more months. Four, tops."

"I know."

There is more silence. But at least his hand wanders onto my back. If Jamie is touching me, then everything will be okay. "I'm sorry about the movie tonight."

"We could go to a matinee."

"Sure," I agree. But neither of us gets up to check the times. Instead, I start dropping little kisses inside the collar of his shirt. He resists me for a minute or two, because he's pissed off that our evening is wrecked. But I keep it up. And ultimately, I'm irresistible. I trail my lips down his collarbone, then down the broad planes of his pecs. I part the halves of his shirt and nuzzle his nipple, then start to suck.

He shifts on the sofa, his legs falling open. I kiss my way down his body and onto the bulge in his sweatpants.

Jamie drops a hand in my hair and sighs. He's a little sad, but also turned on.

We don't make it anywhere near that movie. After I blow him on the couch, we retire to our bed where we alternately nap and fool around all day. And when I finally have to get up and pull myself together for a benefit I have no interest in attending, he's too relaxed and sexually satisfied to care that much.

At seven, I'm cursing at my bow tie while he watches me from the bed. "You are smokin' hot in a tux," he says. "Even if your tie game is pretty weak."

"Help," I whine, starting over for the third time.

He gets up and knocks my hands away. "The trick is to start sloppy and tighten everything up later. Kind of like giving a blowjob."

I snort with laughter. Who knew that my childhood crush would ever learn to give a blowjob? Throughout high school, Jamie was my fantasy. The big blond hottie whose long fingers are fixing my tie still astonishes me every time he touches me. I hold very still because I want this to last. He can fiddle with this thing all night long if it means I have a front-row view of his brown eyes—so surprising on a blond guy—and his golden, chiseled cheekbones.

"There," he says softly, his breath on my face. He gives the tie one more tug.

I reluctantly shift my gaze to the mirror, and my tie is perfectly centered and straight. I have no more reason to stay at home now. "Thank you," I say quietly. When I say this, it means so much more than just for tying a tie.

He cups my cheek. "You're welcome. Now go. Behave.

Wave on the red carpet or whatever. When they ask you who you're wearing, make some shit up."

"Good idea." I lean forward and kiss him once. A quickie. Then I beat it out of there before I can reconsider.

SEVEN
WES

At the benefit I'm miserable.

I'm no stranger to parties, but I hate this kind—a bunch of people in penguin suits trying to impress each other. At least the food was good and the liquor is tasty, even if the pour is on the stingy side. My glass is empty again so I look around. There are always multiple bars set up at events like this. The trick is to zero in on the underutilized one, where the lines are shorter. There's a long line at the bar near the door, so I scan the room and find what I'm looking for in a corner.

Five minutes later I'm sipping a single malt and wandering back to my teammates. Even when they're out of sight, you can still hear them. I can track Eriksson's chortles and Blake's guffaws.

I'm avoiding Blake because I'm irritated at him. Maybe that's juvenile, but my goal for the night is just to get through it. I already heard him say something about hitting the bar after our forced appearance here is over. That's out of the question. Once the speeches are made, I'm slipping out the back.

"Hey, Wesley." Eriksson greets me with a hard thump on the back. "You having fun?"

To lie or not to lie? That is the question. I'm pretty fucking sick of the lies I tell all week long. "Not particularly. This isn't my scene."

Eriksson's eyes widen. "The single man doesn't care for a room full of rich women in skimpy dresses? I used to clean up at events like this. Seven years ago I took home a pair of twins who tag-teamed me all night." His smile is drunken. "Those were the days."

My teammate looks pretty banged up, and it's only ten. His eyes are red, and he looks exhausted. "You okay?" I blurt out. He's looked like hell all week, honestly. I don't know why I'm just realizing that now.

"Course I'm okay. Except my wife told me this morning she wants a divorce, and then she took the kids to her sister's place. I missed another counseling session, apparently. So she's throwing in the towel."

Jesus Christ. "I'm so sorry, man. Maybe she just needs a night to think things through." Is that what you say to a guy whose life is falling apart? I don't have a clue.

Eriksson shrugs. "This lifestyle. It isn't easy, you know? But enough of my bullshit. What do you have against parties?"

"Not all parties," I say quickly. "This kind of thing just gives me flashbacks to my childhood. My mother spends all her time planning shit like this. See these flowers?" I point at one of the ostentatious centerpieces. There are millions of them, and since it's February in Canada, they would have been flown in from the tropics. From the ceiling hang swarms of fake butterflies, each one suspended on some kind of invisible fishing line. "Someone spent a big chunk of change decorating this place. Because the rich people who spent four grand a head to come here tonight expect to be dazzled. I've always wondered why we can't all just stay home and write a check in our underwear. More of it goes to the actual charity. Boom. Fundraising problem solved."

Eriksson tips his head back and laughs. "You cynical bastard. I fucking love you. But you're here already, so stop making that face like the tie is choking you."

I give the tie one more tug, because that fucker *is* choking me. "What is this benefit for, anyway?" I'd missed that crucial bit of information. And since these parties always look the same, there aren't any clues in the decor. Unless the party is meant to benefit florists and faux butterflies.

"Psoriasis research," Eriksson says. "Apparently it's a real scourge."

"What?" I snort. "The skin condition?" I scan the crowd again, but the only skin I see is on nubile young women with backless dresses. The research must be working great.

"Heads up," Eriksson tips his head toward a group of gorgeous girls moving toward us through the crowd. "You're single, and I might be. Might as well admire the models. It's for a good cause, right?"

After a nice slug of my whiskey I paste on a smile. But then I realize that I actually know one of these girls. "Kristine! What the hell are you doing here?" I knew her in college—she used to date my friend Cassel's brother. I haven't seen her in three years—not since she broke up with Robbie.

She gives me a big grin. "When I saw your team on the program, I wondered if you'd be here. Little Ryan, the *famous* rookie forward. Why can't I say that with a straight face?"

I grab her and give her a hug, and my hands meet skin everywhere. Her shiny bronze-colored dress is so skimpy she's practically naked. "Good to see you, Krissi. How you been?

You're back in Toronto?" I'd forgotten she was Canadian. She'd been in Boston when I used to visit the Cassel family on college breaks.

"In the first place, I'm not Kristine. I'm *Kai*."

"What? Who's Kai?"

"I am, dumbass." She gives my ass a pinch. "Kristine wasn't fashionable enough for my agency. They changed my name."

Right—modeling. I'd forgotten she was making a go of that. "You let them change your name? That sounds extreme." *Says the man who hides his sexuality to play in the NHL.* Okay, so a name change isn't that weird. "Kai is kinda butch. I like it."

She laughs. "Come dance with me. Let's liven this place up."

"Sure," I say immediately. Talking to Kristine/Kai has put me in a better mood. It reminds me of simpler times, when she and Robbie and Cassel and I would look for trouble in the stodgy Boston bars. I wish we were there again instead of here, but you can't have everything. And dancing with an old friend makes the swing music the six-piece band is playing more interesting to me than it was a few minutes ago.

I take her hand and lead her to the dance floor.

JAMIE

I'm folding some laundry on the sofa, half-watching a basketball game and poking at my phone. None of these things is very interesting.

The movie I wanted to see has one last showing, forty

minutes from now. If I'm going to see it, I have to decide in the next five minutes.

Will Wes be pissed if I go alone? Probably not. Not much, anyway. And if it's great I can stream it again with him when it's released for home video.

I fold two more T-shirts and try to decide. The movie ticket doesn't cost much, but then there's popcorn and overpriced soda. And two subway rides. It's not free, and I try to save any spare dollars for nights out with Wes. The rent I insist on paying is almost more than I can afford, so I'm broke a lot of the time.

Also, it's cold out there. Toronto has winter winds that just slice right through you. Living on the West Coast my whole life, I never really understood just how brutal a winter could be. Maybe that sounds like a lame reason to stay home, but the wind chill factor doesn't tip the scales in the movie's favor.

If Wes were here I'd go in a heartbeat, though. Weather be damned.

Still dawdling, I tap on Instagram. And—this is trippy—Wes is in the first picture I see. The shot is on the team's account. Someone from the publicity staff is busy taking photos at the party. In the picture, Wes is smiling at a really hot young woman in a copper-colored dress. Their arms are wrapped around one another. The caption says, "Rookie forward Ryan Wesley dancing with model Kai James at #PartyForPsoriasis."

Wes is swing-dancing with a model, while I sit here literally folding his underwear.

That's it. That's the shove I need to get off the couch and go out.

TWENTY MINUTES LATER, I'm getting off at the Dundas stop on the Yonge line. The frigid wind slaps my face when I emerge onto the street from the subway station. I hurriedly slip into my gloves and lift my hood, but my entire face is half-frozen by the time I make it to the theater.

When I try to buy a ticket at the box office, the acne-ridden kid at the counter delivers the bad news. "I'm sorry, but that showing has been cancelled."

"But it was listed on the theater website," I balk.

"I know, but *Morph-Bots* opened this weekend and every show has been sold out since last Friday. We haven't sold a ticket to *The Long Pass* in days, so the theater manager decided to use the auditorium for an extra *Morph-Bots* showing." He awkwardly rubs his pimple-covered chin. "Would you like a ticket for *Morph-Bots*?"

If he says the words *Morph-Bots* one more time, I'm going to lose my ever loving shit.

"—there're a few seats left. All in the front row, but..." He shrugs sheepishly, as if realizing he's not making a good case for this stupid robot movie.

"Naah, it's all right. Thanks anyway."

I shove my hands in my jacket pockets and amble away from the ticket counter. Crap. Now what? I came all the way here, but there aren't any other movies I'm interested in seeing.

With a heavy feeling in my chest, I leave the theater. I've just stepped outside into the cold when my phone buzzes in my pocket. It's a text from Wes. My heart squeezes as I read it.

Wish you were here.

Does he? Or is he relieved that I'm not, because it means not having to answer any uncomfortable questions from his teammates and fans?

Fuck. That's not fair. I'm an ass for even thinking that,

but these days it's getting harder and harder to keep this up. I wasn't raised to hide who I am. My parents encouraged all six of us kids to be *proud* of our identities, to follow our hearts and do what makes us happy and to hell with what anyone else thinks. All my siblings have taken that advice to heart.

Tammy married her high school sweetheart at eighteen, turning down a scholarship to an East Coast school in favor of community college, because her husband Mark and the Canning clan were the most important things to her.

Joe was brave enough to be the first Canning to file for a divorce, even though he'd admitted to me how embarrassed he was about it, and how it made him feel like a failure.

Jess churns through both boyfriends and careers like she's trying to set a Guinness Book record. But we don't judge her. Not much, anyway.

And me? For twenty-two years I dated only women, until life decided to throw me a curveball. I fell in love with another man and I embraced that. Being bisexual isn't a walk in the park. Trust me—I learned the hard way last summer that not everyone in this world is as open-minded and supportive as my family. But I chose happiness over other people's skewed opinions and cruel judgments. I chose *Wes*.

But now I have to hide that choice. I have to pretend that Ryan Wesley isn't my soulmate. I have to look at goddamn Instagram pictures of him dancing with hot chicks and pretend I'm not jealous.

Wish I was there too, I text back. Because it's true. I wish it was *me* at that charity benefit with him tonight.

"Canning?"

I spin around in surprise, instinctively tucking my phone into my pocket just in case Wes's name is visible on the display. Which pisses me off even more, because there I go hiding again.

Coby Frazier, one of the assistant coaches on my major juniors team, walks up to me with a warm smile. He's tailed by Bryan Gilles, an associate coach for one of my boss's other teams. Gilles is a quiet French-Canadian with a full beard and a love for plaid—the parka he's wearing tonight is actually plaid-patterned and the tails of the shirt under his coat? Also plaid.

"So you *do* exist outside the arena," Frazier teases. He slaps my shoulder in greeting. So does Gilles, who nods at me. "You got a hot date?"

I shake my head. "My date canceled at the last minute. And then I was going to catch the movie anyway, but apparently it's not playing here anymore."

"You should watch *Morph-Bots*," Frazier urges. "We just got out of the seven o'clock show. It was fucking awesome. I can't believe the shit they're doing with CGI these days."

I shrug. "I'm not into the whole robots fighting other robots craze. Always end up falling asleep."

Frazier grins. "How about cold beers and hot girls? You into that? Gilles and me are heading to the bar—come with us, eh?"

Since I moved to Toronto and started my new coaching job, my colleagues have showered me with invitations. *Come out for beers, man. Let's grab some grub. Come over for a barbecue this week, the wife would love to have ya.*

I've turned down most of the invites, because if I can't bring Wes, what's the point? Besides, it's a lot easier to hide the fact that you like dick if you keep everyone around you at a distance.

Tonight, I don't say no, because beers with the boys sounds

like a great distraction. It's either that or go back to my empty condo and stalk Wes on Instagram all night.

"Sure, I'm down," I tell the guys.

My phone buzzes in my pocket before I even finish my sentence. This time I ignore it, and follow Frazier and Gilles down the sidewalk toward the bar.

EIGHT

WES

"No one knows? *Really*?" Kristine/Kai gapes at me in our quiet nook in the corner of the ballroom. After nearly an hour on the dance floor, we finally decided to take a breather and now we're rehydrating. Or rather, dehydrating, because my scotch and her cosmo ain't exactly helping our daily water intake.

"No one," I confirm.

She shakes her head in disbelief, and her mane of dark curls falls over one bare shoulder. "Not a single one of your teammates?"

"Nope."

"But everyone on your college team totally knew you were gay." She lowers her voice at the last word, her gaze flitting around to make sure nobody can overhear us.

"That was college," I say quietly. "The NHL is a whole different ball game, baby."

"Puck game, you mean."

I grin. "Puck game," I echo.

Kai takes a sip of her drink. "That sucks, Ryan." She

sounds dismayed now. "Do you really think it would be a big deal if it came out?"

"The media would be all over it, hon. You know that."

She makes a disgusted sound. "Well, that's fucking ridiculous. Gay marriage is legal now. It's been legal in Canada for *ages*. Why are there still so many bigoted jerks in this world? And why aren't we shipping them all to Antarctica?"

A chuckle pops out. "Because we're nicer than they are."

"Maybe we shouldn't be. Maybe we should judge and persecute them right back so they know what it feels like."

I appreciate her support and sweet show of solidarity, but truth is, she has no idea what it feels like. Jamie is the only one I can share the frustration with, because he's the only one who's truly in this with me. And even then, we don't talk about it often, because it just depresses the shit out of us both.

"What are you two whispering about here in the corner?" Blake appears with a tumbler in hand and his trademark grin. His green eyes do a slow sweep of Kai's barely clad body before shifting over to me. "And why haven't you introduced me to this goddess, Wesley? I thought we were buds."

As Kai blushes prettily, I quickly introduce the two of them, and the three of us spend the next few minutes chatting until she excuses herself to use the ladies room. The moment Blake and I are alone, he gives me an exaggerated wink. "So."

"So," I echo.

"Nice job, Wesley. Though I'm kinda bummed you beat me to her. She's smokin'. That sweet mouth... Cheezus. I can think of a few places to put it."

"I'm sure you can."

"Can *you*, though? You two look pretty cozy. I'm jelly."

A prickle of paranoia creeps up my spine, and I choose my

words carefully, because Blake worded that oddly. Or did he? He probably just wants to know if Kai is available. If I've staked a claim. I hastily sip my scotch. "Naah, it's not like that. She used to date my teammate's brother. She's like a sister to me."

His face lights up. "So you're saying there's no dibs?"

"No dibs, man." I glance at the still-crowded dance floor and wonder how much longer I need to be here. The speeches ended ten minutes ago, but nobody seems to be leaving, and I don't want to be the first to bail.

"You think she's DTF or L-FAR?"

"L-FAR?" I echo blankly.

"Looking for a ring."

My lips twitch. Goddamn. Blake Riley is far too amusing for his own good. "I think you're safe," I tell him. "She's focused on her modeling career right now. I don't think she's aiming for anything serious."

"Sweetest words I've ever heard, brosky." He proceeds to chatter on about how much he loves being single, and it isn't until several moments have passed without a response from me that he stops talking and slants his head.

I feel like a bug under a microscope at Blake's suddenly intense scrutiny.

"I screwed up, didn't I?" he says.

I wrinkle my forehead. "What do you mean?"

"You didn't want to come to this party tonight." His examination continues, eyes going serious. "I shouldn't have assumed you wanted in. Ass, you, me, right?" He waves a sheepish hand. "I ruined your night, huh."

He puts this as a statement, not a question. And that paranoid tickle at my neck is back. "Black tie isn't really my thing. It reminds me of my parents' crowd."

Blake cocks his big head to the side. "You said you don't get along with your folks. What's that about?"

"Eh," I hedge. "They like their society soirees more than they like me."

He's still watching me. "My bad, Wesley. I'm sorry."

I shrug, searching for a way to put this conversation to rest. "I'm here now, penguin suit or not. And the women are sure easy on the eyes."

There's a long pause, and then Blake speaks again. "What's Jamie doing tonight?"

The tingle becomes a chill, which actually hardens my spine. Why is he bringing up Jamie? And he called him *Jamie*, not J-Bomb or some other light-hearted nickname that relegates Jamie to casual roomie territory.

"I don't know," I mutter. "He probably went out."

Blake keeps watching me.

The need to flee hits me hard, and I'm probably harsher than I should be as I snap, "Look, it's fine. I'm not thrilled to be here tonight, but it's been an okay time, all right?"

Luckily, we're interrupted by our teammates before Blake can respond—or keep prying. Eriksson leads the pack with Forsberg and Hewitt in tow. Clearly all three have been frequent visitors to the open bar tonight, because they're loud and rowdy as they join us.

"We're hitting up The Lantern House," Eriksson announces. He jabs the air in front of us. "You're coming."

"Sorry, man, but I've got plans," Blake drawls. He peers off in the distance, a slow smile stretching his mouth. "And there she is now."

Forsberg hoots as Blake ambles away from the group toward the stunning brunette who's just reentered the ballroom. Kai greets him with a dazzling smile, and it isn't long before the two of them are tangled together on the dance floor.

Good. This is awesome. Blake is officially occupied for the night, which means there's no chance of him showing up at the apartment when I get home.

If that had occurred to me earlier, I would have spent the whole evening introducing him to women.

Eriksson, however, isn't put off by Blake's desertion. He slings one big arm around my shoulders and says, "Guess it's just the four of us, kid. C'mon, let's get our pub on."

Aggravation clamps around my throat. No fucking way. I'm not going to a pub with these guys, not when Jamie is waiting for me at home. Not when I already allowed this goddamn benefit to ruin our night. If I head home now, at least Jamie and I could have a few hours together before bed. We've both got early practices tomorrow.

"Sorry, I'm passing, too."

But I underestimated Eriksson's tenacity. Or maybe I just hadn't realized how much my friendship seems to mean to him. "Aw, don't bail on me. This day has been shit from the moment I woke up." His voice goes awkward. "I need my team to rally around me tonight."

"You got it, bro," Forsberg says. "Can't believe I'm passing up easy pussy for you tonight. But even I can respect the bros-before-hos rule every now and then."

How I hate that phrase. But the pathetic expression in Eriksson's red-rimmed eyes triggers a rush of guilt. The man's wife just told him she wants a divorce, for chrissake. And I'm standing here telling him to fuck off because I want to go home and snuggle with my boyfriend?

"Okay," I finally say, reaching out to pat his arm. "I'm there."

NINE

JAMIE

My new friends choose The Lantern House, which turns out to be a pretty big place. We snag a high table in the back, and Frazier wades through the crowd to get us a pitcher. The thump of music and the buzz of the chatter around me lifts my spirits. It startles me to realize how infrequently I get out to a bar like this. For a twenty-three-year-old guy, I'm practically a shut-in these days. Gilles tells a funny story about his team getting lost in Quebec, and I find myself laughing more easily than I have in a while.

I've missed this. Wes and I visit restaurants together sometimes, but it's just not the same as carrying on at a bar for a few hours.

"Play some darts? That board just opened up." Gilles points toward the back.

"Let's do it," I agree.

He lays out the rules for a three-man game, and we start shooting. And with that comes the inevitable smack talk. "You're a goalie, Canning. Betcha can't hit the bullseye," Frazier crows.

When I do, he has to buy the next round.

Maybe it's inevitable, but three attractive guys playing darts on a Saturday night will attract the ladies. It isn't long until a trio of young women is watching, cheering us on.

Frazier and Gilles camp it up even more. We're into our second pitcher when Frazier dares Gilles to let him shoot an apple off his head with a dart. The girls dissolve into giggles. And thank fuck nobody can find an apple, because I really don't want to spend the rest of this evening in an emergency room with Gilles and the dart in his eye.

At any rate, the girls sort of descend on us when we give up the dartboard. The assertive brunette claims Frazier, who's hotter than Gilles, with his dimples and impressive forearms that I really shouldn't be noticing. The brunette isn't as cute as her two blond friends, but she's got a bossy vibe that's sexy in its own way.

Apparently one of the blondes has a thing for plaid, because she soon attaches herself to Gilles's arm. Even though I've quite intentionally avoided eye contact with all three of them, the law of the jungle applies. The third girl moves in, planting herself in front of me, nodding whenever I speak. She puts a hand on my back and laughs when I make a joke.

It's not the first time someone has hit on me in a bar, so it's not like I'm going to panic. And she doesn't seem like the pushy type, either. I can buy a girl a couple of friendly drinks for an hour and then pull an oh-look-at-the-time-I-gotta-run. But part of me is just really weary of the charade. Because there is someone in my life and I'd feel completely differently about the next hour if he was here with me.

You can't have everything you want, though.

That's my last thought before I happen to turn my head and scan the front of the pub. My eye snags on a cluster of tuxedos near the bar. I recognize one of them immediately. The back of Wes's head is all I can see from here. Just dark, spiky hair closely shorn where it approaches his neck. And I know that neck. I like to put my mouth on the smooth skin right there, and when I suck on that spot, he moans.

The blonde next to me is talking, her hand on my arm now. But I can't even hear what she's saying, because I'm so distracted by the pickle I'm in. Fumbling into my pocket I pull out my phone and open up my text messages. *Behind you*, I send to Wes. I want to warn him that I'm here. *Turn around.*

He doesn't, though.

Meanwhile, my new BFF Tracie has me in one hand and a pint glass in the other. Suddenly this night out isn't fun anymore.

WES

Eriksson is a mess.

I've never seen him so sloppy drunk. He's in turn gregarious, angry and right on the verge of weepy. "Another round, guys?" he slurs. "Not like I have anyone to go home to."

He is killing me. Eriksson is one tough motherfucker. I once watched him push his own loose tooth back into place right on the bench in the middle of a game after taking a hit to the face. He played the third period with a smile on his face and blood dribbling down his chin. But toughness, apparently, does not extend to having your family walk out on you. He's dangling off an emotional ledge, and I don't think I could catch him even if we were closer friends.

It's getting late and he's getting drunker. What to do? I

keep praying that one of the others who knows him better will step forward and take charge—put him in a cab, or take 'im home for the night.

Eriksson is like a slow-moving train wreck that I'm forced to watch.

Unhelpfully, fans keep approaching us. A group of guys in tuxes in a pub is always going to stand out. But Toronto is a hockey town, and the faces around me are famous ones. Drunk well-wishers keep coming up and asking for autographs. One girl asks me to sign her tummy. This I do without actually touching her with my hands. "It tickles!" she shrieks.

"My house is, like, empty," Eriksson moans.

I'm going to lose my mind within minutes.

There's another fangirl shriek, and I feel another small clot of fans descending. A brunette steps in front of me. "Omigod, you're the rookie Ryan Wesley! Loved your goal on Montreal last week! Will you sign my phone case?"

"Sure," I say as she invades my personal space. I smile anyway, because what is the alternative, really? Then I raise my head to see who else is crowding us—and get a shock.

Jamie is standing five feet away, staring me down with angry laser eyes. He's being dragged toward me by a slight, blond girl.

"Don't you want to meet the team! You're hockey players, too! This is so exciting."

Three girls swarm, and two of their male companions hang back at a more comfortable distance, their hands in their pockets and "aw, shucks," smiles on their faces.

Then there's Jamie. He raises an eyebrow as if to ask, *How the hell do we get in these situations?*

The pushy brunette grabs one of the other guys. "This is Frazier and Gilles and Canning!" she says brightly, as if we're all going to be BFFs now. I recognize those guys' names, too. They're Jamie's co-coaches. "Say hi, boys! This is awesome."

Her companions shake hands with my very tolerant teammates, even if Eriksson sways a little. Jamie keeps his arms crossed. And I can't stand it anymore. I hold out a hand to him. "Hey—how are you? Long time no see." I give him a wink, waiting for a smile.

Jamie takes my hand and gives it a pump. "It's really been too long," he mutters.

"*Wait!*" The blonde who's sticking close to him squeals. "You *know* Ryan Wesley? No wayyyyy!"

Why yes. Biblically. "We go way back," I say. "Hockey camp."

Her pretty little mouth falls open, and I see her look at Jamie as if seeing him for the very first time. Her eyes widen and her hand tightens on his arm.

I hate seeing it there.

"You've been holding out on me!" she squeals, then punches him lightly in the chest.

"Is that so." Jamie's face probably looks friendly enough to everyone in this bar but me. You'd have to know him as well as I do to see how irritated he is.

She steps closer and tips her chin up toward his. The maneuver is unmistakably flirtatious. "What *position* do you play?"

I let out a snort before I can think better of it. But she doesn't notice, anyway. This chick wraps her arms around my man and sort of backs him away from the group.

Jesus, I can't stand the sight of it. So I turn my back. If I thought the night was grim ten minutes ago, we're talking suicide alley now.

"Hey, Forsberg." I reach through the scrum to appeal to the

man Eriksson's been skating with for the last three years. "What's your plan for our friend, here?" If he won't raise his hand to solve this problem, I'm gonna make him do it.

"Guess I should take 'im home."

You think? I give it three more minutes, and when Forsberg doesn't act, I nudge him again. "It's only gonna get harder if he drinks more."

"'Spose you're right." Finally—*finally*—he collars Eriksson and says, "Time to go, buddy. We did enough damage tonight already."

No kidding.

I turn around to see how Jamie is making out, and holy shit. He is almost *making out.* The blond girl has pancaked herself against him, and her hands are wandering toward his ass. I'm completely unprepared for the surge of helpless, jealous anger that chokes me at the sight of their two golden heads so close together. Seriously, I feel like hurling a bar stool against the wall.

Jamie is attracted to women. Even after eight months together, it's still hard for me to come to terms with that. I've seen the way he checks out girls on the street sometimes, and it kills me. Not that I'm a saint—I've checked out other guys before, too. It's human nature to appreciate the hotness of others. But it's so fucking scary to think that I'm competing with both men *and* women for Jamie's affections.

You're not competing for him, dumbass. He's already yours.

The reminder calms me down. Slightly. But as I watch, a few more details of the scene between Jamie and this girl begin to stand out. Jamie is actually squirming with discomfort, not lust. And the hand that I thought was holding hers is actually trying to peel her palm off his butt cheek. "'Scuse me," I hear him say. "Gotta hit the head."

Swear to God I hear a sucking sound when he pries her off his chest. Then Jamie darts toward the restrooms faster than I've ever seen him move, even on skates.

And just like that I'm following him. I don't give a shit who sees. The knot of jealousy in my gut is more urgent than my fear of being discovered.

Some guy who's exiting the john holds the door open for me. I push inside the shadowy room, where I find Jamie standing at the sink, washing his hands. "Hey," he says in surprise.

I say nothing. I grab his elbow and nudge him toward one of the three stalls. I practically shove him inside and bang the door shut. Then I push him up against the dented metal wall and kiss him. Hard.

He grabs my face in two wet hands and gives as good as he gets. He jams his tongue in my mouth and practically bruises me with his lips. It's an angry kiss. I hear myself grunt with surprise and anguish.

Don't get me wrong—it's hot as hell. But we're not about angry kisses, Jamie and me. We're more of a pants-the-other-guy-tickle-his-ass-and-then-laugh-as-we-fall-on-the-bed couple.

But not tonight.

I smack my hips into his, and the stall wobbles. I attack his mouth. My hands clutch at his shirt. He tastes like beer, but there's a cloying whiff of perfume that clings to him. I taste him even deeper to try to lose that foreign scent and shake off the disasters of the night.

But we hear the sudden sound of voices. They rise and

swell and then quiet down again as someone opens the door and lets it fall shut again.

We freeze, mouth to mouth. Our eyes lock at too-close range, distorting the view, so Jamie appears to be a pissed-off blond cyclops.

I ease my mouth off his, but our foreheads remain pressed together. And we're both trying not to pant from anger and exertion.

Whoever's outside the stall whistles drunkenly to himself. I hear the telltale liquid rush of pee hitting a urinal. It's probably only a minute later when the dude zips up and leaves. But it feels longer, because I have to stare into Jamie's ornery eyes. They're asking me why it has to be this way.

The bathroom door falls closed again, muffling the bathroom to silence, but it's another moment before we speak. "Tell your friends goodnight," I say roughly. "Let's go home."

"You first," he snaps. "You're the celebrity who can't walk through this place without getting stopped."

I want to argue the point, but that will only delay our trip home. So I do what needs to be done. I exit the stall and the bathroom. Only two of my teammates are left in the bar, and I say goodnight. Then I go outside to wait for Jamie on the sidewalk.

He takes longer, probably saying goodnight to his coworkers. I realize I haven't met *any* of the guys he works with every day. How fucked is that?

My mind serves up the memory of that chick rubbing herself against him. I make myself a little bit ill wondering if she's trying to persuade him not to leave alone. I know he won't do it, but I'm nauseous even so.

Finally he emerges, hands in his pockets, a dark expression on his face.

I stick my hand in the air, hoping for a cab to swing past and put an end to this crappy night. To my relief, one slows in front of me immediately. I open the door and gesture for Jamie to get in first. When he does, I practically sag with relief, right on the Toronto sidewalk.

We don't talk on the way home, and when we get into our apartment, Jamie heads right for the shower. Either he smells that perfume, too, or he's prepping for some angry make-up sex.

When he finally emerges, I'm in bed. Naked. Ready.

But Jamie puts on a pair of flannel pants and punches his pillow before getting in, back to me. Still hopeful, I roll toward him and kiss his shoulder. "I'm sorry, baby," I say. "Let me make it better."

"My head kind of aches," he mumbles.

If I were the crying type, that would have done me in.

Instead, I kiss his shoulder one more time. Then I roll onto my back and start counting the weeks until the end of the season. I don't think I can take this anymore. Not if it makes Jamie unhappy.

TEN

JAMIE

The next morning passes in a slow grind of tension and frustration.

Wes and I are not doing so great. He knows I'm upset over what happened last night. Running into him at that pub, having to pretend we're old acquaintances instead of lovers. No, *partners*.

To make matters worse, Wes's dad calls the afternoon after our debacle. Since Mr. Wesley never bothers to call, I get tense the moment I hear Wes say, "Hi, Dad. What do you need?"

The man never calls unless he needs something.

"Uh-huh," is all Wes says after listening for a moment. "I suppose it's possible."

This tells me nothing. I scrub down our kitchen sink as if I'm angry at it, wondering when he'll get off the phone and tell me what's up. And when he doesn't do that immediately, I find myself blasting the water in the sink. Then I whistle to myself. I'm making these noises because Roger Wesley doesn't like it that his son lives with a man. I don't exist to that asshole, so it's fun to remind him that I do.

Fun, if pathetic.

But Wes only moves out of range, carrying his phone into our bedroom where he can hear better.

So my childish quest to be acknowledged ends without satisfaction. But hey, I have a very clean sink.

When Wes finally reappears, I'm so cranky that I don't even ask what the old man wanted, because I'm not sure I can speak calmly.

He sits down at the bar and watches me until I finally give up the charade and throw down the sponge. "What?"

A beat passes before he speaks. I have never felt as raw as I feel right now. I've just discovered that falling in love has a dark side. When you're mad at the love of your life, it's impossible to feel joy.

"My dad called," he says finally.

"I got that," I say, but my tone is kinder than the words.

He nods. "Remember his buddy at *Sports Illustrated*?"

"Sure. The guy wanted to do an all-access kind of series about your rookie season."

Wes nods. "Well, now that my rookie season looks fruitful, he's pretty bummed that I said no. So he's pressuring dad to pry an exclusive interview out of me."

"Can't you just say no?" He had before.

My boyfriend stares at his hands. "This time he's working both ends of it. He's leaning on Frank to get him the story."

Ah. Frank is the PR guy, and Wes never says no to him, because he thinks the whole coming-out thing will go easier if Frank's on his side. "So...how about this—tell the guy that if he waits until June, you'll give him a story worth waiting for."

Wes looks up at me quickly. "I can't do *that*. It would be like dangling a mouse in front of a python and asking him not to strike. He'll just start digging. With that kind of hint, how hard would it be for him to find what he wants, then just break the story without my help?"

Shit. "Okay. That won't work."

"You think?" His voice cracks. "Babe, this is all I think about. I've been through every possible scenario. It's not for lack of trying, all right?"

I know he feels cornered. I get it. The problem is that I don't see why that will just go away come June. I'm worried that he won't go through with it. That the idea of a media circus will be so abhorrent to him that he won't be able to bring himself to pull the trigger.

What the hell will I do then? If Wes decides he needs another year of professional hockey under his belt before he comes out, I don't think I'll be able to suck it up.

Suddenly our apartment is just too small. "Going for a run," I announce.

"Right now?" he asks. Usually we spend his pre-game hours together unless I'm away at a game or practice.

"Just for a little while," I mutter, not looking him in the eye.

After a quick change, I stick earbuds in and leave the apartment. There are treadmills in the "health center" on the roof of our building. I set a machine to a blisteringly fast pace and pound my frustrations into the rubber conveyor belt.

I know you're supposed to talk this shit out. The problem with that idea is that I know just what Wes will say. He'll promise me that in June the secrets are over. But now that date seems so arbitrary to me. Why not May? Why not July?

Why ever?

Even though I know Wes is a man of his word, I can't help but worry. It's a hard thing I'm asking him to do. I hate being the one who makes him do it, too. If it goes poorly, he might actually resent me.

I will fucking *hate* that.

A half hour later I'm sweaty but no less miserable. As I head back down to our apartment, I wonder what I'll say if Wes wants to talk about it.

As it turns out, we don't talk about it.

Getting off the elevator on our floor, I hear pounding. "Wesley! You crazy beast! Open up!"

Blake Riley is standing in front of our door.

"Hey," I say, because I'm not smart enough to retreat to the gym for another mile or two until he gives up.

"J-Bomb!" Blake's expression lights up when he sees me. "I have the most vicious hangover. It's like a sheep with fangs, gnawing on my head!"

"A...sheep?" What? I nudge him out of the way and open the door to our apartment.

"Dude, you need a shower," Blake motor-mouths as he follows me inside, heading for the kitchen. "I need two pizzas and a quart of coffee. How's your team doing, man? What do you like on your pizza?"

"Um..." I don't know which question to answer first.

"Sausage or mushrooms?"

At least that's a multiple choice question. "Both?"

"I knew I liked you. Go shower. I'll make coffee," the guy says from the center of my own kitchen.

A bathroom door opens from deep inside our apartment. "Babe?" Wes calls.

Fuck! "What do you need, *Ryan?* And Blake wants to know what you like on pizza!"

Blake looks up from his phone. "Your nickname is Babe? Like that pig in the movie?" He snorts.

"No, moron," Wes says as he rounds the corner. "Like Babe Ruth."

"You grumpy, Wesley? Hungover, too? I'm ordering pizza." He puts the phone to his ear. "Sure I'll hold. But please hurry, we're desperate."

I leave them without another word and take my shower in our en suite bathroom. Blake is too busy talking his ass off to notice. When I come back ten minutes later, he hasn't moved from the kitchen. Now he's holding a cup of coffee in one of the mugs my mom made, and it makes me feel stabby to choose one with the Toronto team's insignia on it instead.

Given the mood I'm in, coffee is probably a poor idea. But I pour it anyway.

It's no comfort to me that Wes looks at least as miserable as I do.

The pizzas arrive during a Blake Riley monologue about the movie *Babe* and the model he hooked up with last night and something about sheep being scary. I'm not listening too carefully. While Blake steps into the hallway to pay, Wes reaches across the counter and puts a hand on mine. "How was your run?"

"Okay." I'm not sure I could spill all the fears in my heart even if Blake *wasn't* here. But his presence sure doesn't help.

Wes sighs, and then Blake is back, and we eat pizza and watch a daytime talk show that only Blake seems interested in.

I make sure to give the death chair a glare as Blake carries his plate over to our coffee table. Wes is not a stupid man. He takes the death chair, dropping onto the ugly upholstery like a man resigned. Then I feel like an ass because he has to play the Oilers in a few short hours, and I hope his whole lower back doesn't seize up from sitting there.

If they lose tonight, I'm going to feel even guiltier than I already do. Yay.

"You ever come to our games, J-bomb?" Blake asks as I finish off the last of my pizza.

"Sometimes," I say with my mouth full. "I have to coach a late practice tonight, though."

"Sweet," he says, taking my plate from my hands. I do appreciate his clean-up skills, though I'm not sure they entirely make up for his barging in unannounced.

As Blake lumbers off to the kitchen, my phone beeps. I lean forward and see the Facebook notification icon. Normally I wouldn't care enough to click on it, not unless it's from someone in my family, but Wes is sulking hard in his chair and I'm sulking hard inside, and I desperately need a distraction before I pick a lover's quarrel right in front of Blake.

I open the app and find a status update from my college friend Holly. It says she's in a relationship now, and there are two photos—pixie-sized Holly on the left and a huge mountain of a man on the right. They make such an unlikely couple—physically, anyway—that I can't fight a snort.

Which of course captures Blake's attention. He's finished cleaning up, and now he's leaning over the back of the couch, peeking at my phone.

"Ooooh," he says in approval, tapping one blunt fingertip on Holly's picture to enlarge it. "And who is this sexy little elf creature?"

"Ah, just a friend from college," I answer. For some absolutely stupid reason, I'm compelled to add, "An ex, I guess."

Blake's gaze shoots toward me in surprise. Or rather, confusion. I can't make heads or tails of his expression. Nor do I miss the tensing of Wes's broad shoulders in my peripheral vision.

"Holly's messaging?" Wes sounds nonchalant. I know better.

"Naah," I say without looking at him. "Status update on Facebook popped up. I guess she has a new boyfriend."

"Good for her." Again, the edge in his tone is only notice-able if you know him as well as I do.

One of Wes's biggest fears when we first got together was that my attraction to women would come between us. I've assured him over and over again that he's the only one I want, but sometimes I wonder if he'll ever believe me. The thing about Wes, he's used to disappointment. Hell, I think disap-pointment isn't something he fears, but *expects*—like he's forever living in a state of when-will-the-other-shoe-drop. *When will my parents officially disown me, when will the world find out I'm gay, when will the team drop me, when will Jamie leave me.*

Usually I do everything I can to offer him that reassurance he needs, but at the moment, my nerves are too raw. I can't give him what he needs right now, and so I remain focused on Blake rather than my clearly agitated boyfriend.

"You were tapping this sweet bundle of goodness?" Blake says slowly.

I nod. "It was more of a friends-with-benefits thing." I get the feeling that he doesn't believe me. Or that if he does, he can't make sense of it.

Worry pricks at my insides. I thought Wes and I had been doing a decent job keeping Blake Riley in the dark, but now I'm starting to wonder how successful we've actually been.

I finally find the courage to seek out Wes's eyes, but he doesn't meet my gaze. His jaw is twitching. And he's white-knuckling the arms of the death chair. Fuck. Why is everything so hard right now? What if it's always like this?

"We should head out," Blake tells Wes.

My boyfriend rises from the chair, still avoiding my gaze. "I'll grab my gear," he mutters.

A few minutes later, Wes and Blake leave for pre-game warm-ups, and I'm almost relieved. The tension between Wes and me is unbearable. Of course, now the apartment is as quiet as a tomb. I'm left alone with my pessimistic thoughts.

It's hard to say which is worse.

THE NEXT MORNING I'm out of the house while Wes is still snoring softly in our bed. I'm not intentionally sneaking out like a thief in the night—well, morning. I have an early staff meeting to get to, and I feel bad waking him up, even if it's just with a quick goodbye kiss. Or at least that's my excuse and I'm sticking to it.

But I don't have a good excuse for why I pretended to be asleep when he got home from the game last night. Cowardice, maybe? Exhaustion?

I'm sure Wes is as tired of the tension as I am. I know he is. All those years we spent at hockey camp together, we had no problem talking to each other. All we fucking did was talk. About music. About where we grew up. Our thoughts on different brands of deodorant and the Superman/Batman schism and about which presidential nominees had the stupidest names.

And now we're a couple, and we've forgotten how to have a conversation. It's like we're two acquaintances making small talk about the weather. Hell, the past couple days, it felt like we *were* just acquaintances, tiptoeing around each other in our condo, fearful of saying the wrong thing and upsetting the other person. We haven't even discussed the night at the pub, for Pete's sake. And sex? Forget it. We haven't so much as kissed since our angry make-out sesh in the pub bathroom.

I don't know how to make things better. I love this guy, I really do. But I didn't anticipate how hard this would be.

I'm still agonizing about it during the coaches' meeting, and I desperately hope my colleagues don't notice how distracted I am as our boss, Bill Braddock, drones on about ordering new equipment and the summer clinic the organization will be running. An hour later, the meeting blessedly comes to its conclusion, and I scrape back my chair, eager to get home. It's a bit ridiculous of me to go back to the condo right now, but practice isn't for another three hours, and the last thing I feel like doing is hanging around the arena.

"Jamie." Braddock's voice stops me before I can dart out the door.

I swallow a sigh, and slowly turn around. "Yeah, Coach?"

"Everything all right?" His tone is light, but there's concern in his eyes.

"Everything's great," I lie.

"You looked a bit distracted this morning." Shit. I guess someone did notice. Bill's gaze sharpens. "I know your goalie is struggling, but I wouldn't want you to take it personally."

I don't. It's just one more thing going sideways in my life. "He'll pull through," I tell Bill. "He has the skills, but the kid is just having a rough patch. Every goalie goes through 'em."

Bill nods thoughtfully. "True. But maybe we need to offer him some more support. I could ask Hessey to spend some time with the kid. Try to help him find his confidence. We don't just breed champions here. We shape young men and women. Luckily, we have all the resources we need to shower on those who are struggling."

A zing of panic shoots up my spine. "Give me a couple of weeks with him," I say more calmly than I feel. I can't have Bill thinking that my coaching isn't enough. What the hell am I here for, then? "If Dunlop gets the impression that he's a problem child, that won't do a thing for his confidence."

Braddock rubs a hand over his chin. "If that's how you want to play it. But your team's morale is low, so the Dunlop kid's psyche isn't the only one that needs massaging. I think a little extra love and attention from the coaching staff might be just the thing they need to pull together."

My heart sinks into my shoes. I don't want a more senior coach to solve Dunlop's problem when I can help him myself. And Braddock is a smart man, but if there's a coach on our team who needs some extra support, it's Danton and his big fucking mouth. I can't believe he doesn't see that. "I'll check in with you next week," I promise.

Bill claps a hand onto my shoulder. "We'll talk soon. I look forward to it." Then he leaves me there to stew in my own aggravation.

I feel like all I've done these past couple months is lose. Lose patience, lose the ability to talk to my boyfriend, lose that indescribable ease that always existed between me and Wes.

But have we really lost it, or just misplaced it? I agonize about it some more as I hop on the subway and head home. Wes has surely left for his morning skate, and I'm relieved at the timing. Then I'm guilty for feeling relieved. And angry for feeling guilty. And annoyed for feeling angry. My emotions don't like me today.

The first thing I notice when I enter the living room is the chair. Or lack thereof. The death chair is gone.

My jaw falls open. I stalk toward the brand new chair that is taking the place of the armchair that's haunted my nightmares for months. Wes must have ordered this yesterday, because I'm now staring at a big, black, cushy contraption that seems to have more knobs and dials than any chair has a right to have.

There's a post-it note stuck on one of the padded arms. I snatch it up and skim Wes's familiar chicken-scratch scrawl.

Dude at the store said this one will be better for our backs. Ten different massage settings. We should use it on our balls and see if it doubles as a sex toy. Fingers crossed.

I read the note again. I look at the chair again. I'm torn between laughing and cursing.

My humor fades fast, though, because...damn it, this is classic Wes, thinking a piece of furniture will erase the tension between us.

I crumple the note between my fingers. Wes is fooling himself if he thinks bruised feelings and growing resentment can be smoothed over by a chair.

ELEVEN

JAMIE

When Friday comes, Wes leaves for a game in New York, and, frankly, I'm relieved again. I hate myself for feeling this way, but I've had a bitch of a time pasting on a happy face this week. I'm not having success with that now either, because my team's scrimmage today is a total disaster.

While Wes's team had won both of their home games this week, mine is on a four-game losing streak since our tourney in Montreal. Morale is low. The boys are angry and frustrated, and it's showing in their game play.

I blow the whistle for the third time in ten minutes, skating toward the two red-faced teenagers who are exchanging not-so-pleasant words in the faceoff. "Cool it," I snap when one of them hurls a rather nasty insult about his teammate's mother.

Barrie doesn't even look repentant. "He started it."

Taylor protests. "Bullshit!"

They break out in another round of heated bickering, and it takes a few seconds for me to figure out what they're bitching about. Apparently Barrie had accused Taylor of being the reason we lost our last game, since Taylor is the one who drew a completely unnecessary penalty that resulted in the other team scoring on the power play. Taylor refused to accept the blame (and why should he? It takes a lot more than one player's error to lose a game) and started chirping that Barrie's single mom is a cougar.

It's obvious my players are not handling our recent losses very well.

"Enough!" I slice my hand through the air, silencing the two teens. I glare at Barrie. "Throwing blame around is not going to un-lose us those games." I glare at Taylor. "And talking trash about someone's mother is not going to make you any friends."

The boys' expressions darken sullenly.

I blow my whistle again, making them both jump. "One-minute penalties for unsportsmanlike behavior. Sin bin—both of you."

As they skate off toward their respective penalty boxes, I notice the unhappy expressions of their teammates. I get it. I hate losing, too. But I'm a twenty-three-year-old ex-college hockey player with plenty of losses under his belt and a thick skin that formed as a result. These are sixteen-year-olds who have always excelled in the sport, always been the best players on whatever middle school or junior high teams they were recruited from. Now they're in the major juniors competing with guys who are as good if not better than they are, and they're not used to no longer being the best.

"Je-sus fuckin' Christ," Danton mutters to me an hour later, as we trudge into the coaches' locker room. "These little faggots are spoiled rotten—"

"Don't use slurs," I interject. But it's like yelling into the wind. His rant doesn't break stride.

"—that's why they keep losing," he goes on. "They have no discipline, no work ethic. They think the wins are just gonna be handed to them on a silver platter."

Frowning, I sink onto the bench and unlace my skates. "That's not true. They've worked their asses off for years to reach this point. Most of these kids learned to skate before they learned to walk."

He makes a derisive sound. "Exactly. They were hockey wonder kids, showered with praise by their parents, teachers, coaches. They think they're the best because everyone *tells* them they're the best."

They *are* the best, I want to argue. These kids have more talent in their pinkie fingers than most players only dream of having, including ones currently playing in the NHL. They just need to hone that talent, build on the skills that already come naturally to them and learn how to get even better.

But there's no point in arguing with Danton. The man is a decent player, but I'm starting to think that his ignorance is a disease without a cure. Frazier told me the other night that Danton grew up in a "hick town up north" (Frazier's words, not mine), where prejudice and ignorance are pretty much passed down from generation to generation. I wasn't surprised to hear it.

I hurriedly shove my skates in my locker and slip into my boots and winter coat. The less time I spend with Danton, the better. Though it bums me out that I can't bring myself to like the man, seeing as how he's the one I work most closely with.

When I step out of the arena five minutes later, I'm disheartened to find that it's still snowing. I woke up this morning to a blizzard raging outside my window. As a result, practice was postponed three hours until the city's snowplows could take care of the mountains of snow that had dumped onto the streets overnight. I ended up driving Wes's Honda Pilot to work because I didn't want to deal with the long walk to and from the subway in such shitty conditions.

I trudge through the snowy parking lot and slide into the big black SUV, instantly switching on the butt warmers and blasting the heat. White flakes fall steadily beyond the windshield, and I wonder if the weather is this bad in New York. Wes texted earlier to say they'd landed safely, but with the snow falling harder than it had this morning, I'm suddenly worried he might not make it back tonight. Or maybe I'm just relieved again. If Wes is snowed in, that means another night of not having to pretend things haven't gone to the shitter between us.

I swallow a groan and pull out of the parking lot, but I'm only five minutes into the slow drive home when my phone rings. Since my Bluetooth is paired with the SUV, I can see on the car's dash screen that my sister is calling. All I have to do is click a button to answer, leaving my hands free to steer the car through the foot of snow on the road.

"Hey," I greet Jess. "What's up?"

Instead of *hello*, she says, "Mom's worried about you. She thinks aliens descended on Toronto and turned you into a pod person."

"Gleep glorp," I say monotonously.

My sister's laughter echoes in the car. "I said aliens, not robots. I'm pretty sure extraterrestrials have a more advanced language than gleep glorp." She pauses. "Seriously, though. Are you okay over there in Siberia, Jamester?"

"I'm fine. I have no idea why Mom's worried—I spoke to her on the phone last night."

"That's why she's worried. She said you didn't sound like your usual self."

Not for the first time, I curse my mother for knowing me so damn well. She'd called while Wes and I were watching *Banshee*—on opposite ends of the couch. It had been another tension-filled night for us, but I thought I'd sounded pretty chipper on the phone.

"Tell her there's no reason to worry. Everything is okay here. I promise."

Unfortunately, Jess knows me as well as Mom does. Of all my siblings, she's the one who's closest in age to me, and the two of us have always been close.

"You're lying." Suspicion sharpens her voice. "What aren't you telling me?" There's a sudden gasp. "Oh no. Please don't tell me you and Wes broke up."

Pain shoots through my heart. Just the thought fills me with panic. "No," I say quickly. "Of course not."

She sounds relieved. "Okay. Thank God. You had *me* worried now."

"Wes and I are fine," I assure her.

Another pause, then, "You're lying again." She curses softly. "Are you guys having problems?"

Frustration has my fingers tightening over the steering wheel. "We're fine," I repeat, grinding out each word.

"*James*." Her tone is firm.

"*Jessica*." My tone is firmer.

"I swear to God, if you don't tell me what's going on, I'm siccing Mom on you. And Dad. Actually, no—I'm calling *Tammy*."

"Aw shit, don't do that." The threat is enough to loosen my lips, because as much as I love our older sister, Tammy is even worse than Mom when it comes to me. When I was born, twelve-year-old Tammy had informed everyone in the family that I was *her* baby. She would carry me around like I was her doll and fuss over me like a mother hen. As I got older, she eased up a bit, but she's still ridiculously overprotective of me, and the first person to come to my rescue whenever I'm in trouble. Or when she *thinks* I'm in trouble.

"I'm waiting…"

Jess's stern voice brings another silent groan. I take a breath, then offer the fewest amount of details possible. "Wes and I are in a weird place right now."

"Cryptic, much? I mean, define weird. And by place, are we talking literal place? Are you at an S&M club right now? Did you join the circus?"

I roll my eyes. "Yes, Jessica, we joined the circus. Wes trains seals and I ride the bears. We bunk with the bearded lady and the guy who swallows swords."

"Is that a gay euphemism? Swallowing swords?" She laughs at her own stupid joke before going serious again. "Are you guys fighting?"

"Not really."

I reach an intersection and slowly pump the brakes until the SUV skids to a stop. Up ahead, I notice an ominous line of cars and a whole lot of red taillights. Shit, is there an accident up there? I've been driving for ten minutes and I'm barely half a mile away from the arena. At this rate, I'll never get home.

"Damn it, Jamie. Will you please stop with this vague bull-shit and talk to me like an adult?"

I press my lips together, but it doesn't stop the confession from flying out. "It's fucking hard, okay? He's not fucking home half the time, and when he *is* home, all we do is hide. We hide in our condo, we hide from the press, we just fucking *hide*. And I'm sick of it, all right?"

Her breath hitches. "Oh. Okay, wow. Those were a lot of F-bombs. Um." Jess softens her tone. "How long have you been unhappy?"

The question catches me off guard. "I'm...not unhappy." No, that's not true. I *am* unhappy. I...I just miss my boyfriend, damn it. "I'm frustrated."

"But you knew going into this that you were going to keep the relationship on the DL," Jess points out. "You and Wes agreed you weren't coming out until the season ends."

"If we even do." The most cynical part of me keeps getting stuck on that. What if Wes decides he's not ready to tell the world he's gay? What if he sits me down and begs me to keep quiet for another year? Or for the entire duration of his pro career? Or forever?

"Wait, has Wesley changed his mind?" my sister demands. "Or did the team ask him to keep pretending he's straight?"

"I don't think so. Wes said the PR department already has a statement prepared for when the news breaks. And I have no idea if he changed his mind. We're not communicating too well lately," I admit.

"Then start communicating."

"It's not that easy."

"It's as easy as you make it." She goes quiet for a beat. "Jamie, you're the most open, honest person I know. Well, you and Scottie. Joe and Brady?" She names our two other brothers. "They act like talking about their feelings is an admission of weakness or something. But you and Scott are like this huge inspiration for me—proof that not all men are tight-lipped jerks. Actually, Wes is pretty open too. I think that's why you guys are so good together. You never, ever shy away from difficult conversations. You always find a way to work through shit."

She's right. Wes and I have known each other since we

were kids. The only time we've ever had trouble talking to one another was when Wes disappeared from my life for three years after we hooked up at hockey camp. I forgave him for that, though. I understood why he shut me out—he'd felt guilty about possibly taking advantage of me, and he'd been confused about his own sexuality. At the time, it was something he'd needed to work through on his own.

But this distance between us…it's something we need to work through *together*. And ignoring the issue isn't going to achieve that. Jess is absolutely right—Wes and I don't usually avoid difficult conversations. But this time we *are* avoiding it, and that's only making things worse.

"I should talk to Wes," I say with a sigh.

"No shit, Sherlock. Now thank me for my supreme wisdom and ask me how *I'm* doing."

I can't help but laugh. "Thank you, oh wise one. And how are *you* doing?"

"Good and bad. I think my jewelry design business is a bust."

I'm tempted to toss out a *no shit, Sherlock* of my own, but I bite my tongue, because I know Jess is sensitive about her career. Or her lack of career, rather. My sister, God bless her, is the most indecisive person I've ever met. She's twenty-five and has had more jobs than I can count. She's also enrolled in and dropped out of half a dozen college programs, and created about a dozen Etsy shops that went nowhere.

"Didn't Mom and Dad lend you money for all those jewelry-making supplies?" I say warily.

"Yup," she answers glumly. "Don't tell them about this, okay? Mom is already stressed out about Tammy's delivery, so I don't want to upset her any more than she already is right now."

My entire body tenses. "Why is she worried about Tammy's delivery? Did the doctor say we should worry?" Our older sister is pregnant again and due to give birth next month. Her first delivery had gone smoothly, so I haven't given much thought to this one. I figured it would be the same as the first.

"No, I think it's just general nerves," Jess assures me. "This baby's a lot bigger than Ty was. I think Mom is scared Tammy will need a C-section. But seriously, you don't need to worry. Tammy's doing great. She's bigger than a house, but totally glowing and all that jazz. Anyway, the jewelry thing was my bad news. Do you want to hear the good news?"

"Hit me."

She offers a dramatic pause, then announces, "I'm going to become a party planner!"

Of course she is. I sigh and say, "Sounds fun."

"You could sound a little happier," she huffs. "I finally know what I want to do with my life!"

Sort of like how she *knew* she wanted to be a chef. And a bank teller. And a jewelry designer. But I keep my mouth shut, because in the Canning family, we support each other no matter what. "Then I'm very happy for you," I say in a sincere voice.

Jess chatters on about her new venture during the entire drive back to the condo, but I have to cut her off when I reach the underground parking lot because there's no service down here. We agree to chat on the weekend, and then I ride the elevator up to the apartment and shrug out of layers upon layers of winter clothing.

I shower and make myself some dinner as I wait for Wes's game to start, and then I plant myself on the couch with a plate of risotto and grilled chicken. I'm going to spend the evening cheering for my man. And when he gets home tonight, I'm going to take Jess's advice and talk to Wes about what I'm feeling.

That can't be so hard, right?

How hard is it? my traitorous brain echoes. And I smile as I take the next bite.

Something magical happens tonight. It's as if all my frustration and distress over my strained relationship with Jamie spills out onto the ice, turning me into an aggressive, determined, *unstoppable* motherfucker. I score a hat trick. A fucking *hat trick*, and the Toronto fans in attendance cheer their lungs out when the final period ends and our team beats New York in their own arena.

The locker room is buzzing with excitement, and nearly every man on the roster wanders over to slap me on the back or, in Eriksson's case, lift me off my feet and spin me around like I'm a toddler. "Shi-it, kid!" he exclaims. "That was the best fuckin' hockey I've ever seen!"

I smirk. "Three goals is nothing. Next game, I'll score four."

He guffaws. "I fucking love you, Wesley. I really do."

Coach pops in to give us a quick you-kicked-ass speech, which is unnecessary because we're already pumped up and riding a victory high. Several sports reporters are allowed into the locker room for post-game press, which is my least favorite part of playing in the NHL. All the interviews get tiresome after a while. Tonight, though, a female journalist corners me and decides to spice things up. Becky somebody—she covers us a lot.

"We've got a new feature here on Sports Tonight," she explains with a huge grin. "We call it Fast Five. Just five fun questions that tell the fans who Ryan Wesley *really* is."

Trust me, the fans don't want to know who I really am.

"So how about it?" she prompts.

Like I can really say no. Talking to the press is a requirement in my contract.

"Hit me," I say.

She gestures to her cameraman and the next thing I know, there's a microphone in my face and she's introducing me as "rookie sensation Ryan Wesley" to the viewers.

"Here we go!" she chirps, as if this is the most fun a person can have. "Coffee or tea?"

"Coffee," I reply, hoping all the questions will be this easy.

"Rock music or EDM?"

"Rock. Duh. I'm on a Black Keys kick right now."

"Awesome!" She grins. "Beach or mountains?"

Like I even remember. Vacations are for other people. "Beach," I say, because Jamie likes the beach, and I want to take him to one. Of course, I want a lot of things I can't have.

"Dogs or cats?"

"Eh, neither? I've never had a pet."

"Wow," she says, as if I've confessed to something scandalous. *If you only knew, little lady*. "Last one—do you go for the blond-haired, blue-eyed girl next door? Or do you like 'em dark and mysterious?"

"Uh, blond hair and brown eyes," I say quickly, happy to be rid of her.

She nods slowly, as if I've just said something fascinating. "Interesting choice. There can't be many women with that coloring."

"Well, Becky, maybe that's why I'm a bachelor."

She giggles, and the interview is finally over.

But when she turns away, I see Blake watching me, one eyebrow raised. So I do the closeted man's instant replay—running through everything I just said, searching for any incriminating nuggets. And I kick myself for telling the world that I like blondes with brown eyes.

Eh. There's no way Blake made that connection. He's probably over there wondering whether he'd be more likely to encounter a seventeen-foot velociraptor on a beach or in the mountains.

I finally hit the showers. By the time the team is on the bus and ready to head back to the airport, our manager makes an announcement from the front. "Guys? We're headed for the Marriott Marquis. Can't get out of La Guardia tonight."

At the same time I groan, Blake lets out a happy bellow. "Party in my room!" He reaches across the aisle to shove my shoulder. "Late flights suck, anyway. Let's order some food and some brewskis. It'll be great."

It won't, though. Because I need to see Jamie. I can't stand the distance between us and it needs to end. I thought getting rid of the death chair would be the perfect opening for us to hash everything out, but the only response I got from him was a grunted "Thanks for doing that." I'd answered with a teasing quip about how our condo was now ghost-free, since he's convinced someone died on that chair, but he'd barely cracked a smile.

Now I'm five hundred miles away from him, once again unable to fix a damn thing between us.

The hotel is only a mile from Madison Square Garden, but that's about a half hour in snowy traffic. And then we're delayed while they find rooms for all of us and pass out keys. Blake's food delivery shows up immediately, though, because he started working on it before we even got off the bus. ("Is this Brother Jimmy's BBQ? I have an emergency. It's bad, man. Only you can save me…")

He's ordered enough for everyone. No wonder the place was willing to deliver in the snow. So I perch on the radiator in his room and put away a pulled-pork sandwich. When I try to kick in some money, he waves me off. "You guys feed me sometimes, right? Your money's no good here. I got someone from room service bringing up a couple cases of beer. Stick around."

That's nice and all, but I need to talk to my man. And holy shit—my man wants to talk to *me*. Even though it's past midnight, I discover that Jamie has tried me on Skype three times in the past hour, which makes me giddy. Maybe I didn't strike out with the new chair, after all.

I sneak out when everyone's attention turns to the television and let myself into my room to find that my duffel bag has been delivered. I toss it onto the luggage rack and hang up my suit. The second I'm in sweats and a T-shirt, I return Jamie's call. "Hey!" I say when he answers. "Sorry it's so late. We're not getting home tonight."

"I figured, babe. Just wanted to see you so bad." He gives me a smile, and I'm so happy it's aimed at me I could cry.

My mouth works open and closed again. I have no idea what to say to get us past the rough week we just had. "I miss you so much," I tell him. Maybe that's lame, because we woke up in the same bed together this morning. But at least it's honest. "I mean, this past week…"

Jamie nods. His brown eyes crease around the edges as his brow furrows. I know that look. He has something on his mind, and I feel a pang of apprehension. Jesus. He wouldn't break up with me over Skype, would he?

Break up with me?

Oh dear God. Did that thought actually cross my mind? Did I really just fucking go from "rough patch" to "the love of my life is dumping me"?

"Babe?" I say in a timid voice that I've never heard leave my mouth before. My heart is pounding faster than ever. "You okay?"

He opens his mouth. "Yeah. I am. But I..." That sexy mouth closes, and then he sighs softly and offers another smile. This one looks a tad forced. "Just tell me about your game, because it was really fun to watch. Honestly, it reminded me why we're in this mess in the first place."

"Okay," I say, trying to wrap my head around the change in temperature between us. "Tonight I just unleashed myself out there. I'm not even sure what happened. It's like the net had a magnet under it just for me."

"Glad I wasn't the goalkeeper." Jamie lifts his sexy arms overhead, and I notice that he's in our bed. That's the wooden headboard I chose and the flannel sheets I bought when winter hit and Jamie began objecting to the cold.

A wave of homesickness hits hard. "I would kill to be there right now." Can't believe I messed up our time together last week. "I'd show you exactly how hot you look."

Jamie grins, and I practically smack myself in the head when realization strikes. "The beard! Where'd it go?" His face is now perfectly clean-shaven.

"Eh." He shrugs. "Got sick of it. Beards itch." He lifts a hand to his cheek and slides it slowly down to his chin.

When his little finger drags across his lower lip, I hear myself growl. "Do that again, Canning," I demand.

He quirks an eyebrow at me. "Why?"

"Because I need to see it."

He must hear something desperate in my tone, because he complies without any more lip. He lifts his palm to his cheek again and closes his eyes. I watch him take a deep breath, and on the exhale, he slides his hand down his jaw. When his fingertips reach his mouth, he slants his eyelids open just a couple of millimeters. Then he slides two fingertips into his mouth and sucks on them.

"Fuck," I breathe. I'm jealous of the fingers, the camera and the bed. "Take off your shirt for me."

For a fractional second I think he'll protest. We never do this. And we just had the shittiest week ever. But Jamie sits up a little, the camera losing him and showing me the ceiling instead. But then I see his arm sweep past, his T-shirt flying up and away. When the camera tilts again, Jamie's golden chest is on full display. He must have the tablet propped on his thighs because the camera angle shows his abs as a ramp up to his pecs. Wide-set copper nipples tease me at the edges of the shot. And one perfect hand lays across his bellybutton, the golden hairs glinting in high-def.

"Touch your chest," I order. I sound like a surly dom in some sleazy video chat. Except it's Jamie at the other end of the scene. And his fingertips are teasing his happy trail now. He spends a moment exploring the light trail of hair up the center of his belly.

My hips shift on the bed and my cock is hard already. I've seen Jamie shirtless a million times. But he's putting himself on display for me. His hand flattens out on his breastbone. He stretches across until his fingertips part over his nipple, and then he shivers.

I hear myself grunt with longing. If I were there, my mouth would be all over that. I'd shove his hand out of the way and suck on that pebbled nub. "Other one," I grind out. "And go slow, Canning."

First, he tips his head back on the pillows, and his eyes fall closed. Then his hand traces a slow path across his chest until he holds his pec in his palm. His thumb and forefinger circle the nipple and then give it a pinch. "Mmm," he sighs, and suddenly I have goosebumps everywhere.

"Canning."

"Yeah?"

"I am so fucking hard right now."

He smiles without opening his eyes. "How hard is it?"

A bark of laughter escapes me. "Lose the rest of your clothes, babe. I want to see you."

First he groans and stretches, making me wait. Then his chocolate eyes open again, and he licks his lips. I lose him on camera again and the room rolls under his motions. A few seconds later the camera tips slowly back toward vertical, and I have a view of Jamie's bent leg, his perfect hip, an oblique taste of his ass in shadow and most of his very bare chest. He must have propped the tablet up on my side of the bed.

His hand is between his legs, but I can only see the curve of his biceps and his muscular forearm. The rest is hidden from view.

"That's just mean," I say, and he grins. "If I were there, I'd…"

"What?" he asks in a rough voice. "Tell me exactly what you'd do first."

"I'd suck on your tongue until you got hard." Jamie's

mouth is his most pronounced erogenous zone. The man can practically come from me chewing on his lips.

"Too late," he says, dropping his leg to the bed. And there's my prize. I groan at the sight of Jamie's erection rising proudly from the thicket of pale, soft hairs at his groin. Even after these eight months, I still feel lucky every time he responds to me.

"God, I want a taste." My voice is gravel. "Are you leaking for me? Get that drop. Use *one* finger." Don't I feel like a bossy motherfucker tonight. My gaze is glued to the screen, though. He's really the one in charge. If that weren't true, I wouldn't be gripping myself over my sweatpants now, salivating at the view on the screen.

He does as I ask. He swipes one finger over his cockhead. Then he looks me right in the eye and licks his finger.

"Unngh," I say, and he sucks on his finger just to torture me. And I fucking love it. "Stroke yourself, now." I can't wait any longer. "Use one hand."

Jamie slides his hand down his chest and takes himself in hand. He gives his cock two good strokes.

"*Slower*," I demand. "That's it," I encourage when his movements turn languorous. His chest rises and falls with each breath, and his forehead is creased with tension. "Do you want to come, Canning?"

"Yeah," he breathes. "Been thinking about you a lot today. Waiting for your game to start…" He strokes himself a little faster. And I'm practically vibrating from the news that Jamie misses me. I haven't messed things up too badly. Or maybe I have, and it's just that our sexual chemistry isn't one of those things. We might be awful communicators lately, but turning each other on has never been a problem for us.

"Cup your balls," I offer. "If I was there, I'd suck on 'em."

He groans, and his eyes grow heavy-lidded. "I'd taste you everywhere. Every fucking place. Lube you up with my tongue." His rhythm falters just a little. His head falls back further, and he widens his legs, as if opening his body to me.

That's when looking isn't enough anymore. My own hand sneaks into my sweatpants, unbidden. I grip my cock and give it a squeeze. Screw it. I rise up on my knees and yank down my sweats. The angle of the tablet on the bed makes my dick appear comically large. It would be funny if I weren't so horny. I pump myself in earnest.

"Want you so bad, babe." My voice comes out as a gasp.

Jamie turns his head to see the screen. His lips part slightly as he tracks the frantic motion of my hand. His fist moves faster too, matching my tempo. For the first time all week, we're in sync. We're not even in the same room, yet I feel closer to him than I have in days, and we're so hot for each other right now that we're both panting and groaning and tugging our cocks with damn near desperation.

"Gonna come," he moans.

"Do it," I moan back. "Shoot on your chest."

He makes a beautiful sound, and a pearly ribbon of perfection paints a line down his abs. His six-pack clenches as he shoots again. And again.

Me too. I fuck my hand hard and fast. I want to be home with him so badly it aches. But the last dregs of my game-night adrenaline still fuel me. All that anguish and longing surge down my spine and I erupt in my own hand.

A minute passes while I calm down. Wordlessly, Jamie disappears from view. I clean myself up and wait for him to reappear.

After a minute or so, he slides into bed, under the covers

this time. Then he rolls to face the camera, his smooth cheek propped in his hand. "I spoke to Jess today," he starts.

I smile. I love Jamie's youngest sister. She's the flightiest chick I've ever met, but boy is she entertaining. "How's she doing? Still designing jewelry?"

He chuckles, and the sound warms my heart. "Nope. Now she wants to be a party planner."

"Of course she does."

"Hey, she might be good at it." But he's still chuckling even as he comes to his sister's defense. Then he goes quiet for a beat, and just like that, my nerves are raw again.

"What's wrong?" I ask gruffly.

I see the telltale dip of his Adam's apple as he swallows. "Nothing. Well, something. Not wrong, really, but just some things I wanted to get off my chest." Another beat. "But it can keep."

My throat is so tight I can barely speak. "Jamie..." That's all I manage to get out.

"You look beat," he says firmly. "You should get some sleep. We'll talk when you get back."

Talk...or break up?

I think he sees the panic on my face, because he lets out another breath, then speaks in a firm voice. "I love you. So much."

My heart does a little flip. He sounds like he means it.

Damn it, of course he means it, I assure myself. We fucking love each other. "I love you, too," I say softly.

A smile tugs at the corners of his mouth. "Good. Now go to bed. I'll see you tomorrow."

THIRTEEN

Wes gets two tickets to every home game, and I'm the only one who uses them.

They're awesome seats—on the aisle a couple rows behind the home team bench. In fact, I'm surrounded by other players' families. The veterans must get more seats or something because there's a whole section of people who screams whenever Lukoczik touches the puck. And the couple who sits next to me at every game are actually Blake Riley's parents. And giant Blake is the spitting image of his…mom. She's big-boned and big-mouthed with floppy hair shot through with gray.

His dad, on the other hand? A skinny professorial type. Genetics. They're nutty. And if Team Riley thinks it's weird that I show up alone for every game, they've never said so.

I've missed the warm-ups and make it to my seats just at the end of the national anthem. I'm quite proficient at "O Canada" these days. Had to learn the lyrics for my juniors team. The coach can't just stand there and mouth "watermelon watermelon watermelon" like an asshole.

Tonight I have a headache, which is unusual. So I stick the straw into a really overpriced soda I bought on the way in and take a deep drink, hoping that a shot of sugar and caffeine will cure it. I need to feel better, because Wes wants to go out after the game.

I do too, because in the three days he's been home, I've been slacking on my whole communicate-with-your-partner mission. I told Jess I'd talk to Wes, and I almost had the night we sex-Skyped the hell out of each other. But that moment of connection, seeing his gorgeous face peering back at me, so full of lust and longing...I hadn't wanted to ruin it by bringing our pesky problems into the mix. And then he came home, and all the real-life sex was even better than jerking off to a computer screen. I didn't want to ruin that either.

Maybe I'm a chicken shit. My sister would definitely agree with that. But things have been good, damn it. Wes and I have been in sync since he got back and I'm too terrified to put us out of rhythm again.

And I can't lie—a night out with Wes sounds like heaven. When I'd asked him where he wanted to go, he'd replied with, "Doesn't matter. Out. You and me. We'll sit at a bar or throw darts or shoot pool."

"Not pool," I'd answered. "My fragile ego can't take that kind of drubbing."

He'd snickered like a dolphin. "Fine. Whatever you want. The game isn't the point, anyway. You're the point."

I liked the sound of that.

Coach Hal has changed up the lines tonight. He does that sometimes. He has Wes on the second line with Blake and Lukoczik. The starters come out swinging tonight—Eriksson practically mows down the other center after the faceoff. As the puck begins its high-speed chase around the rink, I stop thinking about anything else but the game in front of me. My whole world is reduced to these twelve men jockeying for advantage and the weighty little rubber disk that means the world to the eighteen thousand people here tonight.

Wes vaults over the wall for his shift, and I can't help but lean forward in my seat. Ottawa got the puck back and is playing it safe, coddling the puck like old ladies out for a walk with a prized show poodle. They can't score this way, but they can frustrate Wes. His shift is over before he gets a chance to make anything happen.

And so it goes for a while, but I never lose interest. Some of my not-so-subtle family members have asked me if I mind being an NHL spectator instead of a player. I really don't, though I'm not sure they believe me. But I've *always* watched hockey, even when the seats weren't this good. And I skate every day, anyway, with some excellent players.

Life is good. Except for this headache.

Things heat up on the ice. Blake gets a break and sets up an attack. He passes to Wes who slips it right back to him the moment he's open. Blake flips a wrister at the net, and the goalie just barely gets there in time, poking it out of the air awkwardly with the tip of his glove. But that puck is still in play, so both teams converge.

"GET IT BABY SLAP IT SILLY BRING IT HOME TO MAMA BLAKEYYYYYY!" Mrs. Riley is on her feet and yodeling like a maniac.

She's always loud, but tonight it's like a knife straight into my brain. Her husband, though, sits beside her with his knees tucked together and hands folded in his lap. To look at him, he might be in church.

There's a scrum in front of the net which ends when the goalie traps the puck under his glove. No goal.

The game grinds on, scoreless through the first period. I wander around during the intermission, wishing one of the vendors sold ibuprofen. They don't, though. I buy a pretzel, hoping that a little food will perk me up.

When the second period begins, the speed of play picks up. Wes looks aggressive out there, and he gets several shots on goal, but they're rebuffed. I'm not worried. If he keeps that up, it will work eventually. Toronto is outshooting Ottawa. Every time we rush the net Mama Riley spews forth with high-decibel encouragements. "EAT EM FOR AN APPETIZER BLAKEY! SHOOT IT AT HIS EVERLOVING WALNUTS!"

I'm deaf now.

Also, the room is swimming a little in a way that rooms really shouldn't. And when I try to focus on the puck, the glare on the ice burns my retinas.

Eriksson scores deep into the second period, and I am not nearly as excited as usual. In fact, I want to go home. No—I *need* to. Pulling out my phone, I text Wes. *So sorry, babe. Have the worst headache. Going home early. Let's go out tomorrow? Same plan, one day later.*

"RIDE HIM LIKE A DONKEY BLAKEY!" Mrs. Riley is screeching when I get up. I can still hear her all the way to the top of the stands.

THE NEXT MORNING my alarm goes off at five-thirty. I hit the snooze button and take stock. My body feels like lead, though that may be partly because it's weighed down by the muscular thigh of a certain Toronto forward who is passed out while half straddling me.

I never heard him come home last night.

Dozing, it seems as though my alarm goes off again much too quickly. But I heave myself out of bed, because it's a weekday and my boys have a six-thirty practice. These kids play hockey before school, gearing up while the rest of the sixteen-year-old world sleeps. If they can get there on time, then I will, too.

The coffee I buy at the rink forty-five minutes later tastes like water and hits my stomach like battery acid. Really, it must have been a foul batch. My team's practice goes slowly because I'm in agony. My headache is back, sitting low at the base of my skull this time. And my stomach keeps cramping.

Hell. Dunlop looks extra shaky out there this morning. It's only a matter of time before Bill Braddock assigns a more senior defensive coach to work with him. And since we're having a coaches' meeting right after this practice, all my coworkers are standing around watching my goalie struggle.

Could this day get any worse?

After the kids leave, I survive the ninety-minute meeting by propping my aching head in my palm and forcing myself to stay awake. I'm probably coming down with something, but I don't excuse myself. Because A) I'm not a wuss and B) if I ignore it, maybe it will go away.

After the meeting I'm supposed to skate again. Two other defensive coaches and I are teaming up to hold a clinic this morning for some of the older players. When I get out on the ice, though, my stomach cramps again. So I leave the ice, put my skate guards on and head for the john.

The next fifteen minutes are very uncomfortable, but finally my bowels stop exploding. I know this is bad. I have to go home, but home seems really far away all of a sudden. While I'm washing my hands, the light in the room goes yellow and the ambient sound goes dim.

That can't be good.

I take a few steps toward the bathroom door, but it's not working all that well. Maybe if I just had a little rest for a moment, I could do better.

The floor of the men's room at a practice rink is the *last* place in the world a guy should sit down. But hey, it's convenient. I sink down, my back sliding against the tiles. My ass hits the floor.

"Canning?" Danton staggers to a stop as he enters the bathroom. "Hey. You okay?"

Not so much, no. He asks me that again several times, as if I'm likely to change my answer. I tune him out.

Luckily, the asshole disappears, and I close my eyes and try to regroup.

The silence doesn't last nearly long enough. Danton is back—I can hear his weaselly voice. But it's accompanied by Bill's—our boss. Their voices mesh together, and I'm too tired to listen well.

"You just found him here?"

"Yeah. You think he's on drugs?"

"Seriously?"

Someone touches me, and I don't like it.

"He has a *fever*, Danton. A high one. Stay here with him, I'm getting the emergency contact list. You have a phone?"

"Yeah."

It gets blissfully quiet for a minute. But then the voices are back. "Says here that we're dialing...Ryan Wesley? That's odd." Bill laughs. "Same name as that killer rookie forward. Call this number—4-1-6..."

I doze.

"You're not gonna believe this." Danton's voice grates on my consciousness. "The number hits the Toronto clubhouse switchboard. Am I really asking them to find Ryan Wesley?"

"That's what it says on the paper, kid. Must be true."

My last half-conscious thought is: *I'm sorry, Wes.*

FOURTEEN
WES

We're not even halfway through our morning skate when Blake lumbers off the ice and is ushered into the chute by the team doctor. Worry pokes hard at me when I notice he's favoring his left knee. He'd been icing it in the locker room last night after the game, but he assured me this morning that he was A-OK. Said it was just an old injury acting up and that the precautionary X-rays and ultrasound our techs ran came back clear.

I force myself to concentrate for the duration of practice, but I hope to God that Blake is all right. He hadn't looked like he was in too much pain when he'd skated off, but you never know. Hockey players are tough motherfuckers. They could have a broken leg with the bone sticking straight through their flesh and still insist they're fine.

I think the same applies to hockey *coaches*, because Jamie had brushed off his own malady last night. I came home to find him in our bed with a pillow over his head, groaning that he'd never had a migraine like this before. I felt him tossing and turning all night, but he was gone before I woke up, so I'm assuming he's migraine-free now. I damn well hope he is. I was really looking forward to hanging out with him yesterday, and I'm determined to make it happen tonight.

The second Coach blows his whistle to signal the end of practice, I head to the locker room to shower and change, then go on a hunt for Blake. I track him down to the physio room. He's lying on a long metal table, his left leg propped up and an ice pack on his knee.

"What's the word?" I ask in concern.

Unhappiness clouds his face. "They're sending me for an MRI."

Shit. "MCL? ACL?" I pray the answer to that is "neither", but Blake's expression goes even more bleak.

"ACL. They don't think it's a tear. Worst case, a sprain, but it'll still keep me out of action for a while. Two weeks, hopefully. Six at the most."

Double shit. Losing Blake, even for a couple weeks, would be a major hit for the team. He's one of our best forwards. "I'm sorry, man," I say quietly.

Blake is quick to flash that careless grin of his, even though we both know he's bummed out at the prospect of missing any games. "Ah, don't look so mopey, Wesley. Nothing keeps me down for long, eh? I'll be back before you know it."

I raise a brow. "You'd better be. We're going to need you if we make the playoffs." For the first time in years, Toronto is actually in playoffs contention. I like to think that's partly my doing—I've now scored at least one goal in the past six games —but I'm trying not to let myself get too cocky. Hockey is a team sport. No "I" in "team" and all that jazz, right?

"*When* we make the playoffs," he corrects. "Pessimistic asshole."

"*When* we make the playoffs," I echo, which gets me another broad smile from him. "So take care of that knee, you hear me? Don't push yourself to get back on the ice sooner than the docs tell you. We can man the fort until you're ready to—"

"Wesley." The male voice at the door interrupts me, and I turn to see one of our assistant coaches standing in the doorway.

"Yeah, Coach?"

"Call came in for you on the main switchboard." He points to the white phone mounted near the door. "They're on hold. Line two. Sounds important."

He ducks away without another word.

I'm not sure why, but my stomach goes rigid. I don't claim to be a super-intuitive guy. That's Jamie's forte, sensing what people are thinking, instinctively knowing what to do in any given situation. But right now, foreboding is crawling up my spine, and for some peculiar reason, my legs wobble like a toddler's as I walk over to the phone.

I lift the handset to my ear and press the Line Two button with a shaky finger. "Hello?"

"Is this Ryan Wesley?" an unfamiliar voice barks.

"Yes. Who's this?"

There's a slight pause. "Shit, this is actually Ryan Wesley? The Toronto center?"

"I just said so, didn't I?" I can't stop the sharp bite to my tone. "Who am I speaking to right now?"

"David Danton. Associate coach for the U17 Wildcats. I work with Jamie Canning."

I find myself leaning forward, bracing one palm against the wall. Why is Jamie's least-favorite coworker calling me? My heart rate kicks up a notch.

"Canning collapsed about an hour ago," Danton says, and all the oxygen in my lungs shudders out. "We tried calling you when it happened, but I was on hold. And when the ambulance came, I hung up."

An hour ago? *Ambulance*?? Horror clamps around my throat, along with a rush of fear that floods my stomach and brings me dangerously close to hurling all over the pristine white floor.

"Where is he?" I demand. "Is he okay?"

From behind me, I hear a rustling sound. I jump nearly five feet in the air when Blake appears at my side. Concern is etched into his rugged features, but I'm too terrified to pay him much attention.

"We just got to St. Sebastian's. The ER docs are with him now. Last update we got said he's still unresponsive."

Unresponsive?

The handset falls from my suddenly limp fingers. It dangles from its cord, rocking like a pendulum and smacking the wall with each hurried swing. I'm vaguely aware of a big hand grabbing that handset. A gruff voice talking into the phone. I don't know what the voice is saying. All I can hear is the wild hammering of my pulse in my ears.

Jamie is unresponsive. Unresponsive. What the *hell* does that mean? Why is he unresponsive?

An anguished sound tears out of my throat. I lunge out the door, my vision nothing but a hazy, panicky blur. I don't even know where I'm going. I just stumble forward in search of the nearest exit.

I need to get to the hospital. Goddamn it, but I don't even know where St. Sebastian's is. I think if I tried to punch it into my GPS app right now, I'd break my phone. My hands aren't doing so well—they're tingling and shaking and missing the door handle every time I try to push it open.

"Wesley." The voice is tinny. Faraway.

I push on the handle again, and the door finally fucking opens.

"*Ryan.*"

It's the use of my first name that penetrates the fog of terror that's surrounding me like a shield. My dad calls me by my first name, and I was conditioned as a child to always stand to attention when I hear those two commanding syllables. I jerk my head up and see Blake running toward me. Even in my current state, I know he shouldn't be running.

"Your knee," I manage to croak.

He skids to a stop in front of me. "My knee's fine. Keeping me off the ice for now, yeah, but it's not banged up enough to let you get killed in a head-on collision."

I blink. I honestly don't know what he's saying right now.

"I'm driving you to the hospital," he clarifies.

I object weakly. "No—"

"Don't need my left leg to drive, anyway." His tone brooks no argument. "And you're in no condition to drive right now."

I think he might be right. I'm in no condition to open a goddamn *door*, let alone operate a motor vehicle. In the back of my mind, an alarm bell goes off. I can't let Blake come with me to the hospital. He'll see me with Jamie. He'll...know.

But... *Jamie*, damn it. I just need to get to Jamie, and right now Blake is my best chance of reaching the hospital without me mowing down some pedestrians on the way there.

I don't argue as he claps a big hand on my arm and leads me away from the door. I realize I was about to leave through an emergency exit that leads to a cargo area, which is on the complete opposite end of the parking lot I needed to get to.

Blake redirects me down the hall. Neither of us speaks as we ride the elevator to the underground level. Rather than take my SUV, Blake shoves me into the passenger seat of a black Hummer. He gets behind the wheel and hightails it out of the underground.

"The guy on the phone said J-Bomb was brought in with a high fever and abdominal pain," Blake reveals in a quiet voice. "He passed out when they got to the ER. Hasn't come to yet."

Bile burns my throat. Is this his idea of a pep talk? Now I'm ready to pass out myself, because the thought of Jamie— unconscious, sick, *alone*—makes my entire world blur at the edges. I can't even see the road beyond the windshield. Everything is dark and blurry and fading away.

"Wesley," Blake says sharply.

My head snaps up again.

"Breathe," he orders.

I inhale slowly, but I'm pretty sure there's no oxygen in the air. All I'm breathing in is more fear. I don't know how he does it, but Blake and his monstrous Hummer speed through downtown traffic like there aren't even any other cars on the road. When we got into this beast of a car, the Nav screen said our destination was twenty-five minutes away. We get there in sixteen.

The moment we burst through the automatic doors of the emergency room, I'm in a panic again. The large waiting room is packed. Faces whiz past my vision as I race to the nurses' station and slam both hands on the counter.

"Jamie Canning!"

My yell startles the redheaded nurse, who looks at me from behind thick lenses. "I'm sorry?"

"Jamie Canning!" I can't seem to formulate any other

sentence. Just those four, terror-laced syllables, which rumble out for a third time. "*Jamie Canning.*"

Blake speaks up in a calm voice. "We're here to see a patient named Jamie Canning. He was admitted about an hour ago?"

"One second, sir. Let me have a look." Her red-polished fingernails fly over a computer keyboard. Green eyes study the screen, and then she raises her head again and her expression is grim enough to make my heart beat faster. Though I'm pretty sure it stopped beating a while ago.

"He's been moved to quarantine," she tells us.

My surroundings begin to sway again. Or maybe it's my legs. I don't know how I'm even upright. Blake, I realize. He's literally holding me up by the back of my jacket.

"Quarantine?" I croak.

"Flu symptoms," the nurse explains. "There's a very low likelihood of DSKH-DL finding its way to our hospital—"

"DSK...what?" I burst out.

"The sheep flu," she clarifies, and Blake's expression turns to horror. "As I said, it's unlikely, but we're taking every precaution. Are you Mr. Canning's family?"

"Yes," I say without hesitation. Because I am.

Her eyebrows rise. "You're his...?"

Shit. I can't lie and say I'm his brother, because nobody will believe me. And even if I blurt out that I'm his boyfriend in this room full of people, it still won't help. If Jamie and I aren't married, they won't care. "I'm all he's got in Toronto," I say instead. "We live together."

"I see," she says in a patient voice. "Let me explain how our quarantine works. While the patient waits for his laboratory results, family members or their designated appointees can see him, providing they adhere to our quarantine protocol.

That's all we can do until we decide that other patients and visitors are not at risk."

"But…"

"Next!"

Just like that she *dismisses* me. For a moment I just stand there in front of the desk, unwilling to move. How dare she?

Two big hands grasp my upper arms and steer me out of the way. "Come on, Wesley. We gotta regroup." Blake turns me around and parks me against a wall. His paws land on my shoulders. "Where is Jamie's family? You have to call them."

Fuck, I do. I yank my phone out of my pocket.

But Blake yanks it out of my hand. "Don't terrify them, okay? Just because you're freaked doesn't mean they have to be."

"Right. Fine." He gives me the phone back and I pull up the Canning section of my contacts list, and it's not short. But choosing the number for Jamie's mom's pottery studio is an easy decision. *Be calm*, I order myself while I listen to it ring. *No panic.*

"Canning Ceramics, this is Cindy."

In spite of my desire to be calm and collected, the warm strength of her voice flips a switch inside me that I didn't know was there. "Mom?" I croak. Okay—I've never called her that. Not once. Don't know why I did it now.

"Ryan, sweetie, what's the matter?"

I close my eyes and try to pull myself together. "We have a bit of a situation," I say carefully. But I can't possibly fool her, because my voice shakes. "Jamie's been admitted to the hospital with flu symptoms. Last night he had a headache, and today he passed out at work. That's what I know so far."

"Okay, Ryan, take a breath." Why do people keep saying

that? I do it, though, because Cindy told me to. "And now say, 'It's going to be okay.' Say it three times in a row."

"But…"

"I have six children, Ryan. This is an important step for keeping your sanity. Say it. Right now. Let me hear you."

"It's going to be okay," I wheeze.

"Two more."

"It's going to be okay. It's going to be okay."

"Good boy. Now tell me where you are."

I give her a rundown of what the nurse behind the desk told me.

"So you need my permission to see Jamie. How do I reach the right person to provide that?"

"Uh…" *Shit.*

Someone sticks a piece of paper in my face. It's Blake, and he's offered me a card reading Patient Registrar and Permissions, with a phone number.

"Thank you," I mouth into his face. Then I give Cindy the number.

"Okay, honey," she says. "I'll call them immediately. After you get in to see him, you'll call me, okay? Use my cell phone because I have to go pick up my grandson. Tammy is having her C-section tomorrow."

"Oh, wow. Okay. I will. I promise."

"I know, honey. Hang in there. I love you both so much."

There's a giant lump in my throat now. "Love you, too. Bye."

We end our call, and the hospital waiting room comes into focus. It's loud and full of people, some of whom are staring at Blake and me. One teenage girl nudges her friend and points at us.

If anyone asks me for an autograph right now I'll probably explode.

Blake moves his big body, positioning himself to get in between the waiting room and me. "Let's give it ten minutes," he says. "J-Bomb's mom needs to get through to whoever, and then maybe your name will show up on the record. Nurse Nazi over there will have to let you in."

"Right," I say. My head is still spinning. Jamie can't have any kind of weird flu. Where would he have gotten it? On the other hand, then why is he so sick? In my panic, it feels like a problem I ought to be able to solve. I've never felt so helpless in my whole life.

"He's gonna be okay," Blake says, reading my mind. "Healthy guy like that? In a couple of days you'll be laughing about this."

But I just keep hearing the words *collapsed* and *unresponsive* over and over in my head. What if he had an undiagnosed heart condition? My sophomore year in college one of my classmates died playing intramural basketball. He just collapsed on the gym floor. The ref gave him CPR, but he was just gone.

Fuck. Can't think about that. "It's going to be okay," I repeat, just like Cindy told me to.

"*Hey.*" Blake gives my shoulder a shake. "Of course it is. Did Canning's mom make that coffee mug?"

"What?" My head is full of doom, and Blake wants to talk coffee cups?

"I washed the dishes in your pad. The bottom of the mug is inscribed."

Oh. Fuck me. That mug says *Jamie loves you and so do we. Welcome to the Canning clan.* And when I look up into Blake's eyes, I see exactly what I'd been worrying about for months.

He *knows*.

"Blake," I start. Bullshitting him is off the table, so I go with evasion. "It's not a good time to have this conversation."

"Says you." Blake's voice goes to a place I've never heard before. He's actually kind of angry, and I hadn't even known that was possible. "We're about sixty seconds away from fending off a bunch of fans who will decide that it isn't all that rude to approach the hockey players in the emergency room. And they're gonna ask why we're here. I got no opinion at all on what you should say to them. But I'm your friend, and you're supposed to level with your friends."

That's probably true, but I've got a whole lot riding on my secrecy. Blake has the biggest big mouth I ever met, and I'm not sure he can really appreciate the situation I'm in.

We're having a stare down and I win it. Because shutting my trap has become something that I'm really good at.

He sighs and looks away. "Fine. Be that way. But if you're hell-bent on hiding for the rest of your life, at least take off your jacket, man. That thing is like a beacon."

Because he's right, I do it, shrugging off the team jacket and shoving it under my arm.

"Ryan Wesley?" the intercom bleats. "Is there a Ryan Wesley here for Mr. Canning?"

Thank Christ. I spin around and boogie back to the desk. The green-eyed nurse points at a guy waiting there in scrubs. "Go with him."

"I'm Doctor Rigel, infectious diseases." He holds out a hand to shake.

Shaking hands with someone who works on infectious diseases seems a little sketchy to me, but I do it anyway.

Blake is right behind me, too. "What can you tell us?" he asks in his booming voice.

He leads us down a hall, talking as we go. "Mr. Canning is stable," he says, and I practically melt with relief. "He arrived dehydrated and with a high fever. He's getting fluids and an antiviral that fights flu, though we won't have a lab test back for another twelve hours or so. We need to rule out what the media is calling the sheep flu."

Blake shudders so hard they can probably measure it on the Richter Scale. "Dude. That cannot be what J-Bomb has. I refuse to believe it."

"Well…" The doctor rings for an elevator, and we all stop to wait for it. "You're probably right. But it would be irresponsible in the middle of a health scare to treat this lightly. And his coworkers indicated that he travels around Canada for his job, so we need to be sure."

My fear comes roaring back. "He's not used to this climate," I babble. "He's always lived on the West Coast."

Blake gives me a pointed look that suggests I might want to stop talking.

We get onto the elevator. "Good game last night," the doctor says into the silence.

"Uh, thanks," Blake says. "You're gonna let my man Wesley here see Canning, right? There's a couple of box seats in it for you if you do."

The doctor's face goes through several different emotions in rapid succession, from elation to despair and then to irritation. "I would never make a medical protocol decision for hockey tickets."

"Of course not," Blake says quickly. "I only mean that if you're the guy who tells us when J-Bomb can have one visitor, we'd be mighty grateful."

Dr. Rigel nods slowly. "Mr. Wesley can see the patient after he puts on protective gear."

"All right," I agree immediately.

The elevator doors part, and we step off. A sign on the wall reads: Isolation Unit. The doctor brings us into a room straight out of a psychological thriller. It has multiple sides, each side a glass wall into a patient's room. A couple of these rooms have the shades drawn. But a few of them are open, and the people inside look sicker than a person should look.

And then I spot him.

Jamie is lying on his back in a bed, half his gorgeous face covered by a hospital mask, but I know him at a glance anyway. His brown eyes are closed, and he's way too still.

My throat closes up at the sight, and all I can do is stare.

I don't know how long I stand there staring. A few seconds? A minute? Blake grabs my shoulders from behind and squeezes. Hard. That's when I remember to breathe, sucking in a great blast of air.

He gives me a gentle shake. "Stay loose, Wesley. Come on."

"Sorry," I mumble.

Blake shakes his head. "It's all right. This is as far as I go, but I'm going to call you in a couple of hours, okay? Or text me if you need me. Either way, I'll pick you up later. We left your car at the rink."

Shit, we did. I'm not even sure where I am right now. "Thank you," I say, meeting his gaze. "Really, I…"

He waves it off. "No need. We'll talk later."

Blake turns around and disappears toward the elevators.

"Right this way, Mr. Wesley," the doctor says. "The nurses will help you into the gear."

Ten minutes later I'm wearing a long disposable gown,

gloves, a head covering, goggles, disposable slippers and a face mask. It's fucking ridiculous.

"These rooms have two doors," a petite Asian woman—her name tag says Janet Li, R.N.—explains. "You enter this way…" She points at a door off the room with the glass. "And you leave through that far door. All the gear stays in the room just outside the patient's room. There's a lot of signage to help you know what to do. Okay?"

"Got it," I say. I just need to get in there. Screw the signage.

"You'll go in alone right now, but if you need anything or the patient needs anything, use the intercom button on the wall and someone will assist you immediately."

"Thank you."

When she unlocks the door to Jamie's room for me, I dive through it. There's a second door behind that one, unlocked.

Then it's just him and me. Finally. I grab his hand and give it a squeeze. I'm stunned that it's so hot to the touch. They weren't kidding about that fever. "Baby," I choke out. "I'm here."

He is still.

So I start babbling, because I want him to know it's me. I tell him everything that happened to me today. *Everything*. How Blake got injured and I went to find him. How I got the awful phone call. "I was so freaked," I tell him, though Jamie's brow remains perfectly smoothed by slumber.

The masks between us are loathsome. I just want to rip the thing off.

Eventually my story winds down. I park my ass on the edge of the bed, hoping that's okay, and pull his hand into my lap, where I stroke it with my stupid gloved hand.

His eyelashes flicker.

"Canning," I whisper, squeezing his hand. "Hey. Come on, babe."

His pale eyelids part, and when I can see his eyes, I finally believe that everything is going to be okay. His eyes widen, but then his brow furrows.

Fuck, he's scared. I must look like a freak, or at least a stranger. "It's me," I say loudly. "Hey, look." With my free hand I rip off the goggles and then—screw it—the face mask.

His face relaxes, and I smile for the first time in hours. Maybe ever.

"Mr. Wesley! What are you doing?" I turn my head to see the nurse just on the other side of the glass, one hand on her hip, an angry frown on her face. She's holding a phone to her ear, and her voice booms from a speaker on the wall. "You can't take off the protective gear!"

I can, though. She's not going to overpower me. I can take her in a fight. So I shuck off the hair covering, too. Then I get off the bed and stand over Jamie's head. He's watching me with wide, trusting eyes.

"Mr. Wesley!" she barks. "Stop it."

"You don't understand," I say, looking at Jamie, not her. He's the only one who matters. "If he has the sheep flu, I'm already exposed. We share a *bed*."

Then, leaning over him, I kiss his forehead. Even if we're in this chamber of horrors, he still smells like *him*. And this calms me down. "I love you, baby," I whisper in his ear. "Don't worry about a thing." Jamie's eyes fall closed. But I kiss him once more, this time on the lips. Just so he knows I'm still here.

When I look up at the window again, the nurse is gone. For now.

FIFTEEN

WES

The photo hits the Internet six hours after I walk into Jamie's room.

TMZ leaks it first—how do those fuckers always out-scoop everyone??—and after that, it makes its rounds on various hockey websites, celebrity blogs, gossip rags and newspapers that really ought to have better things to report on. Two prominent papers actually feature it on their homepage, where the photo's thumbnail sits higher on the page than an article about the capture of a *terrorist*.

I guess the sight of me, Ryan Wesley, kissing the lips of another man, is a national emergency. And at the moment, there's nothing I can do to put out that fire.

Did I mention I'm in quarantine, too?

Yep, the moment I ditched my protective gear, I signed my own prison sentence. Dr. Rigel had marched into the room in his quarantine suit with the angry nurse at his side. He informed me that since I had potentially exposed myself to what might be a dangerous strain of flu, I would be unable to leave the isolation unit until Jamie's test results came back.

Then his pissed-off nurse took some blood from me and sent it to get tested, too.

Do I have any regrets? Not a chance. I wasn't planning on leaving Jamie's side anyway. At least this way, nobody can kick me out when visiting hours are over. And now that some asshole has outed us without our permission, I can't deny it's nice having an excuse to hide from the rest of the world.

I don't know who snapped the picture, but hoo-boy, they'd struck gold with the intimate moment they'd stolen from us. Me, sitting at Jamie's bedside, pressing my lips tight to his. It was right after he'd regained consciousness, and I'd been so overcome with joy and relief to see those beautiful brown eyes peering up at me that I'd forgotten we were in a glass box with the shades open.

He slept for another hour after that, while I held his hand. Maybe it sounds dumb, but I'd never felt more useful to anyone in my life. If he woke up confused, I wanted him to know he wasn't alone. In spite of the shit swirling through my life right now, I felt calmer than I had in weeks. Because for once I knew I was doing the right thing just when it needed doing.

And when he woke up for real, he was confused. "Where are we?" he said, startling me.

"In a hospital, babe. You're sick. You probably have the flu, but they'll tell us after the test comes back."

"Okay," he said, squeezing my hand. But the more he woke up, the more agitated he became. And when he realized what an odd hospital room this was, it wasn't long before he caught on to the fact that I'd been exposed, too. And now he won't let it go.

"You shouldn't have taken your mask off," Jamie croaks at me. "You're insane, Wes. You shouldn't *be* here."

It's not the first time he's questioned my sanity since he woke up, and now I'm questioning *his* sanity, because where the hell else would I be? Standing on the other side of the glass watching the man I love suffer?

"You're gonna catch this stupid sheep flu," he mumbles.

"First off, we don't know if you even have the sheep flu," I point out. I'm sitting in a chair next to his bed but leaning toward him, my ungloved hand stroking his cheek. His skin is still burning up, which worries me. It's been six hours on that IV, at least. Shouldn't his fever be going down? "Rigel seemed to think it was unlikely, remember? Second, if you do have it, chances are I already do too, because I had my tongue down your throat the other night. Third, I *should* be here. Take a look at this torture chamber, babe." I wave around at the oppressive space. "I'd never let you suffer in here all alone."

He laughs weakly.

Jesus. I'm so relieved he's awake. My first glance of him lying in that bed, so still… It scared the crap out of me.

"Coach Hal is going to shit a brick." He sighs. "What if you miss practice tomorrow morning? And you have a game in Tampa on Thursday night. You can't afford to get sick, Wes."

I stare at him in disbelief.

Jamie falters. "What?"

"Do you really think I'm going to practice tomorrow when you're in the *hospital*?"

"I might be discharged by then."

"With all the precautions these fuckers are taking? Yeah, right. They'll keep you here at least a couple days for observation." My tone sharpens. "I won't be on that plane to Tampa, I hope you realize that. I'm not leaving your side until I know you're out of the woods."

"I was never *in* the woods," he protests.

My jaw falls open. "You passed out at work! You have a hundred-and-three-degree fever! Your skin looks like a boiled lobster and yet you're shaking like a leaf, you're so cold. You're too weak to lift your head!"

Jamie insists, "I'm fine," and I'm tempted to slug him in the face. I don't, though, because he's the one lying in this hospital bed, so I guess I'm the one who needs to act like the adult.

"You're not fine," I say sternly. "You're sick." Possibly with a dangerous strain of sheep poison or whatever the hell it is, but I refuse to let myself believe he might actually have it. Thanks to Blake's worrisome obsession with sheep, I know that at least sixteen people have died of this flu. And all I'm going to say is —Jamie will *not* be number seventeen. I'd sell my soul to the devil before I let anything happen to this guy. He's my entire life.

We stop talking when we hear a loud beep. The door latch releases, and the nurse (who now officially hates me) stiffly enters the room. She's decked out in her hazmat suit and face-mask. I can't see her mouth, but her eyes tell me she's frowning.

"Mr. Wesley. Please follow me," she orders, and I'm concerned by the note of unhappiness in her voice. Oh God. Are Jamie's results back? Does she want to talk to me in private so she can confirm that the sheep got to Jamie?

My heartbeat triples as I stumble off the chair. Jamie looks as worried as I feel, but he doesn't protest as I follow Nurse Death into the secondary room. Once the door closes behind us, she holds out a cell phone. *My* cellphone, which she confiscated an hour ago after she caught me sending a text message to the Canning clan.

Apparently electronics are a no-no in quarantine. Truthfully, I'm glad she took the phone away, because it was lighting up like a fireworks display after the photograph was released. Jamie had still been asleep at that point. Yup, he has no idea that as of an hour ago, a shit storm has been brewing outside our glass cage, and I have no intention of telling him. Not yet, anyway.

My sole priority is to help him get better. If he finds out that our relationship is now being discussed and dissected by thousands of people—hell, probably millions of people? Who knows what it'll do to his already fragile system. I can't take that risk.

"We've been fielding an exorbitant number of calls this past hour," she says flatly. "At least two dozen of them have come from a Frank Donovan. He insists on speaking to you, and frankly, my colleagues and I are getting tired of being yelled at. So we're making an exception for you, Mr. Wesley. You can use your cell phone, but only in this room and only briefly. Now please call Mr. Donovan back before I give in to the urge to look into the cost of a contract killer."

I snicker. Okay. Maybe Nurse Death isn't all bad.

I wait until she leaves the room before pulling up Frank's number, but I hesitate before hitting *send*. Fuck me. I'm not prepared to deal with any of this right now. I had a plan, damn it. Finish out my rookie year, and *then* come out. The story would have been controlled by Frank and myself. Presented to the media the way *we* wanted it to be presented.

But some greedy, nosy, inconsiderate asshole took matters into his own hands. Or...*her* hands, maybe? I suddenly think of Nurse Death. What if it was her?

Then again, it could be any of the nurses I'd seen beyond the glass today. Or the techs delivering test results. The doctors popping in and out of the unit. The family members visiting their quarantined love ones.

Anybody could have snapped that picture. Trying to finger the culprit is like playing a nonsensical version of *Clue*. Nurse Death…in the Isolation Unit…with the Camera!

And does it really matter at this point? What's done is done, and now it's time for damage control.

"Ryan, about goddamn time!" Frank's frazzled voice booms in my ear. "Why aren't you answering your cell phone?"

"The nurses took it away," I tell him. "Not allowed to have phones in the hospital."

"Total myth. Studies have shown the effects of cell phones on medical equipment to be minimal."

Is this really something we should be debating right now? "Frank," I say, veering him back to issues of actual importance. "What kind of backlash are we looking at here?"

"Still too early to tell. Most of the media outlets are hopping on the rainbow train—"

I clench my jaw.

"—waving their gay pride flags and commending you for your bravery in coming out."

"I didn't come out," I mutter. "Someone else did it for me."

"Well, you're out now," he says dismissively. "And now we need to make sure we spin it the right way. The franchise is going to release the statement I prepared after we drafted you. I wanted to give you the head's up about that—it'll go out within the hour."

Frank had sent me a copy of the statement a while ago. It featured a lot of politically correct language, as I recall. *The team is—and always has been—supportive of our players and the rich diversity they bring to the sport of hockey…* Blah

blah blah. *We are proud to call Ryan Wesley a member of the team.*

"We'll give the vultures the night to peck and gnaw at it," Frank says in a cynical voice. "And then tomorrow morning, you'll give a press conference and—"

"What?" I interrupt. "No way."

"Ryan—"

"I agreed to a written statement," I remind him. "A short follow-up to whatever statement you give to the media. I did *not* agree to be on camera." The thought of standing in front of a room full of reporters talking about my sex life and answering questions that nobody has the right to ask me brings bile to my throat.

"That was before pictures of you making out with your gay lover showed up all over the Internet," Frank replies. He doesn't sound angry or disgusted, just matter-of-fact. "They're going to expect more than a two-line press release, Ryan."

"I don't give a shit what they expect!" Frustration claws at my chest. I want to hurl my phone into the wall, watch it shatter to pieces, and then stomp on them for good measure. I feel…violated. And that only intensifies the bolts of indignation whipping up and down my spine. These people have no right to shine a spotlight on me just because I like to fuck men. It's none of their goddamn business.

"Ryan." Frank pauses. "All right. Clearly we should table this discussion until your, uh, partner is discharged from the hospital. For now, I'll release the statement on the team's behalf. Once we gauge the response to it, we'll figure out our next move."

"Fine."

"Should we be concerned about your test results?"

I blank for a second. "My test results?"

"The flu," he says impatiently. "The coaching staff is concerned. You're scheduled to play Tampa in two days."

I draw a breath. "I won't be on the ice on Thursday, Frank. If you want, I will personally phone Coach to let him know, but this is non-negotiable. I'm dealing with a family emergency here."

"Your contract states—"

"I don't care what it states," I retort. "I will *not* be on that flight." I don't give him the chance to object. "I have to go now. The nurses are giving me the evil eye." They're not, but Frank doesn't know that. "I'll call you back once Jamie's test results are in."

My hands are shaking as I hang up the phone. I wasn't prepared for this. Any of it. And even though I'm desperate to get back to Jamie, I force myself to scroll through my text messages, just in case the Cannings have tried to get in touch

And shit, they have. Every single one of them.

Cindy: Richard and I need an update, sweetie (even though we know everything will be okay, will be okay, will be okay!)

Jess: Why won't those hospital assholes let me call you???

Joe: How's my brother?

Scott: How's Jamester?

Brady: Is J OK??

There's even a message from Tammy, who's dealing with her own hospital situation at the moment: *Call the moment u get the test results. Ask main switchboard for my room. Ext. 3365.*

Rather than answer each one individually, I send a group text to the whole Canning clan:

Still waiting for lab results. J is awake and cranky. Fever still high but docs are working on lowering it. Won't let me use my phone in here. I'll msg back when I can.

I skim the rest of my unread messages, which are mostly from Blake. There's also one from Eriksson, but I don't click on it because I'm too scared to know what it says. I'm not sure I'm ready to face my teammates' reactions to the "news." I scroll down further and freeze when I see my dad's name. This time I click.

Dad: You're a fool.

My heart clenches painfully. I'm pissed at myself for allowing those three words to get to me, but…fuck, they hurt.

I'm about to shut off the phone when my Twitter app catches my attention. It says I have 4622 new notifications. Sweet Jesus.

Despite my better judgment, I give in to morbid curiosity and open the app to see what the Twittersphere thinks about this latest development. Ha. #RyanWesley is trending on Twitter. And I got ten thousand new followers since the photo was released. I click on my notification feed and discover that most of the tweets are surprisingly positive.

@hockeychix96: OMG! Your BF is SO hot!

@T-DotFan: Good 4 u, dude!

@Kyle_Gilliam309: Ur an inspiration to us all, Wesley.

On and on it goes. OMGs, cyber hugs and high-fives, people telling me what an inspiration I am to the gay community. Sprinkled among those are tweets of denial, disgust, and disbelief.

@BearsFourEvr: Dicks are for chicks, fag.

@Jenn_sinders: Please say ur not gay!

And in a conversation about fifty tweets long, two female fans decide to tag my username as they conduct a thorough examination of the "proof" of my sexual orientation. They even blow up and crop certain parts of the picture to state their case.

@HeyyythereDelilah: Srsly, that's *not* RW. Look at the eyes. RW's eyes aren't that close together.

My eyes are close together?

@BustyBritt69: It's totally RW! I'd recognize that sexy mouth anywhere.

@HeyyythereDelilah: devil's advocate. Let's say it's RW. Doesn't mean it's RW's *boyfriend*. Could b his brother.

@BustyBritt69: Who kisses their brother on the MOUTH?

@HeyyythereDelilah: I did once. But I was drunk. Thought he was someone else.

@BustyBritt69: Ewwwww! TMI!

Sighing, I close the app and shut off my phone. Nurse Death didn't say she needed it back, so I tuck it into my pocket, then return to the main room, where Jamie's suspicious gaze greets me.

"What was that about?"

I shrug. "She let me use the phone so I could call your parents back."

"Are they freaking out?"

"Nope. Like me, they know there's nothing to worry about." I settle back in my chair and reach for his hand. "You're going to be fine, babe. Those tests are going to come back negative. Just watch."

He nods, but his expression remains uneasy. "You sure everything's okay?" he presses.

I bend and brush my lips over his alarmingly hot cheek. "Everything is just fine," I lie.

SIXTEEN

Fever is trippy. The room has an odd jittery quality, and I'm hot and cold at the same time.

There's only one thing here that's behaving exactly the way I need, and that's Wes. Whenever I open my eyes he's here. Even though I'm worried about his health, his career and every other goddamn thing, I can't deny that it's a comfort to me. Because everything happening to me is just so disorienting.

"How'd I get here?" I ask suddenly.

He looks up from his phone. "Uh, ambulance, I'm pretty sure. Your man Danton called me at the rink, but I didn't hear all the details." He clears his throat. "I think he said something about an ambulance."

I consider this while the walls shimmer weirdly. And then? A huge grizzly bear flattens its giant body against the glass window. I'm staring at it when it yanks the phone off the wall, and a voice booms in at us. "Dude! What a lot of trouble you are, J-Bomb!"

My synapses fire in slow motion, but Wes's groan clues me

in. Blake has arrived. *Fuck*! I try to casually pull my hand away from Wes's, but he holds on tight. "Wes?" I croak.

"Yeah?"

"Is our cover blown?"

"Well…"

Blake's hysteria vibrates the walls. "Is your cover blown? Is a bear Catholic? Does the pope shit in the woods? I just saw both your faces on the ten o'clock news. Nice yearbook photo, J-Bomb."

Wes jumps out of his chair and stalks over to the window. I'm pretty sure he's making a slashing motion at his throat.

"What?" Blake says with a shrug. "He's gonna see a TV, a newspaper or a phone before tomorrow, right?"

Somehow this new information helps clear my head. If we're on the news, that means the whole world is feasting on Wes like a gossip buffet. "I'm so sorry," I say.

Wes whirls around. "No you don't. This is *not* your fault. Not even a little."

I know that's true. But I'll bet this is hella inconvenient. No wonder he's been sneaking peeks at his phone when he thinks I'm not looking. "What does Frank say?"

Wes shrugs. "He's handling it. You don't need to worry." Yet Wes doesn't look nearly as calm as his words.

"You're stuck in here with me. They must be pissed off about that. There's probably satellite trucks in front of the stadium."

"There's satellite trucks in front of the hospital," Blake says gleefully.

We both stare at him. "Seriously?" Wes asks.

"Yup! Had to do a Red Rover to break through 'em. Brought you your jim jams." He holds up a duffel bag. "The super let me into your apartment. I didn't know which tooth-brush was whose, so I just brought everything."

Slowly, subtly, Wes and I turn to catch each other's eyes. We have the same awkward question in mind, I just know it. *Did he open the wrong...*

"Probably shouldna opened all those drawers," Blake carries on, rubbing his chin. "Ya can't unsee some of those toys. But everybody has to have his own kinda fun. Speaking of fun, I also brought you an Italian sub from the deli on our corner. Do you think I can get the bitchy nurse lady to bring this bag in there for you?"

Wes lets out a long, agonized sigh. I might be the one in the hospital bed, but today he's had his privacy amputated. And the wound is a gusher. "Blake, it kind of kills me to say this."

"What, Wesley boy?"

"Thank you for all your help today." My boyfriend rubs the back of his neck, as if saying nice things to our most obnox-ious neighbor is causing him pain. "Really. I appreciate all you did for me earlier."

"Aw," Blake grabs his own chest. "Any time, rookie. And hey—love the new chair. I might have to get one of those for myself. Oh! Miss? Yoo-hoo!" Blake has spotted the nurse, and now he drops the phone and gallops after her.

Wes turns to me and puts his hand on my forehead for the millionth time. His fingerprints are probably permanently imbedded in my face. "Are you freaking?" I ask him.

"No," he lies.

"I'm not apologizing for being the cause," I hedge. "But I'm sorry for all the crap that's coming your way."

He props an elbow on my mattress and brings his hand-some face closer to mine. "This was always going to happen.

Maybe it's like oral surgery. You know you need it, you know it's temporary, but it still sucks for a while."

"Okay. True."

What neither of us says out loud is that we hope it won't prove fatal to his career. Yesterday he was the Rookie Superstar, Ryan Wesley. Tonight he's Ryan Wesley, the First Out Gay NHL Player.

The bolt on the door clicks open, and the nurse and doctor arrive again. But neither of them is carrying the bag Blake had brought for us.

"What's the news?" Wes asks, rising.

"We're going to move Mr. Canning to another room," the doctor says.

That's when I notice—he and the nurse aren't wearing moon suits anymore. "It came back negative," I croak.

"It came back *positive*—for a non-novel flu virus."

"*Not* the sheep flu," Wes repeats, sounding relieved.

"Right," the doctor agreed. "A plain old flu."

They keep talking, but my eyelids begin to feel heavy again. Wes asks the doctor why I'm so sick, and the doctor's buzzwords make me even sleepier, because it sounds like he really had no idea why I've been leveled. He uses phrases like "unusual presentation" and "unfamiliar climate."

Whatever. Now I just want to go home.

"The fever is down to one hundred and one. That's encouraging," the nurse says. She's standing at my head, pushing a thermometer into my ear. "Once those antivirals kick in, you'll start feeling human again."

I feel so woozy right now it's difficult to believe her.

The next time I wake up I'm on my way to a different room on the fourth floor. It's much the same as the old one, except first I have to suffer through an embarrassing ride through the hallways on a stretcher. They actually lift me to the new bed by picking up the sheet I'm lying on and whisking it onto a new mattress.

"Can't I just go home?" I ask whoever's tucking me into the new bed.

"Not until that fever's gone, hon," the new nurse says. She's a big Jamaican woman by the name of Bertha, and I like her immediately. "Tomorrow, probably."

But I thought it *was* tomorrow.

Does that even make sense?

More sleep now.

I close my eyes while Bertha is still fussing with my IV fluids. Wes looms somewhere nearby. And that's all I need to know for now.

SEVENTEEN

WES

After wolfing down the sandwich Blake brought, I spend the rest of the night in Jamie's room, sitting in a plastic chair. I sleep in fifteen minute increments, my head dangling onto my chest. It's more exhausting than just pulling an all-nighter. Live and learn.

Then morning arrives with a startle. There's too much light everywhere, and when my vision focuses I'm staring at Frank Donovan, who's poked his head into Jamie's room.

I stagger out of my chair and move toward the hallway, so he won't wake up Jamie.

"What time is it?" I ask, sounding incoherent even to my own ears.

"Seven-thirty."

Shaking my head briskly, I try to crawl out from under my own exhaustion. "Working early today?" He's standing in front of me in a suit and tie, his shoes shined. His hair combed. We are a study in contrasts.

Frank chuckles. "Turned off my phone at two-thirty in the morning. Turned it back on again at six to find a hundred and fifty missed calls. Every sports news outlet in the world wants to talk to you."

"Too bad they're not going to," I say firmly.

Frank chews on his lip. "Look, I know you're in a tough spot. But it's not enough for the team to issue supportive press releases. My office is doing all it can to say that everything is business as usual with regard to you. But the fans need to see you on the ice with your teammates. That's the only way the public can be sure we mean it. It's that or an interview on Matt Lauer's sofa, sitting beside your coach."

A bark of laughter escapes me. "Hal doesn't want that."

"Hal will do whatever the team needs him to. As will *you*." This last bit is said in an ominous voice.

"Or what?" I ask crankily. "You'll fire me? The gay guy? That's gonna look bad."

Frank taps his foot impatiently. "Don't be that way, Ryan. I'm busting my ass to shut down the swirl of media bullshit. I'm on your side. So put your goddamn skates on this morning and make that job easier."

"When's practice today?" I ask. My wheels are turning.

"Eleven."

I glance over my shoulder at Jamie. When the nurse checked his vitals a couple hours ago, his temperature was down to ninety-nine and a half. Finally. "Okay, I'll skate in practice today. But I'm *not* going to Tampa tonight. If they let him out of the hospital tomorrow, he can't be home alone. We don't have family here."

Frank thinks it over. "Fine. It's a deal. But you'd better call in some backup to come and stay with him. You've got Nashville up next. The team won't let you miss games unless there's a dire family crisis."

I want to pound something whenever he says that. This *is* a dire family crisis. The direst.

"...and the fans need to see that your position on the team is secure. If you stay away, it looks like we're trying to get rid of you. You show up and skate, the story fades faster."

Well now he was singing a tune I could dance to. "All right. I'll figure something out for Nashville," I tell him, just so he'll shut up. "And I'll be there at eleven today."

He lifts his chin toward Jamie's room. "Say goodbye now. I'll drop you off at home so you can sleep for a couple of hours. We need you looking peppy."

Pushy much? I stare him down for a second. But damn it, I'm trapped here at the hospital without my car. "Hang on."

Jamie is awake when I walk back into the room. "Are you okay with me leaving for a couple hours?" I sit on the available few inches of mattress next to his hip. "Does anything hurt?"

He swallows roughly, as if his throat is on fire. "Go. It will be fine."

"You need water?" I look around for the cup with the straw.

"Go," he says more forcefully. "Just..."

"What?" I plant both hands on the bed and look down into his handsome face.

"Just come back later," he says with a smile. "Maybe they'll let me go home."

I lean down and kiss his forehead. Then I pick up my duffel off the floor and go before I can change my mind.

I SLEEP like the dead for two hours at home. Then I shower before heading over to the rink. I'm a little late, but I like it that way. Less time for chatter in the locker room. I'm too tired to hear whatever bullshit my teammates might be saying about me today.

That's something I can't even think about right now. If they're busy trying to assign me to a separate changing area or some bullshit I don't even want to know.

When I walk into the dressing room, all conversation comes to a halt.

Whatever. I don't give a fuck. I toss my gym bag onto the bench and remove my coat. You could hear a pin drop. I hang up my coat and then kick off my boots.

"Wesley, you asshole," Eriksson says. "Aren't you going to tell us?"

"Tell you what?" I growl. My sex life is none of their goddamn business.

"How *is* he? Jesus Christ. The TV news makes it sound like your boyfriend might be getting last rites."

My fingers falter on the buttons of my bright green checked shirt. "W-what?"

Our backup goalie Tomilson speaks up wryly. "I think what Mr. Sensitive is trying to ask is, is your partner okay?"

It's hard to keep my jaw hinged. First off, Tomilson and I have barely exchanged ten words since I joined the team. The veteran keeps to himself, and with two Stanley Cups under his belt I guess he's earned the right not to show up for media events, because I've never seen him at a press conference or party. Blake told me he spends all his off-time with his wife and kids.

Hearing him refer to Jamie as my "partner", and without a shred of judgment, unease or disgust in his voice, brings a sting to my eyelids. Fucking hell. If I start crying in the locker room in front of my teammates, nobody will ever let me forget it.

I clear my throat of the massive lump lodged there. "He's doing better. Fever's down, and I think they're going to release him today." My voice sounds hoarse as I add, "The flu kicked his ass. I've never seen anything like it."

"At least it wasn't that dangerous strain," Tomilson says. "Coach said it was just a regular flu. So that's something, right?"

I nod. Silence hangs over the room again, and I tense on instinct, waiting for more questions. This feels too…easy. Why aren't they hammering me for details about my personal life or demanding to know why I didn't tell them I was gay?

The thing is, though? My college teammates had eventually taken my sexuality in stride. I'd thought it was too easy back then too, and as I stand here waiting for my current team to judge me, I realize what a cynical bastard I've become. Maybe there's more tolerance in this world than I thought. Is that possible? Are my homophobic parents the exception to a rule that's slowly evolving?

A few more seconds of silence tick by, and then Eriksson pipes up again. "It was the shirt, huh?"

I blink in confusion, and he gestures to the green button-down I have on.

"I knew it. Made you gay," he says gleefully.

"Matt," one of our teammates chides, but it's too late, other guys are already snickering, and hell, so am I.

"How many times do I have to tell you?" I grumble. "This shirt is the da bomb dot com. No, dot edu—because it's damn near enlightening."

Forsberg snorts. "It's blinding me, that's what it is." He

ambles over and smacks me on the ass. "Gear up already. Coach ain't gonna go easy on you just 'cause your boyfriend's got the flu. I was late for practice once because mi'lady was sick, and the old bastard made me do a hundred pushups—in full gear. And skates. You know how fucking hard that is?"

"Your lady? I didn't know you had a girlfriend—" But he's already disappeared into the chute, which leaves Eriksson to answer for him.

"He doesn't." Eriksson grins. "Milady is his dog's name."

Okay then. I guess Forsberg has a dog named Milady. Which is just another reminder of how little an effort I've made to get to know the men I skate with every day.

The lump in my throat is back. I gulp it down and quickly change for practice.

ONLY A HANDFUL of press is allowed into the rink this morning, reporters and journalists who were no doubt hand-picked by Frank and his team of publicists. The franchise doesn't typically grant the media access to practices right before game days, but Frank is making an exception today. People need to see me on the ice with my teammates, so that's exactly what we give them.

I'm painfully aware of the cameras that follow me around like the beam of a laser pointer. Every move I make is docu-mented and photographed, and I can practically see the captions below the images.

When Coach snaps at me for missing an easy shot: *Tensions Rise—Hal Harvey and Ryan Wesley battle it out at practice!*

When Eriksson chest bumps me after I give him a sweet

assist: *Matt Eriksson shows support for gay teammate!* Or if we're talking tabloids, I guess the headline would be: *Matt Eriksson and Ryan Wesley—gay lovers??*

When I wave and smile at one of the reporters (after a pointed look from Frank): *Proud to be gay! Ryan Wesley embraces media attention!*

I hate my life right now. I really do. The only saving grace is that the man I love is no longer lying "unresponsive" on some hospital bed. Jamie is getting better. I was so terrified I might lose him, and knowing that he's going to be all right is the silver lining I cling to during this sideshow of a practice.

After Coach blows the whistle to dismiss us, I can't get off the ice fast enough. That gets me another glare from Frank, but he can go fuck himself. I told him I wasn't chatting up the press, and I meant it.

In the locker room, I change out of my gear as fast as I changed into it. When I hear a flurry of activity in the hallway, my stomach drops. Great. I guess Frank is giving the media free access to the facility today. Unfortunately, there's only one way out of the locker room—and it's through the door that probably has a wall of reporters standing behind it.

Tomilson flashes me a sympathetic look as I warily creep toward the door.

"Just smile and wave," Eriksson suggests.

"Give 'em the Queen Elizabeth wave," Luko says helpfully. He then proceeds to do the slow, stilted hand flutter that every member of British royalty has perfected, and everyone bursts out laughing.

"Did you just call me a queen?" I quip.

Luko's smile slides off his face. "N-no! I..."

"No, man. I'm teasing. Swear to God." Shit. I never got a chance to figure out what I wanted to say to these guys. "I don't get offended too easily. And—just for the record—none of you uglies is my type. Except for maybe Eriksson. But I don't want to be his rebound lay."

Eriksson snorts and I make my exit, stepping out the door just in time to hear Coach Harvey deliver a statement that nearly makes my eyes bug out.

"If being queer means skating like Ryan Wesley, I'm going to have to encourage the rest of my players to give it a whirl."

The hallway breaks out in grins and chuckles, which immediately turn into shouts when the press notices me in the doorway.

"Ryan! Do you have a message for any gay athletes who are too afraid to come out?"

"How does it feel to be the first openly gay player in the NHL?"

"When did you first know you were gay?"

"Do you have a response to Coach Harvey's statement?"

I was prepared to utter the words "no comment" today until they lost all meaning, but after just hearing my coach voice his support for me (albeit in a colorful way), I can't stop from addressing the last question.

"Hal Harvey is the best coach I've ever skated for," I say gruffly. "I hope to continue making him proud for seasons to come."

The reporters fire another explosion of questions, but I've said everything I wanted to say, so I duck my head and push through the swarm, letting their eager voices bounce off my back. There are clusters of journalists and media vans stationed in the parking lot, but I ignore them too and hurriedly unlock my SUV. Thank God for tinted windows. I'm sure the cameras caught me lunging into the front seat, but hopefully nobody can see me scrubbing both hands over my face and releasing a tortured groan.

I'm zooming out of the lot a minute later, and my Bluetooth kicks in as a call comes through. Frank's name flashes on the dash.

I hit the Ignore button on the steering wheel. When the phone rings again, I nearly rip the steering wheel off its frame. For fuck's sake. Can't he give me even a second's peace?

Wait, it's not Frank. I relax when I see Cindy Canning's name, and this time I waste no time picking up.

"Hey, sweetie," she greets me, the warmth in her voice doing more to heat the car than the hot air blasting from the vents. "I just spoke to Jamie. He says they won't be releasing him today. He didn't want to call you in case you were still at practice."

Disappointment crashes into me. I was really hoping they'd let him out today. But at least this means Frank can't persuade me to leave for Tampa tonight. As long as Jamie's in the hospital, the only place I'll be traveling is to his bedside.

"I just left practice. Heading to the hospital now."

"Jamie said you're going to miss your game tomorrow?" She sounds concerned.

"Yeah. And the game after that, and maybe the one after." To hell with Frank and his "family emergency" bullshit. This *is* a family emergency.

"Ryan—"

"I'm not stepping on a single plane until Jamie is one hundred percent better," I say firmly.

Her tone is equally stern. *"Ryan."*

"*Mom*," I mimic, before my voice softens. "I'm all he has here. There's no one else who can stay with him while I'm away, and I refuse to let him stay in the condo alone, at least not until I know he's fully recovered."

Cindy sighs. "All right. Let's just wait until he's discharged from the hospital before we make any rash decisions."

I flick the right turn signal toward the highway ramp. It's still early enough in the day that the traffic on the Gardiner won't be too bad. "I'll call you when I have a better idea of when they'll let him go home," I tell Jamie's mom.

"Thanks, sweetie. When you see Jamie, tell him he has a new niece. Lilac was born about an hour ago, nine pounds, two ounces."

"Wow. Congratulations, Grandma! But...Lilac?"

"Tammy had some drugs in her system."

"Ah. Oh, and Cindy? Thank you for what you said yesterday."

"What did I say?" she asks blankly.

"The mantra you taught me," I remind her. "*It's going to be okay.* I said it about three *million* times last night, and it really did make me feel better."

A snort of laughter pops out of my car speakers. "Oh that? I just made that shit up on the fly because you needed it, sweetie."

I can't fight a hysterical laugh. And did Jamie's mom really just say *shit*? That woman never curses. "Well, it worked. I think you saved me from having a nervous breakdown."

"I'm glad I did. Now get off the phone and concentrate on driving. Take care of our boy, and I love you."

"Love you, too."

I disconnect the call and thank my lucky stars that Cindy and the rest of the Canning clan are part of my life. Then I drive to the hospital to take care of our boy.

EIGHTEEN
JAMIE

The hospital kept me another day just to run tests. They drew blood so many times that I had a dream about vampires in scrubs.

So I had to spend another night in this place. While I tried to sleep, they kept coming in to take my temperature every hour. And now I have a dry, hacking cough that keeps me from sleeping even when the nurses aren't prodding me.

At least I convinced Wes to go home to our bed for the night. He's going to miss the Tampa game tonight for nothing, because I'm still fricking here. I want out of this bed and into my own clothes.

"Hey handsome!"

It's about ten in the morning when he turns up to see me, looking well-rested and fresh as a daisy. While I'm skank man with stubble and armpit stink, at least one of us is comfortable.

"I brought you a chocolate croissant and a double cappuccino," he says, kissing my temple before dropping into the chair. "And good news. Supposedly you're being released in a couple hours."

"Great," I say, trying to believe him. "Thank you." I take the coffee cup he offers me and swig it, but my stomach clenches a second later. Fuck. I set it on the table. If I can't even handle coffee, you might as well just take me out back and shoot me.

His smile fades. "What's the matter? What can I do for you?"

I'm already tired of being the one that people do things for. "Just want a *shower*, and I want to go home."

Nurse Bertha clucks her tongue from the doorway. "Gotta kick that fever if you want permission to use the shower. I'm a big lady but not big enough to catch you if you fall."

"You still have a fever?" Wes yelps, clamping a hand on my forehead.

It's a struggle not to push him off me. "Low grade," I grumble. "No big deal."

"I can bring a basin and a cloth and freshen you up," Bertha offers. She taps one brilliant red fingernail against her smile. "Or, I could take a thirty minute break first. Then I'll come by and help clean you up."

"But I'm going home later, right?" I plead. Because that's all that really matters. At home I can do whatever the fuck I want.

"Sure, sugar. The doctor will make his rounds at noon and release you. But I'll see you in thirty minutes." She leaves and I groan, which makes me start coughing. Yay.

Wes bolts across the room and shuts the door. "Okay, up!" he says, taking off his jacket. "Shower time."

"What?" I cough again, because it's hard to stop, even though my stomach is already sore from the effort.

"Jesus, Canning." Wes gives me a smartass grin over his

shoulder, the same one he's been giving me since we were fourteen. "Rules are for breaking. There's no lock on the door, but whatever." When he turns around, I see he's unbuttoning his shirt.

"What are you doing?"

"Don't want to get my shirt wet," he says as his tattoos ripple into view. He tosses the shirt onto the chair and then unzips his jeans.

I'm still hesitating, though, my hands on the sheet that covers my lap. The words are on the tip of my tongue: *We're going to get in so much trouble for this.*

"You want a shower, right?" His eyes flash with humor. "The warm water will help you with that nasty cough. We got thirty minutes, tops. I'm starting the shower."

He disappears into the little bathroom, where I've only been once. Last night, instead of calling for the bedpan, I walked shakily in there to pee. Which I have to do again now that I can hear the water running.

Well then. No time like the present.

I ease myself off the bed and onto the cold floor tiles. I hate the stupid hospital johnny I'm wearing. Can't even look at the thing without feeling disgust.

Note to self—don't ever get sick again. This place is the worst.

And I actually sway on my way to the bathroom. My fever is low, but I haven't really eaten much in two days. When I make it to the toilet, I grip the grab bar bolted to the wall like I'm an old lady.

"Okay. Water's warm," Wes says in a cheery voice. But I know he's watching me carefully, and there's concern on his face.

I turn away and aim at the toilet, taking care of business. Wes pretends to fiddle with the shower faucet in order to preserve my tattered dignity. After I flush the toilet he unties the wretched hospital gown and tosses it onto a hook. I stagger past him into the little shower stall.

"Have a seat," he says casually. There's a shower bench waiting.

I ignore him and walk under the spray. It feels *amazing*. I turn slowly around, just basking in it. But fuck, now I'm *dizzy*.

A warm hand closes around my upper arm. Whether or not I like it, I'm guided firmly onto the waiting seat. I put my elbows on my knees and drop my head into my hands. If I weren't so tired I might even cry. And the water only hits me at an awkward angle from here, damn it.

There is a rustle beside me and then the water moves. When I open my eyes, Wes is naked and standing in the shower stall, too. He's unhooked the showerhead, which is attached to a hose. Humming to himself, he eases it around to rain down on my shoulders. "Tip your head back," he says softly. When I do, he wets my hair.

The water disappears a moment later, and then Wes's hands are lathering up my head. We've showered together a hundred times, but never like this. I hate being dependent on him like this. Leaning forward, I rest my forehead on his hip bone and sigh.

He just keeps going. The strong hands that I love so much skim the back of my neck, my shoulders, behind my ears. He rinses me next, shielding my forehead with his palm to keep the soap out of my eyes. They sting anyway from frustration. Then he kneels in front of me.

When I look up, a serious pair of gray eyes are right there, level with mine. "Hey," he says softly.

"H-hey," I stammer. *Don't mind me, I'm just having a fucking breakdown.*

He grabs my head in both hands and kisses me. I let my eyelids fall closed while I pull him in. His lips are soft and wet. He slants his mouth over mine for real. A warm tongue sweeps the seam of my lips. Then we're making out in a hospital shower, which is just insane. It's not about sex, though. It's comfort kissing. I like it a lot more than a palm on a forehead.

When Wes pulls back, he gives me a secretive little smile. "Tonight you'll be home," he whispers. "In our bed."

Swallowing hard, I nod. I'd better be.

"Lift your arms," he prompts.

When I do, he washes my underarms, skimming my sensitive skin with soap-slicked hands. Those palms continue their journey down my abs and into the juncture of my legs. He nudges my knees apart and washes my inner thighs, his fingertips grazing my balls. He lets his hand linger there, giving me one slow stroke. He's reminding me that life isn't always such a drag, and I'm grateful for the message.

Humming again, he takes the hose and washes away the soap, taking his time, touching me everywhere with admiring hands. "We should probably get out of here," he says eventually.

"Yeah."

The water shuts off, and Wes grabs both towels off the rack where they wait. He ties one around his waist, then drops one over my head and begins to rub my hair dry.

"I got it," I say, lifting my heavy arms to do the work. "Could you see what Blake left me for clothes?"

"He brought flannel pants, so I brought your jeans this morning. Hang on."

Wes dries himself hastily and climbs back into his boxers. I hear him thumping around in the room, jumping into his clothes. He returns with underwear and jeans for me. "Stand up, babe."

Creakily, I do. I dry myself off, but I do it while practically leaning on him. Wes chucks his towel onto the shower bench and then I sit on it to put my drawers on and then my jeans. He holds out a hand that I grab to stand up, and he pulls me into a hug.

If I've ever doubted his love for me, I'm an idiot.

"Come on." He lets me move under my own power into the room, but he thrusts the chair at me. "Sit. You'll feel better if you're out of that bed for a little while."

He's right. I will.

I take a seat by the windows. Wes is digging through the duffel that Blake brought. "Hey, you want a shave?" He holds up a razor and a can of shaving cream.

"Here? Now?"

"You got something else you need to be doing right now?"

"No." I chuckle.

Wes drapes my towel over my bare shoulders. He grabs some kind of little basin thing from a cabinet on the wall. I don't even want to know what it's supposed to be for. He fills it with water and leans over me. He lathers up my cheeks and chin, then inch by inch he shaves my stubbled face.

I can feel his breath on my cheekbone as he leans in to shave me carefully. The water is warm and so is his touch. Getting a shave at the barber shop used to be something dudes did in ye olden days, but now I know the process is weirdly intimate. My face is so sensitive to Wes's touch. I enjoy the way his free hand cups my jaw, his thumb stroking over my cheek to check his work.

When he switches sides, I get a kiss on the back of my neck. "I'm supposed to go to Nashville in the morning," he says as two fingers tap beneath my chin. "Lift."

I lift. "Go. I'll be fine," I say quickly. "I'll order take-out soup and watch TV at home. That's all I need, anyway. A few days of quiet. I'll be good as new."

He's almost finished when Bertha walks back in. "Look at you!" she crows. "Somebody looks happier."

Do I? I guess so. It's good to be clean.

She doesn't say a word about the steam in the air or our damp hair and bare feet. Instead, she gathers the sheets up off the bed and disappears, returning a minute later with a clean set. She puts them on while Wes finishes smoothing the last bits of shaving cream off my face.

"Now sit here again for me," Bertha says, lifting the back of the bed and pointing at it. "They're going to bring you some chicken noodle for lunch while I chase down your release paperwork."

The soup is tasteless, but I eat it anyway in case it's some kind of test of my ability to go home. Wes and I end up splitting the chocolate croissant, and I choke down my half. I have no appetite at all. But I'm tired of feeling so weak.

Wes finds a photo on Facebook of my new niece. And then by some miracle, my release papers turn up. Wes chats with a doctor about all those freaking tests, but I don't even listen. They haven't turned up anything of interest, and I just want to put the nightmare behind me.

The final insult is the wheelchair Bertha brings for me. "It's a rule," she insists. "Just like on TV."

I'm so desperate to leave that I don't even argue. I sit in the damn thing. Wes shoulders the duffel bag and pushes me toward the elevators. Freedom is near! He must feel the same way, because when we get to the main floor, he pushes me at a jog, following the signs toward the parking garage.

When the electric doors part for us, the cold air takes my breath away. I'm not wearing a jacket.

"Sorry," Wes says, squeezing my shoulder. "He should be right…there!"

A Hummer pulls toward us with Blake Riley grinning from behind the wheel. "Why isn't Blake in Tampa?" I ask.

"Knee injury. He's gonna miss…oh, fuck."

I'm just processing Blake's crappy news, so it takes me a second to register the sound of feet pounding across the asphalt.

"Ryan Wesley!" a voice calls. "Tell us how you two are doing!" Then flashbulbs begin to illuminate the concrete walls of the parking garage. "Over here, Wesley!"

"Ignore them, babe," Wes says tightly. He yanks open the back door of the Hummer, then turns to offer me a hand.

"If you help me right now I will *end you*," I threaten.

He lifts his hands quickly, like a busted perp, and I push to my feet unassisted. It's only a couple of steps and I'm sliding onto the leather seat of Blake's machomobile.

Wes ditches the wheelchair and climbs in beside me. He yanks the door closed as reporters swarm the car windows. One of those assholes actually puts the lens up to Blake's tinted window and lights up the interior with his flash.

There's a growl from the front seat, and then Blake eases the car forward a few feet, which does the trick. Nobody wants his feet run over. Blake accelerates as Wes lets out a big sigh. "Jesus."

It's quiet in the car for a couple of minutes as Blake

maneuvers us back onto Toronto's busy streets. "How you feeling, J-Bomb?"

"Fine," I say, but then I start coughing like a TB patient.

Wes is tense and silent beside me, scrolling through what looks like a lifetime of text messages. "Oh!" he says suddenly. "Phew."

"What?" I ask between coughs. A little good news would be nice right now.

He holds up his phone to show me a text from my mom: *Your schedule says Nashville and then Carolina. So we're sending you Jess on the red eye. She arrives in the morning.*

"Wait," I gasp, willing my throat to relax. "What?"

"Jess is coming to take care of you because I'm going out of town. Man, I could kiss your mom. Too bad she doesn't get here until tomorrow, though."

"I don't need Jess. I don't need *anyone*," I correct. Christ. My sister will just hog the TV remote and nag me.

But Wes tucks his phone away and relaxes against the seat. "Too late. Looks like they bought a ticket."

He sounds ridiculously relieved, so I swallow my objections. "Thanks for picking me up," I rasp to Blake in the front seat.

"No problemo! I like driving the getaway car like a gangster. Do you think I'd make a good gangster?" He clears his throat and does a poor imitation of the Godfather movie. "Luca Brasi sleeps with the dishes."

"It's *fishes*, champ," I point out.

"Nah!" Blake snorts. "Can't be. That's not grammatical." He takes a corner really fast, which means that Wes and I get tossed a little toward my side of the car.

Wes clamps an arm against my chest the way you do for

little kids who aren't buckled in. If everyone would just leave me alone, I'd be fine. I really would.

"Dunno if I'd put a horse's head in some dude's bed, though," Blake muses from the front. "Kinda messy."

I beat my head back against the seat and wonder how it all came to this.

Wes is already gone when I pry my tired eyes open the next morning. There's a green post-it note on his pillow, and I groggily reach for it.

Wanted to say goodbye with a BJ but you were so out of it I didn't have the heart to wake you. Call you when I land in Nashville. Blake's on the couch if you need 'im. Jess gets in at eleven. Love you.

His familiar scrawl soothes me, but the words he'd written? Not so much. I don't need a babysitter, let alone two of them. What I *do* need is to get out of this bed, throw some clothes on, and go to my morning practice.

I've got people depending on me, damn it. Braddock may have given me the week off (or rather, he gave me an indefinite amount of time off, until I "get better") but there's no way I'm skipping work. We have an important tournament coming up in a few weeks. The kids need to be ready for it. My *goalie* needs to be ready. It makes me sick that another coach might be working with Dunlop just because I have a stupid cough and—

I nearly hack up a lung as I sit up in bed. Fuck. My eyes water, chest aching as I grip my side and cough so hard I fear I might've cracked a rib.

Heavy footsteps pound in the hallway. In a heartbeat, Blake appears at the door sporting a pair of plaid boxers and a serious case of bedhead. "Cheezus! You all right, J-Bomb?" he demands. "What can I get you? Water? Pain meds?"

I glare at him through another round of wild coughing. When he steps closer, I whip up my hand and choke out, "I'm fine."

Disbelieving green eyes stare back at me. "You're not fine. You sound like you're about to drop dead any second. I'm calling Wesley!"

Luckily, my coughing fit stops at that moment. I stumble out of bed. "You don't need to call Wes," I say tersely. "I told you, I'm fine."

"Oh yeah? Then why you wobbling around like a…what wobbles? A little horse, right? A *foal*." He looks pleased with himself. "Why you wobbling around like a foal? Hey—where you going?"

I stop in front of the door to our private bath. "I'm taking a leak," I say through clenched teeth. "Is that allowed?"

Blake follows me right into the bathroom. To my annoyance, he crosses his huge arms over his huge chest and says, "Wesley said I can't let you outta my sight. In case you fall or something."

Oh my fucking God. "You want to hold my dick for me too?" I mutter.

He chuckles. "Naw, I'll leave the dick-holding to your man. I'll just watch."

There is nothing more mortifying than taking a piss while your boyfriend's giant teammate stands there watching. He then proceeds to follow me around the bedroom as I make a very labored effort to get dressed.

"You don't need to doll up on my account," he remarks as I button up my shirt.

"Not for you," I bite out. "I've got practice in an hour."

"Oh no he di-in't." Next thing I know, Blake is in front of me again. *Unbuttoning* my shirt. My weak attempts to bat his hands away are unsuccessful. "You're not going anywhere except back to bed," he orders. "Or on the couch, if you wanna watch some of the morning talk shows with me. You like *The View*? I do. Those broads are fun. I was on there once, d'ya know that? I hit on Whoopi. Struck out." He pouts. "Bummer, huh?"

"Blake."

He stops. "Yeah?"

"Stop. Fucking. Talking." I'm being rude. I know I am. But holy hell, my head is killing me. My chest aches. My legs can barely support my own weight. Don't my ears deserve some comfort? Can't this behemoth shut up for *five goddamn seconds*?

A hurt look crosses his face. "Ah, okay. Sorry." Then his features harden, and in that moment I can see why he's so formidable in the ice. His don't-mess-with-me glare is terrifying. "But you're not going to practice, J-Bomb. Better wrap your head around that, because it. Ain't. Happening."

BLAKE and I watch *The View*. In silence. I've suddenly got that Joni Mitchell song blaring in my head, about not knowing what I have 'til it's gone. I actually miss Blake's nonsensical chatter. The silence is excruciating. It makes me overly aware of my unsteady breathing, the wheeze in my chest every time I inhale. Whenever I hack, Blake silently reaches over and pats my back through the coughing fit. Once I'm done, he hands me a glass of water in an unspoken command to drink. Fuck. He really is a good guy.

"I'm sorry," I blurt out.

His head tips toward me.

"I'm sorry I told you to shut up, okay? I'm just not used to accepting help from anyone. I'm not used to being…" *Helpless*. I can't even say the word. And now I feel my face getting hot, but I don't know if it's from embarrassment and frustration, or if my fever might be back. My sweatpants and hoodie are kinda damp, now that I think about it. I'm sweating.

"S'all good," Blake mumbles.

I reach over and clap my hand over his shoulder, giving it a squeeze. "No, it's not. I was an ass, and I'm sorry. You're a good friend, Blake."

After a beat, he breaks out in a broad grin. "Damn right I am. Apology accepted, Mr. Cranky Pants. I know you're just grumpy because—" He halts, frowning. "Your hand feels like an oven mitt. Well, if the oven mitt was in the oven getting roasted. Is your fever back?"

"No." He gives me a wary look, but at least he doesn't leap off the couch in search of a thermometer. I don't think we have one, anyway.

He does bring me a glass of ice water and a bunch of pills, which I force myself to swallow. Unfortunately, they happen to be the drowsy kind, so it's not long before I'm snoring on the couch.

I'm not sure how long I sleep for, but eventually I register the sounds of dogs barking. There's a high-pitched Chihuahua and she sounds very pissed off. The Rottweiler she's barking at...maybe he thinks the Chihuahua is in heat? He sounds kinda happy. Do Chihuahuas and Rottweilers breed? Are their offspring called Rottuas?

"Chiweilers," I mumble.

The dogs stop barking.

"Did he just say 'chiweilers'?" a female voice demands. "What the hell is a chiweiler?"

"Rottweiler Chihuahua mix breed," comes a deep male voice. "Fucking duh."

My eyes snap open and I groan when I see Blake and my sister Jessica in front of the couch. They're both staring at me like I've grown horns and a pimp mustache.

Then Jess says, "Jamie!" and throws herself at me, hugging me tight enough to make my ribs ache. "Are you okay, Jamester? How are you feeling? Wow, you feel a little hot."

"Shit," Blake says irritably. "Is the fever back?"

"I've got this—I can take it from here. So buh-bye, you big mountain of man meat. I'm on duty now."

Blake stubbornly shakes his head. "I promised Wesley I'd take care of him."

"I give you permission to break that promise. Now shoo!"

"Guys...would you..." My voice sounds hoarse "...please stop yelling? My head is killing me."

Concern washes over Jess's brown eyes. Followed by the heat of accusation as she spins toward Blake again. "You didn't tell me he had a headache!"

"I didn't know!"

"What kind of nurse are you?"

"The kind who plays hockey!"

Their voices are raised again. I want to strangle them both. Groaning, I sit up and rub both fists against my eyes. "What time is it?"

"One," Jess says. "Did you eat lunch?"

"Um…"

"Breakfast?" she prods. Then she glares at Blake. "You didn't *feed* him? How's he supposed to get well if he's starving?"

"I'm not really hungry," I offer. But it's no use. The two of them are bickering again. This time the argument is over what I'll be eating to regain my strength. Blake's idea involves a trip to Tim Hortons, so he walks out the door.

I slump down on the sofa again, and for many blessed minutes nobody bothers me, because Jess is rattling around in the kitchen cooking something. The ache in my head eases a little. Time slips by, and the only sound is the TV trying to sell me luxury cars and pharmaceuticals.

The peace is shattered when the door opens again, admitting Blake. "I have food, J-Babe!"

"*What* did you call me?" Jess yelps from the kitchen.

"How did you get in?" I slur from the couch.

"Made myself a key," Blake says, dropping it into his pocket. He sets a big box down on the table and pops it open. "Brought you a turkey club on a honey cruller! All the food groups in one handy package."

"A…" I must have misunderstood, because I swear he said he brought me a sandwich on a donut. That is just wrong.

Jess marches toward the couch with a plate in her hand. "Keep that away from him," she snaps. "I made him an organic kale omelet." She thrusts the plate onto my lap and sticks a fork in my hand.

Not to be outdone, Blake plops a scary looking donut club sandwich on the plate beside it.

I want to tell both of them where to shove it, but that will only lead to more arguing. So instead I take a small bite of the omelet. And then a nibble of Blake's creation.

Chewing. Swallowing. These are things I used to find easy. But my head aches and my stomach isn't at all sure about this. I chase another bite of omelet—heavy on the kale—with a syrupy bite of donut.

"That's health food right there," Blake crows.

Jess puts her hands on her hips and begins to argue. And I can't take it anymore. The room spins for a moment before my vision clears, but the rush of nausea that floods my gut only gets stronger.

"*Fuck*," I choke out.

I heave myself off the couch. The hall bathroom seems too far away, but I just make it, slamming the door behind me and then bending over the toilet to ralph my brains out.

I'm still gasping and trembling when I feel warm hands on my shoulders. My vision is fuzzy again. A cold, wet cloth sweeps over my face.

"You need to go back to bed," Jess says softly.

I think she might be right. So I clean myself up for a second and then stumble to my room. I crawl under the covers and listen while Jess and Blake yell at each other over whose breakfast made me boot.

THE WOOZINESS STAYS with me all day. I think I'm pretty feverish, but I don't say anything, because I don't want any attention. Rest is the only thing I need.

Jess claims that we're low on groceries, which may or may not be true. But she sends Blake out with a list, maybe to keep him busy. The two of them forget about me for a while, which is perfect.

I have more fever dreams, though. There are periods of complete confusion when I open my eyes and don't know where the hell I am. I feel cold, my entire body breaking out in shivers as ice flows through my veins. No, wait, I'm hot. It's blistering in this room. Jesus Christ, do we live in a *furnace*?

I frantically rip off my hoodie and sweats, but the fabric just stays tangled around my limbs.

"*Furnace*," I say to the walls. "Feel like a furnace."

The room doesn't answer back.

The next time I wake up, it's dark out. I don't know what time it is, or what day.

I don't know why I'm so out of it. They told me I didn't have the sheep flu. They said it was just the normal flu, damn it. I should be getting better.

So why do I feel worse?

I miss Wes. I want Wes. Did I talk to him today? I don't remember. But I want to hear his voice. Instead, I hear a strange sound, like a Chihuahua and a Rottweiler mating. There are weird little yips and low grunts, and the low hum of the vibrating chair.

Weird.

I'm just trying to make sense of the noises when the phone lights up on the nightstand. Even though I'm bleary, the display clearly says WES, and I'm overjoyed.

"Hello?" I slur into the phone. "Do we have dogs?"

Call me crazy, but all the way to Nashville I worry about Jamie.

Even as the taxi from the airport pulls up in front of the stadium, I just keep picturing things that could go wrong. Maybe Jess's plane will get grounded during her layover in Denver. Maybe Jamie will get dizzy and hit his head and end up lying on the floor in a pool of his own blood…

Damn it. I need to stop letting my imagination run away with me. I'm not usually a worrier. But my spidey sense is uncomfortable, and I can't figure out why. It's probably just the shock of seeing him so sick in the hospital. Maybe I'm not over it yet.

I type Jess's flight information into the airline's app once more and find that she landed safely hours ago.

Unless she missed her connection, and her phone is dead…

The security guard opens my door, and I pay the cab driver and flash my ID for the guard.

He looks up quickly, his bushy eyebrows lifting. "You're the guy on the news."

Unfortunately. "Where can I find the visitors' dressing room?" I ask him.

He shakes off his surprise and opens the door. "Down this hall. You'll see signs on your left."

"Got it. Thanks."

"Good luck out there," he says as I start down the hall.

"Uh, thanks." The new paranoid me actually spends a minute wondering what he meant by that. Do I need extra luck today? Or is it the same thing he says to every player who walks through the door?

Shit. I hope our practice will be sweaty and grueling. I need to get out of my fucking head.

It's not so hard to find the dressing room, because I can hear my teammates' voices as I approach the door.

"So, season ticket-holders are selling their seats on the cheap?" Eriksson's voice asks.

"Not cheap," Forsberg answers him. "But those seats never turn over. There's guys waiting a decade for a season ticket. But the next few games are for sale by the hundreds of seats."

I stop walking so fast that my duffel bag bumps me in the ass.

"But so what, right? It's not like we're gonna play in an empty stadium on Monday."

"Nah," Forsberg agrees. "Frank Donovan said the club is buying all of 'em up at the face price and donating them to some, like, LGSQ group."

"You mean LGBT?"

"I dunno. I'm pretty sure there was a Q in there."

"Ryan?"

I whirl around and spot Frank coming down the hall behind me, another man at his side. "Hey," I say quickly, giving him an awkward wave. Is there any chance he didn't see me standing here outside the door listening?

"Ryan, is everything okay?"

Nope—no chance he didn't notice. "Of course. Never better."

"Great."

The other guy steps forward to offer his hand. I shake it, wondering if I'm supposed to know who he is. "I'm Dennis Haymaker."

Oh. My father's college buddy. "*Sports Illustrated*, right?" I ask, though I'm certain he's the reporter I've been ducking since July.

"Yeah..." He clears his throat. "How is your partner doing?"

"Better." It still weirds me out to talk about Jamie in public. I'll get used to it, but it might take a while.

"Good," he says. "You know, your dad stopped taking my calls all of a sudden."

I laugh before I can think better of it. "Uh-huh. Lemme guess—he stopped returning them about three days ago?"

Dennis smiles tentatively. "About then, yeah."

"Shocker." I chuckle. "I wouldn't hold your breath to have those calls returned. He's too busy scratching my name out of the family bible."

"This is *not* on the record," Frank Donovan stammers. I know he wants me to stop talking. But for the first time, this guy is someone I might want to talk to. That would really be sticking it to the old man—I could give my Big Gay Interview to his college buddy. If I'm lucky, it will make the alumni magazine at Dad's alma mater.

"Well..." Dennis looks grave. "I'm still looking forward to writing about your rookie year."

I can't help but snort. "I'll bet."

"Hey now—I've been waiting for your story for eight months. It's still a rookie season story."

"Is it?" I stare him down.

"Of course it is."

"So we wouldn't be talking about my sexuality?" I say this with a straight face somehow.

"Well…" he hedges. "I'm not going to write some piece of clickbait. But your background was always going to be part of the story. Your college team. Your *upbringing*."

The man is smart. He already knows that I'd like to stick it to Dad. "Fine. We have a string of home games coming up. If Jamie is feeling better, I'll make time for us to sit down."

He almost keeps the glee off his face. But not quite. "I'm looking forward to it," he says, thrusting out his hand to shake again.

"We'll call you," Frank tells him, and he gets a shake, too.

The guy makes himself scarce then, before I can change my mind.

"So," Frank says.

"So."

"Any problems? Anything you need to know about the media coverage?"

"To be honest, I haven't read much of it. Too busy."

He nods slowly. "Okay. I'll have my team compile some clips of the highlights, if you'd like to be kept up to date."

"What if I don't?" I sound like a smartass, but I'm dead serious.

He shrugs. "Your call."

"Hey—what's with people selling their tickets? I heard murmurs."

"Ah." He shifts his weight. That's his tell, I've learned. If I faced him over a poker table, I'd bet heavily whenever he did that. "That's just noise. Nothing will come of it."

"How many season-ticket holders bailed?"

"Not enough to matter. Just a few loud mouths with nothing else to yap about. Next week it'll be old news. We're trying to buy up any tickets for sale—I put an 800 number on the website and everything. Haven't gotten many nibbles. The tickets go too fast on Craigslist."

Huh. I don't know whether to believe him or not. "Okay."

"That all?"

"Yeah."

"I'll let you know if you'll be part of the post-game conference tonight. We'll see how the game goes."

That sounds a little ominous, but I'm not gonna ask.

He steps around me and opens the dressing room door. I follow him inside, and when I do, my team calls out various casual greetings. "How's Jamie?" someone asks.

"Good," I say for the second time in five minutes. "His sister is coming to stay with him for a couple days."

"Nice."

"Yeah," I agree, feeling guilty. I should be there in Toronto myself. But instead I'm here in this unfamiliar room, trying to figure out where they're putting me.

"Over here," Hewitt calls out. He points at a bench, and then I spot my practice jersey hanging there.

"Thanks." I start stripping out of my clothes. Our ice time begins in mere minutes.

"We're gonna run PK drills," he says, sitting down beside me. His skates are on and he's ready to go.

"Okay," I answer, my mind only half on this conversation with our team enforcer. "Why penalty drills?"

"Gonna rack up some minutes if these guys go after you."

My heart sinks all the way to the goddamn floor. "Why do you think they'll go after me?" *Apart from the obvious.* "I mean—won't that backfire?" Now that I think about it, I'll bet the refs are having a pretty high-level meeting today. *Strategies to handle teams who want to smear the queer.*

"They might not," Hewitt says quickly. "I just want to be ready. I plan on taking as many minutes in the sin bin as needed, man. We're not gonna let those assholes get away with anything."

Shit! This is exactly what I was hoping to avoid. If I'd come out over the summer, it would have cycled out of the news before I was put in a position to make my team change their game to defend me.

"Look," I say quietly. "I appreciate it. I really do. But don't jump the first guy who calls me a faggot. There's no point in making this into a gong show if we can avoid it. Keep it reined in at first. Let's just see what happens."

Hewitt nods slowly. Then he thumps me on the back and stands up. "Okay, rookie. I won't go all Hulk on 'em right away."

I SKATE HARD during our abbreviated practice. But when we're sent to the hotel to rest, I can't sleep. A call to Jamie goes unanswered, probably because he's sleeping.

That's good, right?

Everything feels just a little off, though. I'm still worried about Jamie. And I have rarely been so keyed up for a game as I am for this one.

After a restless few hours it's back to the rink and the bustle of getting ready for the game. We're the visiting team, so we get some heckling when we're introduced at game time. I never pay attention to that shit, but tonight I can't screen it out. Are the boos louder than usual? Is my team going to regret me?

The game starts off normally, but my teammates are visibly tense, and I know it's because of me. When my line takes a faceoff, I'm shoulder to shoulder with a guy named Chukas. My eyes never leave the puck as he says, "So you're the faggot, huh? You gonna sport some wood if I pin you against the boards?"

"Only if you kiss me first," I return. Then the puck drops, and it's on. When I'm playing hockey, I shut off all my doubts. I have to. The game requires every bit of my concentration. I love that about hockey. It feels hella good to drop out of my own life for a couple of hours and see only the bodies in motion on a bright white sheet of ice.

By the end of the first period it's clear that this game is neither rougher nor friendlier than any other matchup. Just the same big-league brawl that it always is. By the third period, my team stops looking so clenched up.

It's too little, too late, though, because we only tie the game, when we really could have done better. But for once in my life I'm counting that as a win. There won't be any bruising newspaper headlines about my game tomorrow.

A week ago I scored a hat trick. Tonight I'm scraping by without making the national news. My standards? Consider 'em lowered.

I get back to the locker room dripping with sweat and relieved that the NHL has survived a game with its first out player. I drop my pads and grab my phone even before I hit the showers. It's almost ten and I want to call Jamie before he goes to sleep. I dial him, hoping I'm not waking him up. He answers immediately. "Do we have dogs?"

"What, baby? I didn't catch that."

"Dogs. Chiweilers. We don't have one of those, right?"

A chill climbs up my sweaty back. "Uh, we don't have dogs, no." Is he joking with me?

"I want a puppy," Jamie says. His voice is hoarse. "Always wanted one. My parents said six kids was enough animals in the house."

My brain is playing catch up with this conversation. "Do you have a fever, babe?"

"I dunno. Hot in here, though."

"Where are you?" *Because I'm about ten seconds from calling 911.*

"In bed. Where are you? Shouldn't you be here?"

The chill breaks everywhere across my skin. "I'm in Nashville," I say carefully. "For a game. Where is Jess, babe? She's supposed to be there with you."

"Uh…" he says with a sigh. "Haven't seen her lately."

Then he starts coughing, and the sound is awful. Deep and wet. I just stand there with the phone pinned to my sweating face, listening to him struggle for breath. I've never felt so helpless in my entire life. "Jamie," I say finally when there's a break. "Are you…"

He hacks again.

Frank Donovan is trying to get my attention now. He's pointing at his watch, and then the showers. He must want me at his post-game press conference.

I wave him off, or I try to. But he camps out in front of me. So I ignore him. "Jamie," I plead when he stops coughing again. "I love you, but I have to hang up and call Jess. Has she heard that cough?"

"Dunno," he mumbles. "Sleepy now."

"Okay," I say, my mind reeling. What am I going to do? "Sleep well if you can. But if your sister needs you to go to the emergency room, you're gonna go, okay?"

"Nah," he whispers. "Night." The line goes dead.

"FUCK!" I shout.

"What's the problem?" Frank asks.

I'm too freaked out to answer him. I dial Jess and listen to it ring. When her voicemail eventually picks up, I disconnect and try again. Nothing. "Hey, Eriksson?" I call.

"Yeah?" He's toweling off in front of his locker.

"I need a favor. Try to raise Blake on your cell. It's an emergency. I need him in my apartment."

Eriksson doesn't ask questions. He jams a hand in his suit coat pocket and pulls out his phone.

I redial Jess. Where the hell is she? On the fourth try, she answers. "Wes?"

"Where are you?" I demand.

"At your house!" She sounds oddly breathless.

"Really? Because I just spoke to Jamie and he's *delirious*. He thinks we have something called a Chiweiler. And his cough sounds like a death rattle." I shudder just saying it. "Where's Blake?"

"Uh, Blake? I'm not sure."

But in the background I hear sudden strains of "Who Let The Dogs Out," which is Blake's ringtone. "Hey. Is that him?"

"He just walked in." Now she sounds flustered.

"Okay, listen. Jamie needs *help*. He said he was in bed. Get Blake to break the door if it's locked. You might have to take him to an emergency room."

"Oh my God," she gasps. "I'll call you back in ten."

"Is everything okay?" Frank asks when I've hung up.

"No, it fucking isn't. You know any doctors?"

"Doctors?" He gazes at the ceiling, considering the question. "We retired a team doctor about three years ago. He lives in Rosedale. Why?"

"There's something wrong with Jamie. He has a fever and this awful cough. Fuck. I should never have left town."

Frank's face sags. "Sounds like pneumonia. Maybe he's come down with a secondary infection. He should go to emergency."

"I KNOW!" I holler, and everyone in the room—including a few reporters—turns to stare at me. "I know," I say more quietly. "Get me this doctor's phone number. I need help."

TWENTY-ONE

JAMIE

One Week Later

It's déjà vu all over again.

Another release from the hospital. Another wheelchair. Another crowd of media vultures lurking outside, and another speedy getaway in a hired car that Wes has waiting outside.

The last week has been hell. I found myself in that fucking hospital *again*. But I was out of it for the first three days. On the fourth day I woke up to find both my mother and nurse Bertha staring at me with worried expressions on their faces.

Never get pneumonia. Just don't. It's a real bitch.

But my fever is gone for good now. Mom flew back to California this morning with Jess, and I can't say I'm not relieved, especially about the latter being gone. I love Jess, but she was *not* in a good place this week. She felt so incredibly guilty that I'd gotten a high fever on her watch that she stuck to me like Velcro the whole time I was in the hospital. My mother had to send her home a couple of times when I couldn't take any more of her overbearing brand of love.

Wes and I don't speak as we step out of the elevator. My legs feel a bit wobbly, and I stumble when we're halfway down the hall, but when Wes tries to take my arm, I scowl at him. I'm sick to death of being fussed over and treated like I'm an invalid.

Without a word, his hand drops to his side. We reach our apartment. Wes jams the key in the lock and pops the door open. Inside, he throws the bag with my stuff in it onto the floor and then stands in the middle of the living room, staring at me.

"You need anything?" His voice is gruff. "Food? Shower? Tea?"

Tea? Like I'm a little old lady whose delicate stomach can't handle good old coffee?

Bitterness rises in my throat. I force myself to swallow it down, because it's not fair to Wes. It's not his fault I got laid out on my ass with pneumonia. And I know what a panic he's been in this past week.

He played another two games on the road before he could even come to the hospital to see me. Not that I noticed in my passed-out state. But the team wouldn't give him a hardship leave because my sister and mother were converging on the hospital.

He told me this morning that he doesn't even remember those games, he was so pissed off and worried, calling Jess and Mom and Blake every free moment he had.

I should be kissing his feet for being a concerned, loving boyfriend. But I'm not. I'm just...mad. At him. At my body. At fucking everything. And the drugs the hospital pumped me full of this week are wreaking havoc on my system. I started a course of steroids this morning, and they're making me feel strange. It's like a superficial high that doesn't quite match the anger and resentment churning in my stomach.

Wes watches me warily. "Babe?"

I realize I haven't answered the question. "I don't need anything," I mumble. "Gonna take a nap."

Disappointment crosses his expression. He doesn't have a game today, and I know he was probably hoping to spend some time together. But I'm not good company right now. I'm sick of being sick. I hated being in the hospital. I hate that I can't go back to work until…until who fucking knows when. I called Bill last night and he ordered me not to even think about coming back for at least another week.

I don't need another week. I just need my life back.

"Okay," Wes finally says. "I'll just…" His gray eyes dart around, then land on the hall table, which is stacked high with mail. "Open the mail, maybe pay some bills."

A scornful remark almost flies out. *Do you even know how?*

Since we moved in together, Wes hasn't taken care of any house-related shit. Laundry. Bills. Cleaning. I do it all, because he's too busy being an NHL sensation to—

Enough, an internal voice commands. Maybe it's my conscience. Or the part of me that is madly, deeply in love with this man. Either way, I'm not being fair again.

So I inject genuine gratitude into my response. "Thanks. That would definitely make my life easier if you did that. And keep a lookout for the hospital bill—" I stop and gulp, because it just occurred to me that a two-week hospital visit might very well drain my savings account. Maybe even max out my credit cards. I'm not a Canadian citizen, so I'm not sure if my insurance will cover the entire stay.

"Oh, there won't be one," Wes says, waving a hand. "I already paid your deductible. Insurance covered the rest."

I clench my jaw. He paid my bill?

Wes frowns when he notices my expression. "What's wrong?"

My voice comes out harsher than I intend. "Let me know the amount you paid and I'll transfer the money into your account."

He's quick to protest. "It's not a big deal, babe. I've got plenty of cash. Why put financial strain on yourself when I'm perfectly capable of—"

"I'll pay you back," I grind out.

There's a long pause. Then Wes nods. "Okay. If that's what you want."

"It's what I want." I don't know why I'm being so snappy. It just grates that Wes settled my hospital bill without even telling me. I get that he's got oodles of money, but I'm not his...his fucking *mistress*. We're partners, and I'll be damned if I let him pay for everything.

After a beat of hesitation, he steps forward and touches my cheek. He strokes my clean-shaven skin. I actually got to shave this morning. By myself. Woo-fucking-hoo. But I guess I should be thankful for small mercies.

"Jamie." His voice is hoarse. "I'm glad you're better."

A lump clogs my throat. Goddamn it. The relief in his eyes spurs a rush of guilt. I know I've been an ass to him this week. I snapped at him when he came to visit me. I balked when he suggested that maybe my mom and sister should stay longer. I resented him when I watched him on the hospital TV, skating like a champion and scoring goals while I was flat on my back, pissing into a bedpan. And now I'm picking fights about *money*, of all things.

"Me too," I murmur, leaning into his warm touch.

He rubs my bottom lip, then presses his mouth to mine in a soft, fleeting kiss. "Okay, go nap. I'll be out here if you need me."

I'm about to ask him to join me, but his phone rings before I can open my mouth. Wes's hand leaves my face and slides into his pocket. His gorgeous face creases in frustration when he sees who's calling.

"Frank," he mumbles to me, then steps away to take the call.

I linger long enough to glean that Frank the PR Wonder is on Wes's case again about interviews. Or rather, the lack of interviews, because Wes is still refusing to talk to the media. He was supposed to finally do that *Sports Illustrated* interview, but then I got sick again and he postponed.

Just another bullet point on the long list of things fucked up by my illness.

I duck into our room and sit on the bed, leaning my head against the stack of pillows. I'm not tired. The steroids I'm taking to clear my lungs ensure that I'm wide awake and unnaturally alert, so sleeping isn't an option right now. I only told Wes that because...damn it, I'm being an ungrateful ass again. But I need space. I need one frickin' hour to myself, without nurses hovering over me or Wes asking me if I need something.

After five minutes of staring at the wall, I open my laptop and check my email. Holy shit. There are *hundreds* of them. My mom confiscated my phone in the hospital because she said I didn't need anything distracting me from my recovery. At the time, I bitched like a pre-teen girl whose texting privileges had been revoked. Now, I'm glad she did it. My inbox is overwhelming.

There are messages from my college teammates—some asking me if I'm okay and some wondering why I didn't tell them I was gay. *Dudes, the joke's on me, too.*

There are Get Well Soon e-cards from my family and friends, but those are overshadowed by the scary amount of emails from media outlets. Every sports magazine I've ever heard of. *People.* Local and not local newspapers.

As I scroll through the interview requests, my stomach feels queasy. My life—my *sex* life—is under a microscope, and I don't like it. It suddenly gives me a new appreciation for Wes, because I realize his spotlight is twice as large as mine.

Another message catches my eye. It's from my boss. He sent it when I was in the hospital the first time.

Dear Jamie,

You tried to tell me about an issue with your co-coach and homophobic language, but I didn't listen as well as I should have. I'm truly sorry. Our policy is unambiguous—no employer or player should have to put up with discriminatory language or a hostile work environment.

Please allow me to help you do now what I should have helped you do then. Attached is the form for filing a complaint. As soon as you feel well enough to do so, fill it out so that we can properly investigate your complaint.

I've learned a difficult lesson this week, and I'd like to amend my previous response to your inquiry.

Sincerely,

Bill Braddock

I have no idea how to respond. Making a complaint now seems so petty. Since I was keeping my bisexuality a secret before, I'll look like some kind of spy. Like I was taking notes while they weren't paying attention.

Danton shouldn't get away with spreading hate, but I have to walk back into that rink in a few days. I don't want to give all my coworkers the impression that I've been writing down everything they ever said in the locker room.

I'm rereading the email for the fourth time when Wes enters the bedroom.

"Why don't you put that away and get some rest?" my boyfriend suggests. His grip is firm as he takes the laptop from me and closes it. "You look tired."

Damn it. I *feel* tired. I hadn't five minutes ago, but now my eyelids are starting to droop. The act of checking a few measly emails drained me of energy, and that feeling of helplessness jams in my throat again. I hate being weak. I *hate* it, and the anger drives me to snap, "Yes, Mom."

Hurt flashes in Wes's eyes.

Guilt pounds into me again. "I'm...sorry," I whisper. "Didn't mean to snap at you."

"It's okay." But he still looks upset as he quietly leaves the room.

Jamie isn't doing well.

It's been three days since he was released from the hospital. Physically, I can see him getting stronger. He's not sleeping as much during the day. He cooked breakfast this morning without keeling over in exhaustion. He's left the condo to go for short walks. But when I dragged him out to our favorite diner—the one we found the first morning after Jamie moved in with me—it was a total disaster. Right after we placed our order, some college kids hustled over for our autographs— plural. Then a couple of other people took photos. Jamie got all pissed off and started coughing.

We left without eating. And when I suggested a trip to this Chinese place we like, he said, "Let's just order in."

His body is healing, that I know for sure. But I have no clue where his head is at or what he's feeling. He's shut down on me. He alternates between snapping at me and apologizing to me for snapping at me.

I can't remember the last time we kissed. *Really* kissed, and not just the quick pecks we've been giving each other this week. I think it might have been during his first hospital stay. Yes…in the shower. That had been a damn good shower.

The one I'm in right now? Not as good. I'm in a stall with saloon-style walls, which means that I've got two teammates on either side of me. Staring at me. Not in a pornographic, check-out-his-dick way, though honestly, I'd prefer leering to their looks of deep concern.

"You don't talk to us anymore." The rushing water all around us doesn't muffle the note of accusation in Eriksson's tone.

"Sure I do," I answer as I soap up my chest.

On the other side of me, Hewitt is quick to contradict my statement. "Naah, you're being antisocial."

They want me to be *social*? When my boyfriend is at home moping and snapping at me every chance he gets? They're lucky I'm even showing up to our games. My mind has been so focused on Jamie it's a miracle I still remember how to play hockey.

"Blake says your man's doing better," Eriksson prompts.

I wash the soap off my body and reach for some shampoo. "Yeah. He is."

"So then what's with the glum face?"

My reluctance to confide in them has me taking an extra-long time lathering up my hair and rinsing it out. I hope it's long enough for them to forget the question Eriksson had tossed out, but they're still watching me when my eyes finally snap open.

"Come on, Wesley, spill. What's going on at home?" Eriksson gives a self-deprecating laugh. "Can't be any worse than what I'm dealing with right now."

The reminder of his marital problems chips away at my hesitation. Fuck it. My teammates have gone out of their way to support me since the "news" of my sexual orientation broke out. They've constantly asked me how Jamie is doing. They've had to deal with my sour face at every away game. They've been nothing but kind, and I feel like an ass for continuing to keep my distance from them.

"Jamie's depressed," I confess.

Those two words seem to suspend in the steamy air. I haven't said it out loud. Hell, I haven't even thought too hard about it, but now I realize how true it is. Jamie isn't just moping. He isn't just bummed out. He's *depressed.*

More words stream out of my mouth before I can stop them. "He still can't go back to work, and last night his team won another game without him. He doesn't have his full strength back. He can't work out—it's against the doctor's orders. He can't leave the building without getting harassed by a reporter or two." My throat closes up. "I think he blames me for everything."

Fuck, that's the first time I've said *that* out loud, too. It makes me sick that it might be true, that Jamie might blame me for the media storm that refuses to die off.

Frank still calls me several times a day. The franchise has released numerous statements to make up for my refusal to talk to the press. My face and Jamie's are on every sports blog. During our last home game, there were protesters outside the arena, wielding signs with Bible passages and nasty slogans.

Life…sucks. It really fucking sucks right now.

"I don't know how to make it better," I mutter. I shut off the water and grab a towel, wrapping it around my waist. "And it's not like I have any reinforcements to call who can cheer him up. We don't know anyone in the city—other than you guys," I hastily add when I see their hurt faces. "But most of Jamie's friends are on the West Coast, where he went to college. His family's in Cali, too, and they can't exactly drop everything and fly to Canada to be with him. His mom and sister already did that when he was in the hospital."

Eriksson and Hewitt follow me into the locker room. Their faces are sympathetic. "That's rough, man," Hewitt says.

"Yup." I turn toward my locker so they can't see my desperation. Rough is an understatement. Rough, I can handle. But this? Seeing Jamie upset and being unable to help him?

It's not rough.

It's *torture*.

WHEN I GET HOME from practice, Jamie is in our bedroom, his nose buried in a book. A science book about endangered species, if I'm reading the title correctly.

I find myself tensing instinctively, because these days I don't know what I'm going to see on Jamie's face. That shuttered expression? The don't-talk-to-me scowl? The guilty cloud? The sad frown?

Today I get none of the above. I greet him with a strained smile before pulling off my hoodie. And I'm startled to see a flash of desire in his brown eyes.

My dick instantly thickens behind my zipper. It—and I—can't remember the last time we had sex. Not since the first hospital stint, at least.

"How was practice?" he asks, setting the hardcover on the night table.

"Good. How's the book?"

"Interesting. Did you know that some captive male pandas can't figure out what to do when the female is in heat?" He grins, and damned if my heart doesn't soar to my throat. It's so rare to see him smile lately.

"Bummer."

"It is, though. Because they need to breed them in captivity. So there's this zoologist who made a panda sex tape and played the video for the males who couldn't get it done. Who knew that panda porn was a thing?"

Laughing, I undo my jeans and toss them on the nearby armchair. Jamie stares at my black boxer-briefs, then my bare chest, then says, "Come to think of it, you look especially fuckable today."

I'm so happy I almost cry. I'm not stupid—I know that sex isn't an easy fix. I know it won't miraculously cheer him up and erase the awfulness of these past few weeks. But it's a start.

I lunge toward the bed, and he laughs at my eagerness. The husky sound goes right to my dick. I miss his laughter. I miss my easygoing, always-ready-with-a-smile Jamie, and his familiar smile has me mauling his mouth with mine.

My kiss is desperate with excitement and longing and *oh God I missed you* all rolled into one hot, breathless package. His tongue enters my mouth and steals my sanity. His hands caress my chest, thumbs sweeping over my pecs, my nipples, before sliding down my abs toward my waistband.

"Off," he mutters, tugging on my boxers.

I release his mouth long enough to wiggle out of the underwear and throw them across the room. Jamie's flannel pants and T-shirt follow suit. I'm a tad worried that he might get cold, might get sick again, but he presses his warm, naked body to mine before I can cover us with the blanket.

His lips find my neck, kissing and sucking on my skin like

it's covered in sugar. The deep, growled noises he makes tickle my ear, tingle in my balls.

"Missed this," he whispers.

"Me too." The words come out choked, thick with emotion. Christ, he doesn't even know how much I've missed it.

He pushes me onto my back, and I'm a hot, shivering mess as he kisses his way down south. When his mouth engulfs the tip of my cock, my hips buck, seeking more. Seeking *him*.

Jamie slowly takes me in deeper and deeper and deeper until he swallows up my entire length. The only sensations I can register are *wet* and *warm* and *fucking awesome*. But then I remember the way he'd coughed so violently last week, and I touch his soft hair, stilling him.

"Are you sure you're up for this?"

His strong jaw tightens.

Crap, wrong thing to say.

For some reason, Jamie's become sensitive about looking "weak." I *don't* think he's weak, though. I never have. He was just sick, end of story. But no matter how many times I've told him that, it's still a sore issue for him.

"The cough," I clarify hastily. "'Cause if your throat's still sore, there're other ways you can make me come…"

He relaxes, his tongue coming out to circle my cockhead.

My lips curve wickedly. "Actually, the more I think about it, the more I like the alternative." I allow him one more lick before tugging him up by the shoulders and pushing him onto his back.

"What's the alternative?" he says thickly.

I'm already reaching for the nightstand drawer for some lube. "Having that big cock pounding my ass until I shoot."

A lust-filled groan escapes his throat. "Mmmm. Yeah. That sounds really hot."

I probably don't take as much time as necessary to prepare myself, but I'm too damn impatient. It's been so long. *Too* long. I want him so much my mouth is dry and my palms are damp. My fingers shake as I slip two of them inside me, rubbing and twisting while I hurriedly climb onto Jamie's lap.

His chest is flushed red with arousal, his eyes burning as he focuses on the movement of my arm, then on the erection jutting from my groin. His dick is just as hard, and I moan when he wraps his hand around it and gives it a slow stroke. The engorged head peeks out from his fist, leaking pre-come. My mouth goes even drier. So I moisten it by bending over to suck the pearly liquid from his tip. Then I lift my head and lick my lips.

Jamie jerks. "Damn it, Wes, I *need* you."

My heart does a funny little flip. He needs me. I know he's talking about sex right now, but a part of me hopes he means something else, too. He's refused to accept my help this week. Anyone's help, really. He's refused to admit he *needed* help. Maybe this is his way of admitting it now.

Either way, I give him what he wants. I give him *me*, raising myself up and then lowering my ass onto his hard cock. The sting of pain confirms that I wasn't entirely ready for this, but I don't care. I welcome the burn. I welcome every inch of the man I love, leaning forward to kiss him as he gives an upward thrust that steals my breath.

"Ride me," he orders. "Ride me hard."

This time I don't obey. I go slow instead. Painfully, deliciously slow, dragging out each rise and fall of my hips until his features are creased with impatience and need, until he's moaning and squirming and begging for more.

Jamie clutches my hips with damn near desperation. He tries lifting his own hips, but I continue to tease him, planting kisses along his neck and collarbone, sucking on his earlobe, nibbling on his lip. I want to savor every second of this. I want to lose myself in the feeling of being stretched by him, filled by him.

But then he touches my cock.

The evil gleam in his eyes makes me curse. The moment he starts jacking me off, my body takes on a life of its own. Suddenly I'm riding him with fervor, unable to maintain the lazy tempo.

"Want you to come all over me," he mumbles. His hand speeds up, thumb pressing against the underside of my cockhead with each hurried stroke.

Jesus Christ. He's trying to make me explode. He *does* make me explode. With his hand on me and his dick in me, it's impossible to stop the release that barrels toward me like a jet on the runway. I come with a harsh cry, and he jacks his hips up while his strong fist milks me dry.

He squeezes his eyes shut and shudders from his own release, letting go of my dick and wrapping both arms around me. My chest is glued to his thanks to our sweat and my come. His heartbeat hammers wildly against my pecs. It feels...too fast. Should his heart be beating that fast?

I quickly sit up, worried that he might have overexerted himself, that my selfish need to be with him might cause him to relapse.

Jamie must read my mind, because the pleasure in his expression fades and a slight frown touches his lips. "Don't say it," he warns.

I swallow. "Say what?"

"Whatever you were going to say." He yanks me down on

him again, wrapping one arm around my shoulders. "I'm so sick of that look."

"What look?" Do I even want to know?

"The *worried* look. It replaced your sex look less than a minute after you blew your load."

It's not like I can deny it, because that would be a lie. "I have a sex look?" I ask instead.

"Yeah. Your eyes go a little out of focus, and your tongue hangs out a little."

I snort into his armpit. "Sounds sexy."

"It is when I'm the object of it. But I wouldn't make that face for *Sports Illustrated* when you do your big interview."

When he talks about the press, Jamie sounds...*bitter*, I think. I've never used that word to describe him before. Ever. Now my spine prickles with unease, because I don't know what to do about it. And yesterday I'd told him that the reporter wants to do it as a broadcast now—not just a print interview. "Baby, do you want me to cancel on them?"

He shrugs. "You can't."

"Uh..." Can't I? This is all uncharted territory. Dennis Haymaker is going to ask about my relationship with Jamie. And it's just occurred to me that whatever I say, I need to clear with Jamie first. "I have to talk to him about hockey, 'cause it's in my contract. But I'd like your thoughts on what else I should say, or not."

"Why?"

"Because we're *partners*." I lift my head. "Right? We're together. And it's *our* relationship. You should have a say in what we tell everyone about it."

He turns his head away, toward the windows. "Say whatever you want."

My gut tightens. I've just been "whatevered" by the love of my life. "Jamie," I whisper.

He doesn't look at me.

"I think the pneumonia isn't the only thing that's wrong. And I want you to talk to me about it."

"I'm fine."

You're not. You're depressed. The words are on the tip of my tongue. But I have him in my arms for the first time in weeks. And I can't bring myself to mess it up with a Big Serious Talk.

I clear my throat and try another tactic. "What would be fun for you right now?"

"*Right* now?" he asks.

"No, um…" I choose my words carefully. "Just generally. What are you looking forward to?"

He stares at the ceiling. "Sunshine would be nice. I want to go to California."

My heart shimmies. Jamie wants to *leave*. I heard him say "sunshine," but I can't help but hear it a different way. I take a half second to think through my travel schedule. We're headed to Minnesota and Dallas. Nowhere near a beach. "Okay, uh, there's eight weeks left in the season. Why don't you look at some tickets for the summer? We could take a nice long trip out there to see your folks? You could teach me to surf."

"Okay," he says slowly. "I'll do that."

I bury my face in his neck. Maybe planning a vacation will perk Jamie up. Maybe the sex will help get his endorphins going again. Maybe the fact that he wanted me today means he'll start feeling better. I hope it will.

Hope is all I've got.

The next day I'm lying on my back on our sofa, studying the ceiling. I've been here for a while now. Wes is at practice, and the apartment is so fucking quiet that every thought I have echoes too loudly in my head.

A couple hours ago I looked at some flights to California. But depending on whether Wes's team makes the playoffs, that's still two or three months away. I just couldn't see the point of planning a trip now.

It's like I've forgotten how to feel excitement. Or—the fever I had burned all the happiness out of me. Even the high I got yesterday from sex with Wes faded fast.

The day stretches out in front of me. I have nothing to do and nobody to talk to. Lunchtime comes and goes, but I'm not even hungry. It doesn't take any energy to be a complete bum, so my stomach has forgotten how to crave food.

Disgust makes me get up and stroll over to our wall of windows facing the waterfront. The lake is a dark, cold color, and I get a chill just looking at it. But down below, I can see people bundled up and hurrying through the March afternoon. Cars stop and start on Lakeshore.

The whole world is busy except for me.

My phone buzzes on the kitchen counter. It does that a lot. I walk over and study the incoming message, but it's only an automated text reminding me that my team has a game starting in thirty minutes. Even though I'm on leave, those messages keep coming just to remind me of everything I was missing.

I wander into the kitchen, choose a carton of yogurt and eat it. Cooking seems like a lot of trouble lately.

That done, I throw away the container and confront the empty hours ahead of me. For once my stir-craziness actually overpowers my listlessness. If I don't go somewhere right now, I will lose my mind.

Grabbing my phone, I shove it into my pocket. Then I find my coat, adding a hat and scarf just so Wes won't get mad if he sees me out in the cold.

I don't even know where I'm going until I get into the elevator. But then it hits me—I'm forbidden to work, but I'm not barred from the rink. I can *watch* my guys play, right? It's a free country.

It takes me a half hour to get there, between the subway and a pretty long walk. My chest is rattling when I finally see the building ahead of me. I stop to cough, because I don't want to be hacking like an idiot in the stands. I hate the sound of it, and the way my stomach muscles ache from the now familiar workout of clearing my lungs.

Laughing hurts worst of all. Good thing I don't do that very often.

When I finally reach the rink, the game is already in progress. But that's fine, because it allows me to sneak in unnoticed. My guys look sharp out there, too. I climb the bleachers and take a seat on the top row. The rink isn't huge —it only seats a couple thousand people. But it's weird to be so far away from my guys during a game. I should be down there behind the bench, where Danton's pin-shaped head is weaving back and forth as he talks to the team and calls the lines.

I miss being involved. I feel like an outsider up here. And helpless. Another coach has taken my place. Gilles is working with Danton, coaching my defensemen.

Hell, it's working, too. My guys are doing a good job of keeping their chins up, finding the pass before they're beset by opponents on the back check. And my goalie looks alert and ready. His stance is more relaxed than the last time I saw him play, like he's shaken off his fear.

The teams are well matched, and the game is scoreless through the first period. Dunlop makes a couple of beautiful saves, but he doesn't have to work all that hard. Not yet.

Things get scrappier during the second period. Our team gets some good shots on goal, but they're answered by some brilliant defense. And then our star center puts one in, and my smile is really wide for the first time in weeks.

My hands are in tense fists as the game grinds on. The opponent steps on the gas, bringing everything they've got. Dunlop has his hands full for a little while. But he doesn't choke. I'm so proud of him I could burst. Then our team draws a penalty and I'm holding my breath for two minutes, hoping Dunlop doesn't fall apart.

But he is a rock. He saves two during the PK. And he holds the line for the entire third period.

When the buzzer goes off, the score is still 1-0, and Dunlop has shut the other team out. I'm limp with relief. It's great to see them win.

And then? All the happiness drains out of me again. Just like it always does now.

Below me, Danton and Gilles gather my guys together. They are a clot of happy victory, patting each others' shoulder pads and smiling, their faces red and sweaty. I feel like Scrooge when the ghosts of Christmas make him watch scenes from his own life. I should be down there, congratulating kids and giving a post-game wrap-up. But another coach has taken my place, and now they're *winning*. Dunlop looks about a hundred times happier than after my last few games with him.

Why the hell did I come here? This was the worst idea ever.

I need to leave. But the stands have emptied out, and my team is still visible. So I sit there a few awful minutes longer, waiting for them to hit the showers so I can make my exit unnoticed. I don't even know what I'd say to those kids right now. *Nice game. Glad I got pneumonia so you could win a few.*

The truth clobbers me. *I'm unnecessary, and I'll probably be fired.* If that happens, there won't be any more job for me in Toronto.

Then what?

Suddenly I can't be in the building any longer. I stand up and jog down the bleachers, heading for the door. There's nobody in the hallway, and it seems like I have a clear path to freedom. But then somebody shouts my name.

"Canning!"

I spin around on instinct, and it's Danton jogging toward me. He skids to a halt. "Hey." His face is red.

"Hey." *I have nothing to say to you.*

"Listen. You shoulda come to me."

"What?" I look into his angry, beady eyes and almost

laugh. He can't mean that I should have *confided* in him. We are *not* friends.

"You had a problem with me, you shoulda spoken to me about it. Now I got Braddock on my ass. You went behind my back to him. And I didn't mean *shit* by anything I said. It was just smack talk about the other team. You *knew* that. I never called *you* a faggot."

My blood pressure spikes hard. I've never felt anything like it. All of me is shaking. "Doesn't matter who you say it to. It's still wrong."

"But I didn't treat you bad! I'm not like that. I wouldn't have been an ass to you if I knew you had a boyfriend."

That's it. That's all the bullshit logic I can take in one day. I grab Danton by the shoulders and shove him roughly up against the wall. "You stupid asshole. Don't mistake me for someone who cares what you think of me."

His eyes widen in shock, but I'm not even half finished. I give him another shove and the back of his head actually bounces against the cinder blocks. "That shit that falls out of your mouth? The kids hear everything you say. You're an authority figure. Now they think it's okay to call someone a faggot just as long as you don't actually know them. And it's. Not. Okay." I am practically spitting in his narrow little rat face.

There's movement at the edges of my vision, and to my horror, I see Bill Braddock coming down the hall.

Oh my fucking god.

I yank my hands off of Danton. Yeah, it's bad to say "faggot" to your team. But it's also a dealbreaker to slam your co-coach up against the wall and scream in his face. There's a page in the employee handbook which specifically forbids the laying on of hands.

See how easy it will be to fire me now?

The door is only ten yards away, and suddenly I'm striding toward it. Bill Braddock yells my name, but I don't stop. I beat it out the door and then jog down the sidewalk. I run a hundred yards or so before my lungs are burning. My pace falters and I stop. Then my chest is wracked with coughing.

Fuck. I can't even run. I'm useless, even to myself.

When I'm able, I walk to the subway. And nobody follows me.

Tonight we're playing Pittsburgh. They're a great team, but I'm confident we can kick their asses. Our morning skate went well, and Blake is back on the ice.

Even better, when I exit the stadium for our pre-game hours of rest, there aren't any nutbars picketing the stadium, and I haven't heard about black-market ticket sales in a couple days.

Could the frenzy be winding down? I fucking hope so.

This morning when I left, Jamie had the playoffs calendar in one hand and a travel reservations website open on his laptop. On my way out the door I asked him to think if there were any resorts he might want to visit in Cali. "Or how about a couple days in Hawaii before we see your family?" I'd asked.

"Sounds expensive," he'd mumbled.

But I wanted him to think big. After this grueling year, we deserve to have some fun. While I drive home I think about paddle-boarding with Jamie on a beach somewhere. And ordering beers with wedges of limes jammed into their tops. I'd mentioned Hawaii, but Mexico is also fun.

I'm whistling as I let myself into our apartment. Inside the door, the first thing I notice is that it's messy. There are several glasses on the countertop, and magazines cascading from the coffee table to the floor. That's not exactly a big deal. But Jamie is kind of a neat freak most of the time, and lately he just doesn't care. That worries me. A lot.

"Babe?" I call as I often do when I arrive.

There's no answer, but I hear the sound of a zipper from somewhere inside the apartment.

I drop my coat onto our coat tree (something Jamie bought when he grew sick of finding my coat on the couch). A few quick strides bring me down the hall and into our bedroom.

Jamie is bent over a large duffel bag. *His* duffel bag. He's tucking a shaving kit into the end part.

"Babe?" I say again.

He startles, then straightens up quickly. *Guiltily*. "Hey," he says, his voice gruff. "Didn't hear you come in."

Obviously. I don't say it, though. I'm too busy doing the math. There's a print-out on the bed. BOARDING PASS, it reads. Air Canada. His computer is zipped into its case beside it. His phone and charging cord lie beside them on the bed. "Where are you going?" I croak.

"Home," he says, then quickly adds, "To see my folks. I told you I thought I needed some time in California. I can't go back to work yet, right? Might as well visit."

"Um…" Something is just really wrong with this. His face is pinking up, too. "Were you going to tell me? Were you even going to say *goodbye?*" It comes out sounding jagged and scared. But I *am* scared.

"Yeah," he says. "Of course. I knew you'd be home about now."

Warning bells are blaring. Jamie is standing five feet away, his hands stuffed awkwardly in the pockets of his jeans. I've never been in a relationship before. But this isn't how it's supposed to work. "Are we breaking up right now?" I blurt.

Jamie looks startled, as if he didn't expect me to say it out loud. "No," he says after only the slightest hesitation. "No. This is just a vacation. I..." He clears his throat. "I just need to see my folks."

But I can't help but hear, *I just need to be away from you.*

My heart is pounding in my ears. Do I yell at him now? Is that the right thing to do? I don't know what Jamie needs. If I knew, I'd give it to him. A loud, pushy display of my love would be one way to go.

But what if this trip is what he really needs? What if some sunshine will fix him? Indecision keeps me rooted to the floor, and my throat is hot and achy all of a sudden. I grab my water glass off the bedside table and drain it while I try to figure out what to say.

His phone rings on the bed. He grabs it and answers. "Thank you," he says after a minute. That's the whole call.

"Who was that?" I croak out.

"The, uh, cab company. The car will be here in ten."

I fight off a whole-body shiver. "If you needed a ride to the airport, why didn't you ask me?" *What the HELL is happening here?*

His expression turns guilty again. "Dunno," he said, studying his shoes. "Just thought it would be easier this way."

He's right. Because I'd probably make a scene at the airport. I'm pretty close to making one right now. "I don't want you to go, Canning."

Jamie cringes. "I gotta…" He chokes on the word. "Gotta just try something, okay?" When he raises his eyes again, they're wet.

Now I'm more panicked than ever. I stumble toward him and wrap my arms around him. He hugs me back, at least. My throat locks up completely. *No no no no* I chant inside. I'd yell it if I knew it was the right thing to do. But how do I deny him a trip to his parents? Tomorrow I'm leaving for Minnesota. It makes no sense for me to beg him to stay and then hop on the team jet for five days.

Fuck.

So I man up and do what is right. "Take care of yourself," I whisper. "You're really fucking important to me."

He hugs me a little tighter and takes a shaky breath. "You too."

Okay. I can do this. "I love you," I say, taking half a step back.

"Love you, too," he mutters.

He doesn't look me in the eye.

Fuck.

Fuck.

Fuck.

He putters with the last few items on the bed, zipping them into wherever they go. The cab company texts him that the driver is downstairs ahead of schedule.

Awesome.

I walk him as far as the door of our apartment. I kiss him on the cheek and hug him one more time.

Then I let him walk into the hallway alone. If I go downstairs I'll just make a fool of myself.

Instead, I put my forehead against the cool steel of our door and listen to the sound of his footsteps retreating.

One more time I go over it in my mind. A trip to Cali to see his parents. He can't go to work anyway. He said we're not breaking up. It's a vacation.

So why does it all feel like I just let my heart leap out of my chest and take a cab to the airport?

TWENTY-FIVE

WES

After our 3-2 win over Minnesota, I heave myself into the first row of seats on the bus. I should be riding the same high as the guys around me, but I'm not. I've been a basket case for two days now. It showed on the ice tonight—I didn't score a goal. Didn't get an assist. I skated my ass off, but I couldn't seem to summon up any magic.

Jamie took all the magic with him when he left me.

He didn't leave you. He's on vacation.

Bullshit. He left me.

Lemming boards the bus and accidentally locks eyes with me. I know it's an accident because he quickly looks away again. He passes the open seat next to me and heads toward the back.

Yeah, not all of my teammates are psyched to sit next to the gay guy. It turns out that growing up in Beantown wasn't enough of a common bond with Lemming after all.

Ten minutes later the bus pulls up in front of a five-star hotel in downtown Saint Paul, and my teammates and I trudge off the bus and into the lobby. I'm in a sour mood as I head up to my room. I change out of my suit and into sweats and a hoodie, but sitting around in the empty suite only bums me out, so I decide to go down to the hotel bar. Eriksson and some of the other guys planned on going to a strip club tonight. They invited me, but didn't look surprised when I turned them down. They've come to accept my antisocial grumpiness, I guess.

I ride the elevator down to the lobby, and I don't care that I look like a slob. The suit-and-tie routine is reserved for travel and after-game press, but the spotlight isn't on me right now and if I want to have a goddamn drink in my sweats, then I damn well will.

I slide onto a tall stool at the long, shiny counter and order a whiskey, which the male bartender delivers in speedy fashion. Maybe he sees the desperation in my eyes. But he doesn't try to go all *Cheers* on me and initiate a heart-to-heart, which I appreciate.

Sipping my drink, I check my phone to see if Jamie has texted. He hasn't. Frustration bubbles inside me, hotter than the burn of the alcohol as it slides down my throat. He called me when he landed in San Francisco, but other than a few "I'm fine, folks are doing great" messages, I haven't talked to him.

I wonder if he's rehearsing the breakup speech he's going to give me when he gets home.

My heart cracks at the thought. I slug back the rest of the whiskey and order another. The bartender delivers it with sympathetic eyes.

After about five minutes of sitting in stone-faced silence, I pick up my phone again, my fingers trembling as I find Cindy's number and press send. It's nearly midnight in Saint Paul, but only ten on the West Coast.

Jamie's mom answers right away. "Hi, sweetie! You must be tired after that exciting game! Why aren't you in bed?"

I smile despite the massive lump in my throat. Cindy Canning is the mother I never had. It's so humbling to have someone actually give a damn whether I'm getting enough sleep. "I'm not tired," I tell her. "But you watched the game, huh?"

"We all did. Jamie almost punched the TV when that jerk tripped you in the second period."

My heart does a happy flip. Jamie watched the game. He got mad when an opponent tripped me. That has to mean something, right? Like maybe he's *not* going to dump me?

Cindy's uncanny mind-reading abilities must have been triggered by my moment of silence, because she says, "He was very proud of you tonight."

My throat squeezes shut. "I…didn't even score a goal."

She laughs softly. "You don't need to score goals to make him proud, Ryan. It's enough for him to see you on that television screen, playing professional hockey." She pauses. "Why don't you just ask me whatever it is you called to ask?"

Mind reader, damn it. "Is he okay?" I blurt out.

"He will be." Jamie's mother goes quiet for a second. "I'll admit, he's not entirely himself, but I think that might have something to do with all the medication he was on."

I furrow my brow. "The painkillers?"

"I was thinking of the steroids they gave him. I'm no doctor, but I can't imagine all those meds not having any sort of side effects. He's sad, a bit withdrawn, but I wonder if coming off the meds has contributed to that."

Worry pokes at me again. God, I can't stand the thought of my laughing, easygoing Jamie being sad and withdrawn.

"But the fresh air has helped," Cindy says, her tone brightening. "He's out with his father right now, actually, taking a night stroll. And he spent yesterday with the twins, helping Scottie pick out a new surfboard. Sometimes the best medicine for what ails you is just a healthy dose of family."

My eyes feel hot. I thought Jamie was *my* family. I thought his family was *our* family. It kills me that I wasn't enough for him, that he had to seek comfort from the Cannings when I've spent weeks freely offering my comfort to him.

"I'm glad he's doing better," I choke out. "Just…keep taking care of him, okay? And don't tell him I called to check up on him. He doesn't…" I bite my lip. "He doesn't like it when I worry. It pisses him off."

"Oh, sweetie, that's not true. I know he appreciates your concern. It just shows how much you love him."

She reassures me for a few more minutes, but I still feel like total shit when we finally hang up. I miss Jamie so fucking much. I hate being apart from him, which is stupid if you think about it, because what's really changed? Regardless of where he is right now, Toronto or California, we'd still be apart. I'd still be in Saint Paul on this road game.

I can't wait for this season to be over.

"Buy you another round?"

The male voice startles me. I steady myself before I fall off the stool, turning to see a blond guy sitting beside me. He's gesturing to my empty glass. I don't remember downing this second drink, but a third isn't an option. Frank would lose his shit if someone reported seeing me sloppy drunk at the hotel bar.

"No thanks," I say absently.

The guy keeps watching me. He's in his early thirties, handsome, and making no effort to hide the fact that he's checking me out. And not in a "Are you NHL player Ryan

Wesley??" sort of way. His gaze conveys pure sexual awareness.

"Do you want to talk about it?" he drawls.

I grit my teeth. "Talk about what?"

"About whatever put that ravaged look in your eyes." One muscular forearm rests on the bar as he twists around slightly, angling his body so he's facing me. He's in a dress shirt and trousers. I suspect he's a businessman. "What was it? Messy breakup?"

My molars nearly turn to dust. I'm grinding them that hard.

As my silence continues, he chuckles and leans even closer. "I'm sorry. I know I'm coming on strong. But..." He shrugs. "I know who you are. Ryan Wesley, right? I've seen your mug everywhere these days, so I know your deal, that you have a boyfriend and all that." He sounds a bit sheepish. "But that look on your face...it tells me that maybe you *don't* have the boyfriend anymore...?"

I don't answer. He's got balls, I'll give him that. Hitting on me even though he's aware I'm in a relationship is a bold move. Unfortunately for him, it's not the kind of boldness I appreciate.

He proves to be even bolder when he reaches out and touches my wrist, stroking lightly. "And if that's the case, then I'd be more than happy to—"

"Get lost," a sharp voice snaps. "He's taken."

My head whips around to see Blake looming over us. His green eyes glitter menacingly, and the glare he levels my suitor with has the desired effect. Mr. Bold hops off his stool, shrugging carelessly. "Worth a try," he says before wandering toward the exit.

Blake usurps the guy's chair and directs the glare to *me*.

"What the hell are you doing, man? Stepping out on J-Bomb? What is the *matter* with you?"

I roll my eyes. "I'm not doing a damn thing. I was about to tell that asshole to get lost before you showed up."

My teammate's massive shoulders relax. "Oh. Okay. Good."

"I thought you were going to the strip club with Eriksson."

He nods. "S'posed to. But then I got out of the cab, saw the sign and got right back into the cab."

That spurs a chuckle. "Why'd you do that?"

"Dude, you know what the place was called?" He pauses dramatically. "The Black Sheep!"

My chuckle turns into a full-blown laugh. It's the first time I've experienced genuine humor since Jamie left for Cali, and I'm not surprised that Blake is the one to elicit this response from me. Somehow, in the short time I've known him, this guy has become my best friend. I'm glad to have him back on the ice with me. And unlike some of my other teammates, Blake genuinely has no problem sitting next to me on that damn bus.

"Now, if that ain't a sign from the universe to stay far, far away, I don't know what is." He shakes his head in dismay. "Swear to God, Wesley, sheep are the devil."

"I know they are," I say sympathetically, patting him on the arm.

Blake glances behind the counter. "Barkeep! Beer me, por favor!"

My lips twitch as the bartender comes up and lists all the beers they have on tap. Blake takes an interminably long time deciding, a process that involves two lager jokes, a pun about hops and a detailed account of the first time he ever drank Heineken. The bartender looks dazed by the time he hands Blake a glass of a local craft beer.

Me, I'm trying hard not to bust a gut.

"What?" Blake narrows his eyes at me. "Why are you grinning like that?"

"I…" I shrug. "I just missed you, that's all."

His entire face lights up. "Missed you too, brosky. Does that mean you're ready to stop sulking?"

Just like that, my good humor fades. For a moment, I actually forgot that my boyfriend deserted me, and the reminder of Jamie's absence is like a skate blade to the jugular.

Blake sighs. "Guess not." He raises his bottle to his lips, sipping thoughtfully. "You talk to J-Bomb?"

"A couple texts."

"Did he say when he's coming home?"

Pain shoots through me. "He *is* home," I mumble.

"Bullshit." Blake taps his fingers on the counter, while his other hand toys with the label of his beer bottle. This man is the poster child for ADD. "His home is Toronto. With us."

"Us, huh?"

"Yup. You and J-Bomb are my best friends. We're the three amigos." He pales. "J-Bomb knows that, right? Or does he think I'm only friends with him because of you? 'Cause I'm not."

"I know that." I wonder if Jamie does, though. He's been so miserable in Toronto all these months. When he's not with me, he's alone. I think the only time he went out with his work colleagues was the night we ran into each other at the pub. And it's all my fault. He's been isolated because of *me*, because of *my* need to hide our relationship, because of *my* career.

But that's not who Jamie is. For as long as I've known him, he's had friends and family surrounding him. He's been popular, adored by everyone he meets, and why *wouldn't* they adore him? He's the nicest, friendliest, most endearing person I've ever met.

No wonder he left. I doomed him to a life of isolation.

"It's too bad we don't play Anaheim until April," Blake muses. "We could've surprised him in Cali."

I nod bleakly because I've already done that math. But we're heading to Dallas tomorrow, not Anaheim. And after Dallas, we're back in Toronto, where this time I'll be the one sitting alone in our condo while Jamie gets to bask in the love and support of his family.

My whole body trembles as I slide off the stool. "I'm going to bed," I say woodenly.

Blake is clearly ready to argue. I don't give him the chance. I just lumber off, walking to the elevator with a cloud of misery hanging above me.

TWENTY-SIX
WES

When I let Frank Donovan and the reporter talk me into an on-camera interview, I knew it would feel humiliating. But I didn't count on *makeup*.

I'm gritting my teeth while a dude named Tripp brushes something across my cheekbones with a sponge, humming to himself while he works.

My father would die a thousand deaths if he could see it. And somehow this cheers me.

When Tripp steps back to admire his work through a pair of black-framed hipster glasses, I ask, "They make everyone wear this, right?"

He snickers. "Yeah, hon. It's not because you're the gay guy."

Get out of my head. I hate it when people read me like that. And it's only going to get worse, because I'm about to sit down for an intimate chat with a few million TV viewers. Shoot me already.

"Good to know," I mumble.

Frank walks into the room looking all hyped up. At least someone is cheery about this ridiculousness. "Ready?" he asks.

"Sure," I say. Because what's the alternative? I promised Dennis Haymaker I'd do this. My team wants me to. And as a side benefit, I'm sticking it to Dad. Better just get it over with. "We're done here, right?" I ask Tripp.

"One sec." He leans in with a giant brush and I close my eyes just in time to be thoroughly dusted with some kind of powder.

"Gross," I cough out when the assault is over.

"Aw. Big tough hockey player can't handle a little powder? We don't want you looking shiny on camera." He giggles.

"You are having way too much fun," I grumble.

"True! But I don't usually have a hottie like you in my chair." He yanks the black nylon cape off my shoulders. "Up you go. Knock 'em dead, Ryan Wesley."

"Thanks." But I'm not looking to knock anyone dead. I just want to get through this hour-long probe of my soul and get on with my life.

Frank leads me to a sound stage which is set up to appear intimate. There are two macho-looking leather chairs angled to split the difference between facing each other and facing the eighty-seven cameras pointed at them. Just outside of the faux room sits a hundred thousand dollars' worth of broadcasting equipment.

How quaint.

They've dressed me in a dark suit jacket and dark-wash jeans. Expensive but boring shirt, open at the neck. I'll bet someone in PR spent hours trying to figure out how to make me seem masculine and hip and casual and interesting but ordinary all at once. They probably have a computer model for this shit.

Whatever. At least I'm not being strangled by a necktie right now.

"This is your seat," Frank says, indicating the chair on the left.

I don't ask how they chose that, either. I just sit.

"Now, remember," Frank says, rubbing his hands together. "Look at Dennis, or look at the camera. This one." He points at a camera which is just a few degrees to the right of where my interviewer will sit. "If you gaze around the room, you'll look shifty. Avoid the upward inflection. Don't raise your voice at the end of sentences."

A little of my natural cynicism escapes. "Too queer?"

He rolls his eyes. "No. Too insecure. Which you aren't. So don't sound that way."

"Fine."

It's weird being the guy the camera is pointed at. I never asked to represent gay dudes everywhere. And I don't really feel up to the task. Let's face it—I lead a pretty self-centered existence focused on winning hockey games and spending as much time with Jamie Canning as possible.

Right now I'm failing at both those things. So this interview comes at a moment when I feel like I have very little to offer anyone.

My self-flagellation is cut short by the appearance of Dennis, who's dressed like my twin, but with shinier hair and more self-confidence. "Ryan! Good to see you." He pumps my hand and then sits down. "How are you feeling? Ready to answer a few questions?"

"Sure," I lie. "I read through your list."

"Is there anything on there that's off limits?" he asks, straightening the lapels of his jacket.

"No." Frank already warned me about the so-called list of

questions. Dennis won't necessarily stick to it. Since this inter-view is pre-recorded, I can always say, "Nice try, asshole," and they'll edit out the question. The contract I signed stipulates that I can strike out any topic that's not on the list, but it's up to me or Frank to flag it.

"Great," Dennis enthuses. "Let's get started."

A producer comes forward to talk to us about timing and camera angles. I try to pay attention, but I'm wondering what Jamie is doing right now and whether he'll watch this inter-view tonight. Jamie used to be my happy thought. His smile was the thing I pictured whenever I was stressed out.

It still is, I remind myself. I just hope he's smiling, wher-ever he is.

Warm lights come on, and Tripp runs in to blot our faces one more time with a crackly piece of tissue paper. He gives my shoulder a squeeze on his way out.

Then the producer says, "Rolling."

Dennis Haymaker pivots toward the camera. "I'm here tonight with Ryan Wesley, rookie forward for Toronto's winning team…"

As his introduction rolls on, I feel my face freeze into a self-conscious mask. What kind of dumb idea was this, anyway?

But at least he starts off with softball questions. "How long have you wanted to play hockey?"

"Always," I say easily. "When I was five my mother had my bedroom redone in the Bruins colors, because I'd taped up action shots all over my walls, and she was sick of fighting it."

He takes me through the early years, when I played Peewee and Bantam. I haven't thought about that stuff for years. I tell the story of finishing a tournament game with a broken arm, because this is my interview and I can make myself sound like a tough kid if I want to. I *was* a tough kid. "I was bummed out to miss the awards ceremony to go to the ER. I wanted to see the trophy after all that."

Dennis laughs. "Ouch. What did your parents think about your obsession and the danger? Did either of them play hockey?"

Now I have to laugh, too. The idea of my dad sweating over anything but financial transactions is comical. "No sir, they did not."

"Are they your biggest fans?"

I guess we're going there now. "Not so much. My parents and I aren't close."

"Why is that?"

Here it comes. I give a nervous chuckle. "The truth is we've never been close. That time I broke my arm? It wasn't my folks who took me to the ER."

Dennis looks genuinely surprised by this plot twist. "Who was it?"

"My father's driver. A guy by the name of Reggie. See, my dad liked to watch me win hockey games, as long as it didn't take too much time away from his busy schedule. They sent me to all the away games with a driver. And Reggie was my favorite. I used to look into the stands after we scored and see him cheering. He'd be standing there in his blue blazer, yelling for me. I always thought he liked hockey, but now I have to wonder if my dad slipped him an extra twenty bucks to cheer for me. I had no idea that was a weird way to grow up, though. I was ten. That was just normal to me."

"So…" It takes Dennis a moment to formulate his next question. "Your dad was too busy to take you to the ER with a broken arm?"

I shrug, because we're getting off topic. "I don't know.

Maybe Reggie just took me out of common sense. You don't deliver the boss's kid home with a broken bone, right? Sounds like a good way to get fired. I didn't care who took me, anyway. Even at ten I knew you were supposed to man up and not cry in front of the x-ray tech. It didn't matter to me who was in the waiting room."

The journalist clears his throat. "What other ways were you expected to man up, Ryan?"

That question was not on the list, of course. But I don't stop the interview. "Well, Dennis, you're not supposed to fall in love with your roommate from hockey camp. That was another no-no in the Wesley household. But I've never been good at following rules."

His expression turns dire. As if we're about to discuss the Iran disarmament. "When did you tell your parents you were gay?"

Man, are these lights hot, or what? I resist the urge to wipe my hand across my forehead, but just barely. "I was nineteen and in college. I was prepared for shouting and cursing or whatever. But they just sort of refused to hear it."

"What did your father say?"

"Well…" I cleared my throat. "I think he said, 'your tie is crooked.' And last summer I told my father that I was living with my boyfriend, and he said, 'I have a conference call. Gotta jump!' He just refuses to hear whatever doesn't work for him."

"How did that make you feel?"

I almost roll my eyes. "What do you expect me to say? It's not ideal. But there are guys whose families throw them out on the street, and there are kids who are beaten. So I'm not going to complain."

"When's the last time your parents called you on the phone?"

"Um…" I give in and rub the back of my neck. I feel twitchy answering these personal questions, but this is what I signed up for. "I think I heard from them in February. My father wanted to schedule dinner the week my team played Boston. But after my boyfriend got sick and my face was plastered all over the Internet, he rescinded the invitation."

"I see," Dennis says, and he tilts a sympathetic face toward camera number two.

Gag me.

"Tell me about your boyfriend. He must be pretty special. You're taking a lot of flak for being with him."

I smile, because I like thinking about Jamie. But these questions will be the hardest to answer, because I want to respect Jamie's privacy. "We became friends at thirteen when we started going to the same hockey camp every summer. He's a great guy, and a great defensive coach. And he puts up with me, mostly."

"You weren't always a couple, though?"

I shake my head vigorously. "It took me a good nine years to tell him how I felt. But it was worth the wait. See…" I catch myself staring off into the studio's darkness while I try to form my thoughts. Like a good little interviewee, I look Dennis in the eye. "I trust who I am with Jamie. He's known me since I was a pimply thirteen-year-old when we used to argue about video games. He doesn't see me as Toronto's rookie forward. He doesn't care about my scoring average. I don't try to impress him." *Except with my ability to deep-throat. But we won't talk about that on prime time.*

"He's your family," Dennis suggests. "More than your real family."

"Absolutely," I agree.

"Do you think you'll get married?" Dennis asks with a smile. "Wait—am I putting you on the spot?"

That bastard. He's poking me in a sore spot just to lock in his ratings. But I stay cool. "Oh, it's not me you're putting on the spot. It's Jamie. I'd marry him in a hot second, and I'm sure he knows it."

"Have you asked him?"

Dennis is pushing his luck, and he's well aware of it. I should save face with Jamie and bail out of this line of inquiry. A beat goes by while I consider my options.

In for a penny, in for a pound. "I haven't asked him. In case you didn't notice, we're having a pretty rough year. It would be, like, 'Hey, babe, I know that ever since you landed in the hospital someone sticks a camera in our faces whenever you leave the house, and the whole world suddenly wants to dissect our sexuality. So wouldn't you like to put a ring on this?'"

My interviewer chuckles. "So you're saying the right moment hasn't come up?"

"It most definitely has not."

After that, Dennis turns to the subject of hockey and my teammates. And since hockey is the easiest thing to talk about in the world, I finally relax.

The last time I came to California upset, my mom let me sulk in peace. But not this time.

Yesterday I helped her stock the shelves at the church food bank for three hours, then we made deliveries all afternoon. Today I mowed and edged an elderly neighbor's giant lawn and pruned my mother's rose bushes.

I practically hacked up a lung out there in the back yard from all the exertion, but Mom just whacked me on the back and told me to keep cutting.

And that's not counting all the time I've spent with my siblings.

The weird thing? It's working. I still don't feel like my old self, and none of my problems are solved. But moving around has helped me a lot. The more I work, the less I worry. And my appetite is back. We ate dinner an hour ago, but already I'm foraging for a snack.

"Ryan called last night."

I freeze at the kitchen counter, my hand poised over the cookie jar. My mother sits at the table, serenely sipping her tea as she watches my face. I wonder what she sees in my expression. Joy? Terror? Regret? Frustration? I'm feeling all of that, so I'm curious which emotion is most obvious.

Regret, I imagine. Because boy, do I harbor a ton of regret for the way I handled my departure from Toronto. After the disaster at the rink, I just couldn't stay in that apartment one second longer. I came home and ran one more airline ticket search. When I spotted a last-minute fare to San Francisco, I didn't even hesitate. And hey—it cost a lot less than the trip that Wes wanted to plan. A jobless guy can't afford a beach resort.

It wasn't Wes's fault that I really needed to get away, but the look on his face still haunts me.

My hand closes around one of my mother's seven-grain cookies with raisins. They're healthier than a cookie really should be. But when in Rome. "What did Wes say?" I finally ask, taking a bite.

Mom sighs. "He wanted to know how you're doing. Sounds like he hasn't heard much from you."

Ouch. I've been ducking him out of guilt. Now I only feel worse. "He hasn't," I admit.

"And why is that?"

"Well…" I grab a napkin and join her at the table. "I don't know how to explain what's wrong. I've been really unhappy, but I don't want him to think it's his fault."

Mom swirls her cup around, her expression thoughtful. "But if you don't tell him, he'll just assume it's his fault anyway."

The cookie suddenly tastes like dust, but I'm not sure it's the cookie's fault. "So what you're saying is that I'm an asshole?"

She laughs. "No, and don't use that word at my table."

"Sorry," I say through the cookie. I get up and head to the refrigerator for milk before this thing kills me. And I can't die, right? Not before I've hashed things out with Wes. I dump the rest of the carton into a big glass and chug it.

She's studying me when I come back to the table. "So what are you going to do?"

"Talk to him?"

"Besides that. If you're unhappy, there must be a reason."

Or a dozen of them. My life in Toronto is a tangled knot that I don't know how to untie. I haven't told a soul about the emails I've gotten from Bill Braddock. The worst one arrived before my plane even left the tarmac in Toronto:

Dear Coach Canning—

I regret to inform you that Danton has filed a complaint against you for the altercation after the game today. Attached please find his signed complaint form. You have fourteen days to respond before the disciplinary committee makes a final decision. Since you're on sick leave, it wasn't necessary for me to consider any further actions at this point.

And Jamie—please call me. You haven't responded to my earlier suggestions to report your colleague's misbehavior. If you don't tell your side of the story, it's hard for me to help you.

Your team continues to perform well, and it's my sincere hope to see you skating with them very soon.

—B.B.

He sent a couple of follow-up emails, but I've been too embarrassed to respond.

"My job isn't going well," I mumble at Mom. "I might be unemployed before summer."

"I'm *sorry*, honey," she whispers. "That can happen to anyone. But I'm sure it's scary when it's your first real job."

I feel a shiver of horror just thinking about it. When I got this job I thought, *this is it!* My future was all figured out.

Not so much.

"If the coaching job doesn't work out, I'm so stuck. Another team won't want me. My work visa is specific to my organization. I can't just waltz in anywhere and get hired. What the hell am I going to do?" Christ, I haven't *ever* said this out loud. It sounds even worse in my parents' kitchen than it does in my head.

She reaches across the table to squeeze my hand. "It happens, baby. You can't take it personally."

Oh, but I can. How else am I going to take it?

"Does Wes know?" When I shake my head, her gaze only becomes more pitying. "You have to talk to him. Now seems like a good time."

It isn't, though. "His big interview airs tonight. He sent me a text saying it's okay if I don't watch."

"Oh, we're watching," Mom says cheerfully. "Who could stay away?"

My stomach rolls because I'm nervous for Wes. What if the interviewer was an asshole? What if they edited it so that *Wes* sounds like an asshole? I feel sick for him. He never wanted this kind of attention.

Mom drains her tea and checks her watch. "And we don't have long to wait. Time to make the popcorn?"

Forty minutes later I'm sitting on the couch beside her, my

hands fidgeting and sweaty. My dad is in his recliner reading a newspaper.

Maybe I *shouldn't* watch. Wes's message said: *It wasn't too bad, and I didn't say anything remotely personal about you. I promise. But don't watch if it makes you uncomfortable. Life is too short, right? Call me later. I miss you.*

My phone is in my pocket, torturing me. I miss him so bad. But whenever I imagine explaining my work woes, I want to throw up. If I get fired, it will be more embarrassing than hearing my name on TV. And if I can't get another job, what then? Will we have an awful slow-motion breakup when he realizes I can only get a job in the states?

And will I regret giving up my shot in Detroit only to be fired in Toronto?

I'm way too young to have a midlife crisis, damn it.

That's when Wes's face appears on the screen, wearing a deer-caught-in-the-headlights expression, and there's no way I'm bailing now.

"Aw," my mother says beside me. She sits up a little straighter. "We love you, Ryan!"

"You know he can't hear you, right?" my father asks from behind the op-ed page.

I hold my breath for the first ten minutes of the interview. The story about the broken arm just kills me, because I've never heard it before. I think I *met* Reggie, too. I'm pretty sure he drove Wes to camp that first summer, and then picked him up again.

Until right now I don't think I ever really understood how alone in the world Wes is. I mean—when we're together, he's not alone, right? So how would I know?

Oh.

Fuck.

Fuck me.

He's alone *right now* because I made it that way.

As the interview goes on, I sink lower and lower down into the sofa. My mother makes these little noises whenever Wes makes another self-deprecating joke or mentions his father.

By the time Wes says that I'm his real family, I pretty much want to punch myself.

And when the reporter asks Wes if he wants to get married, I stop breathing entirely.

"Wouldn't you like to put a ring on this?" he jokes. Then he laughs to himself, as if he's already convinced it's a pipe dream. He wears the same cocky smile I've always seen on his face. But now I know how much pain it hides. It was right there the whole time, too. But I didn't understand, because my man is really good at appearing confident.

My parents are both staring at me.

"What?" I croak.

My mother bites her lip. This woman who always knows the right thing to say is silent for once, which only makes me feel worse.

I can't take it anymore. I get up and go into my childhood room, taking a seat on one of the twin beds. When Wes spent Christmas here, it was weird waking up to see him asleep in the opposite one. He looked as peaceful as I'd ever seen him.

Goddamn it. What have I done to us?

I'm ready to do something about it now, if it's not too late. I whip out my phone and find the old email with Wes's itinerary on it. Fuck, he's in Dallas for at least another day. They have a game there tomorrow night. The private jet won't get him back to Toronto until the following afternoon.

But there's always FedEx.

That idea gets me up and rummaging around in the closet

of my old room. On the top shelf, under some of Scotty's old football pads, I find something that will do.

A box.

It's not perfect. Somebody drew on it with marker, but it's about the right size, like a cigar box.

I dump out some old hockey cards of mine and then examine the empty interior. I want to let Wes know that I'm with him. When he gets this, he'll understand. This was always our way of saying how much we care. I'm embarrassed that I haven't done anything like this for him in a long time, either.

The last time a box had traded hands, he'd sent it to me at Lake Champlain, the week before we moved in together. *Jesus Christ.* The truth rolls through me like an icy breeze off Lake Ontario. It was I who broke the chain. Not him. Me.

I've just spent the last couple of months feeling like I was the one who tried harder in our relationship, and he was the rookie. I thought that doing a few extra loads of laundry made me better at the whole thing.

Not so much.

Though I can still fix it, right? I know what to do.

But minutes pass while I stare at the tidy, empty corners of the box, wondering what I have left of myself to put in here. There was a time when all our troubles were small enough to fit inside a box this size.

Defeat chases my confidence around and around in my head while I come up with ideas and then quickly discard them. A gag gift won't cut it this time. And I've already given Wes a lifetime's worth of Skittles. I need to give him a *sign*.

It needs to be a big deal. And it needs to fit in the box.

Right.

I'm almost ready to give in to despair when the answer

comes to me. And it's so fucking obvious that I let out a laugh right there in the empty room.

Pulling out my phone, I tap my sister's name.

"Jamester!" she says. "Did you watch? Omigod—"

"Jess!" I cut her off. "Go to the mall with me? I think I need your help."

"Um…did you really just ask for my help? I must alert the media."

"Shut it. Are you free or not?"

"Pick me up in fifteen."

I jump into my shoes and yank open the bedroom door, only to find my mom standing on the other side, her fist poised to knock. "Can I borrow the car? It's really important."

"Of course," she says without hesitation. "Let me grab the keys from my purse."

TWENTY-EIGHT

WES

We win our second consecutive road game. But while everyone else piles onto the bus in high spirits, I just slouch in my seat, stare out the window, and wear what Blake has officially dubbed my Downer Donny frown.

I'm allowed to be down, though, because I still haven't heard from Jamie. I don't even know if he watched the interview— he hadn't responded to the text I sent him after it aired. I covertly messaged both Cindy and Jess after Jamie's radio silence, but they both answered that they "weren't sure" if Jamie had seen it.

I wish I didn't have to go back to Toronto tomorrow. All I want to do is hop on a plane to California and see Jamie, but I know management will kill me if I do. Frank told me this morning that my interview drew in a crazy amount of viewers. The team's media department has been flooded with more interview requests, and Frank wants me in Toronto during this next stretch of home games. I need to be "available" in case he schedules any press conferences. I don't see why that matters, because I don't plan on talking to any more reporters, not unless it's about hockey. My personal life is officially off the table for the foreseeable future.

"Knock it off, Donny." Blake punches me in the shoulder, then proceeds to place his thumb and forefinger on either side of my mouth and literally turn my frown upside down.

"Sorry," I mutter.

"You should be. You're bumming me out, and you know I'm not happy unless I'm happy."

I stare at him. "That's the dumbest thing you've ever said."

"Naw. I've said dumber."

True. Luckily, my phone buzzes, sparing me from listening to whatever cheer-Wes-up speech he's prepared. A glance at the screen shows an unfamiliar Boston number. I immediately regret being so gung-ho about the interruption. All my Boston friends are programmed into my phone, so I'm either dealing with a reporter who somehow got my number, or worse— someone who's connected to my dad.

But I pick up anyway, because I'm tired of listening to the Downer Donny voice in my head. "Hello?" I say in a guarded tone.

"Is this Ryan?" The male voice sounds oddly familiar. A deep baritone with a comforting rasp to it. Shit, where do I know that voice from?

"Yes. Who's this?"

"Well, hot damn, kiddo. I can't believe I actually reached you."

My forehead wrinkles. "Who—" I stop suddenly, a wave of nostalgia washing over me. *Kiddo*. Lately, only Jamie's mom calls me kiddo. But before that, I used to hear it from… "Reggie?" I say in shock. "Is that you?"

"Yesiree. It's good to hear your voice, Ryan. Been a long time."

Since I graduated from high school, I realize. Reggie retired when I was in my senior year. "Too long," I say gruffly. "How've you been?"

"I'm great. Loving retirement. But I didn't call to talk about me." He pauses. "I saw your interview on TV." Another pause. "He didn't give me a dime."

I swallow. "What?"

"Your old man. You said you wondered if he slipped me some cash to cheer for you at the games. He didn't." Reggie's tone is impossibly gentle. "Almost got fired for that, actually."

I'm hit with another jolt of shock. "What do you mean?"

He makes a disgusted noise. "Drivers are s'posed to wait in the car. The first game of yours I watched, I mentioned to your old man afterward how well you'd played. He threatened to can me if I ever left the car again."

Of course he had. My father is a grade-A asshole. "But..." I frown to myself. From the corner of my eye, I see Blake listening intently to my side of the conversation. He's not even trying to be sneaky about it. "But you kept coming to the games."

Reggie chuckles. "Nobody ever said I was smart, kiddo. But I figured, how was the old man gonna know? I sure as heck wasn't gonna mention it again. And you never did either, so..."

Something inside me cracks, flooding my chest with emotion. This man had faced my father's wrath—had put his *job* on the line—just to watch me play hockey?

"Never been prouder, watching you on the ice," he continues. "I just wanted you to know that. Didn't want you thinking I got paid to do it, or that it was a chore for me, because I didn't, and it wasn't."

My throat closes up. "Oh. Okay."

"I watched your college games too, whenever they were televised. And this season? Jeez, kiddo, you're setting records left and right." His voice is gruff. "I'm damn proud of you."

Oh hell. I might actually cry. On the bus. In front of all my teammates and my coach.

I blink rapidly, trying to stop the tears from spilling over. "Thank you," I whisper.

"You're a good kid, Ryan. Always have been." I can almost see the crooked smile on Reggie's wrinkled face. "Just keep doing what you're doing, you hear me? Forget the old man. Forget the critics and the nosy busybodies. You live your life the way you want to live it, and you keep doing what you're doing. And know that you've always got people in your corner, people who give a shit about you."

I blink some more. "Thank you," I say again.

"Nice win tonight," he adds, and then he disconnects the call.

My hand shakes as I set my phone on my thigh. Blake peers curiously at me. "Who was that?"

"An old friend." My throat is so tight I don't know how I manage to answer. "He was just calling to say hello."

Blake nods fervently. "Blast from the past, huh? Those are awesome. Well, not always. Sometimes they *suck*. You know who called me out of the blue last week? This douchebag I knew in high school—know what he wanted? For me to bang his girlfriend."

I'd been fully prepared to tune Blake out. Until I heard *that*. "Are you serious?" I gape at him.

"Serious as leprosy." Blake gives me a disbelieving look. "Turns out this chick's dream was to bone a pro hockey player, and the douchebag thought it would be a nice birthday present for her."

"Wow." I suddenly narrow my eyes. "Fucking hell. Please don't tell me you said yes."

Blake just grins.

I groan. Loudly. "You are a sick, sick man, Blake Riley."

The grin collapses as he breaks out in laughter. "Aw, relax. Of course I didn't say yes. I'm not *that* much of a slut."

"Bullshit," Eriksson's voice wafts over from across the aisle. I guess I wasn't the only one enthralled by Blake's blast from the past. "You're a dog, Riley."

"Woof!" Blake calls back.

Eriksson howls in return, which makes Forsberg join in, and then half my teammates are howling like a bunch of idiots until Coach Hal finally rises from his seat and says, "Shut the fuck up, dumbasses." He sinks back down, and I hear him muttering to our defensive coordinator, "It's like dealing with children."

I choke down a laugh. Yeah, I suppose he's right. We *are* children. Overgrown, testosterone-filled children.

I'm still in surprisingly good humor when the bus finally pulls up to the hotel where we're staying. I thank the driver and follow Blake down the steps, already loosening my tie as my dress shoes hit the pavement. Frank won't like it that I'm slobbing up before I'm in the privacy of my room, but I don't give a flying fuck what Frank—

Crap. Maybe I *do* care. There are half a dozen reporters in the lobby. Cameras flash and a couple of microphones get shoved under my nose. I stifle a groan. I'm not in the mood to talk to the press, and I inwardly curse Frank for not warning me that last night's interview would summon the media to swarm our hotel.

Of course, they don't ask a single question about tonight's game. Eriksson and Blake shoot me sympathetic looks as one of the reporters harasses me about my "gay relationship". I'm seconds away from snapping that a relationship is a relationship and he doesn't need to qualify it with "gay", but I suddenly feel Blake's hand on my shoulder.

"Bar," he murmurs.

I clench my teeth. Screw that. I don't need a drink right now. I just need to disappear upstairs.

Shaking my head, I mutter, "I don't feel like drinking—"

Blake cuts me off and says, "*Bar*." Firmer this time.

With a frown, I shift my gaze toward the bar area in the lobby, and my heart soars and plummets simultaneously.

Jamie.

Jamie is *here*.

He's seated at a table near the counter, his brown eyes searching the crowd until they lock with mine. My heart somersaults before landing in my throat.

What is he *doing* here? And how the hell am I going to get to him without giving the press a photo op that will no doubt embarrass us both?

I'm torn between sprinting toward him and texting him to meet me upstairs, but Jamie takes the decision out of my hands. As I watch wide-eyed, he gracefully rises from his chair and makes his way toward me. His long stride eats up the marble floor beneath his sneakers. His blond hair ruffles as he rakes one hand through it. He's holding something in his other hand. I squint. Fuck me. It's the box. Or rather, it's *a* box. Not the one that exchanged hands multiple times last summer, but close enough.

I stare at him, wondering what this means, wondering why he's not in California, why he flew all the way to Dallas—

Shit. The vultures have smelled blood.

Several curious heads turn in Jamie's direction as he

crosses the massive lobby. A flashbulb goes off, but still, he doesn't stop. He keeps me trapped in a serious stare and erases the distance between us, and then he's in front of me, those brown eyes twinkling playfully as he leans closer and—

Kisses me.

Panic and joy streak inside me as his lips briefly touch mine. There's no tongue. No overt passion. But when he eases back, the desire in his expression is impossible to miss. Jesus. I hope the cameras didn't capture that lust-filled glint, but Jamie seems completely oblivious to the proverbial spotlight that's narrowed in on us.

"Hey," he says softly.

I miraculously find my voice. "Hey. What…what are you doing here?" Beside me, Blake is grinning so widely I'm surprised his face doesn't crack in half.

"Can we, uh, talk privately?" Jamie's head swivels as he finally notices all the people staring at us.

"Of c-course," I stutter.

Blake clamps a hand on my shoulder. "There's another set of elevators back there." He tips his big head toward the distant end of the bar.

Jamie doesn't waste any time. He grabs my hand and tugs me in that direction.

I follow, and we weave around high tables until the elevator doors appear. His hand feels so good around mine that I forget to push one of the buttons until he gives my fingers a squeeze. "You gonna tell me the floor number?"

"Uh, nine. I'm pretty sure." We stayed here one night already, but when you visit as many hotels as I do, it's hard to keep track. I fumble into my jacket pocket for the key card.

Jamie grins and punches the button.

A minute later we're swiping into room 909. When the door clicks behind us, I have a moment of true uncertainty. It's not cold feet. I know what I want to do. It's just that I don't know how.

I've never told anyone that I wanted to spend the rest of our lives together before. I know he loves me, but it's still a risky conversation.

So I do a lap of the generous hotel room, with its sleek hipster furniture and floor-to-ceiling windows. "Nice place," I say, checking out the view.

When I turn back to Wes, he's watching me. "It's nicer now than it was before." Shrugging off his suit jacket, he tosses it at a chair. He hasn't turned on any lights, but his handsome face is illuminated by the glow of downtown Dallas. Ryan Wesley in a suit, ladies and gentlemen. There are very few sights as impressive as this one.

I'm staring. And I've still got the box clutched in my hand. "Okay," I blurt out. "So I made you something with my sister's help, and I got on a plane. But now I'm worried you'll think it's crazy."

"Well…" He clears his throat. "I promise I won't. I'm just so happy to see you." He steps into my personal space and puts his arms around me. "I thought you weren't coming back. Maybe that's dumb, but…" He shoves his face into my collar and takes a big breath of me.

All right. So I'm starting with an apology. My free hand lands on his back. "I'm sorry I was a dick. That…sucked." Eloquent. *Not.*

"Don't apologize. You didn't do anything wrong. I just panicked."

"No, *I* did." I take a deep breath and lean against him. "I have a situation at work. I screwed everything up and I didn't want to tell you. It's embarrassing. I was worried about money, too. So I just shut you out. How shitty is that?"

His warm hands wander my back. "Baby, you were too sad to think straight. If you're feeling a little better now, that's all I really care about."

My first impulse is to argue with his diagnosis of the problem. I don't want to be the guy who fell apart. But I *was* that guy. And maybe my mom is right about the steroids messing with my body chemistry. But whatever the reason, I lost it there for a little while. It's not fair to Wes if I deny it. "I think I'm getting better now," I say instead.

"Good." His grip tightens. "That's all I want, okay? That's everything."

There isn't a shred of doubt in my mind that he means it. I don't know how I got so lucky to find someone who loves me as thoroughly as Wes does. How many people ever find that?

Time to man up, then.

I take a half step back, forcing Wes to relinquish me, and

look down at the box in my hand. He's going to think it's ridiculous.

Taking a deep breath, I decide that's okay. It doesn't matter. It's an important gesture, and it got me all the way to Dallas to apologize, right?

I'm staring at the box now like it contains a venomous snake.

"Do I ever get to open that or what?" Wes asks with a laugh.

Wordlessly, I offer it to him. He weighs it in his hand and then looks at me. "Not heavy," he says. "Doesn't rattle." He lifts the lid to reveal the tissue paper we cushioned it with. Hell, it's probably broken, which makes the whole idea even stupider than it already was.

I'll just go hide under one of those thousand-dollar leather chairs now.

Wes's big hand pulls back the tissue. He squints at the thing inside. Then he carries the box over to the window to see it better. "It's…made of purple Skittles?"

"Yeah." My voice is like gravel.

He picks it up in two fingers, the one-inch circular shape outlined against the city lights. "It's a…?" He bites off the question, as if afraid to guess wrong.

"Ring," I croak. "You…I…" My mouth is like sandpaper. "In that interview, you said you wanted…" Deep breaths. "To get married some day. And I think that's something we should do."

For a second after I get the words out he stands so still that he might be a figure in a wax museum. The ring—in all its clumsy glory—is held aloft. It took Jess and me a whole lot of Skittles and patience before we figured out which of her craft glues would stick, and how long we had to wait before adding each successive bead. It all seemed quite sweet and hilarious last night.

Now I wasn't sure.

Wes's chin dips, and something goes wrong in my stomach. He's backlit against the cityscape so I can't see his face. I take a few steps closer, even though I'm afraid I really fucked things up. But I have to know.

He opens his mouth, but nothing comes out. And then his eyes well up, all shiny in the window light. "Really?" he rasps.

I take the silly thing out of his hand and drop it in the box. I set it down on the desk. "Yeah. I mean, not right away if you need some time to get your head around it..."

Two strong hands grab me by the shirt and haul me into his arms. "I don't..." He takes a deep breath that sounds a lot like a choked-back sob. "Don't need time to think about it. Wanna marry you this summer before you change your mind." His arms clamp around me, extinguishing all the space between us, and he puts his head on my shoulder. I feel his chest hitch a couple of times as he tries to hold himself together.

"Hey," I whisper. "I'm not going to change my mind."

"But you..." He clears his throat yet again. "It's a bigger decision for you than me. You could have, you know, a wife and kids. A family."

"Babe, I have a family. A big one. I never sit around and think about moving to the suburbs and procreating."

"You might, though," he says, his voice hoarse. "I wanted to give you a while to get used to the idea of being with me and not having...that."

"Who says we can't?" I point out.

He blinks.

"If we decide we want to have kids someday, there are ways for us to do that, babe. Adoption. Surrogates." I lightly pinch his ass. "Stop acting like you're dooming me to a life of childless misery."

That makes him chuckle.

"I *love* you," I say firmly. "I never stopped, even when things felt bleak. And then I watched your interview and I just needed to be right here. The, uh, plane ticket wasn't very budget friendly, but…"

He finally leans back to look at me. His face is kind of wrecked, but he's never looked better to me. "I'm going to send that reporter a nice bottle of scotch. And a box of cubans."

Then he kisses me. He tastes like tears and *Wes*. I dive right in. Damn, I missed this. The way he kisses me like he's trying to make a point. And now I know what the point is.

We're supposed to be together. Why not make it official?

Suddenly my body decides on a whole host of ways we're supposed to be together. I press against his hard chest and deepen the kiss. He grabs my hips and groans.

It's only a nanosecond later when I'm yanking on his tie and unbuttoning his shirt. He's unzipping my jeans and steering me toward the bed. Before I can blink, I'm on my back, my shirt off and my jeans at my ankles, and Wes's hot mouth is taking deep pulls on my dick.

Pleasure darts from my shaft to my balls. I tangle my hands in his messy hair and thrust deeper into his mouth, floored by the eagerness, the *passion*, he's giving to this blowjob. He licks and sucks and nibbles every inch of me, and I groan when he pops his finger into his mouth before dragging it down the crease of my ass.

At the teasing penetration, my hips jerk upward. Wes chuckles and eases his finger deeper, until the pad of it is stroking my prostate. My entire body trembles. Tingles. Burns.

He spends a maddeningly long time torturing me with his mouth and finger—no, fing*ers*. He's got two inside me now, rubbing that sensitive place and bringing white dots to my eyes.

"Wes," I murmur.

He raises his head. His gray eyes are smoky with desire. "Hmmm?" he says lazily.

"Stop fucking teasing me and start fucking *fucking* me," I rasp.

"Fucking fucking you? Did you really need two fuckings?"

"One's an adverb and one's a verb." My voice is as tight as every muscle in my body. I'm about to go up in flames if he doesn't make me come.

His laughter warms my thigh. "I love the English language, dude. It's so creative."

"Are we really having this conversation right now?" I growl when his teeth sink into my inner thigh. His fingers are still lodged inside me, but no longer moving.

"What would you rather talk about?" He blinks not so innocently, knowing exactly how close to the edge I am.

"Nothing," I sputter. "I'd rather talk about nothing!"

Wes makes a tsking sound. "That doesn't bode well for our impending marriage, sweetheart. Communication is key."

I glare at him. "Then tell your mouth to start communicating with my dick, dude. Because if you don't make me come in the next five seconds, I'm going to—"

"Going to what?" he mocks, and I moan in dismay when his fingers slip out. Chuckling, Wes climbs up my body, grabs both my wrists and shoves them up over my head. "Tell me what you'll do, Canning."

"I…" My eyes glaze over. It's hard to think when he's rubbing his trouser-clad lower body over my aching erection. I try to push out of his grip, but my man is a strong mother-fucker. He keeps my wrists locked between one hand and the headboard. His other palm strokes my bare chest, fingers lightly grazing one nipple.

He grinds against me until I'm growling with impatience. But I can't move my hands. I can't yank his pants off and take his cock in my hand. I can't do anything but lie here as this big, beautiful man rubs off on me like I'm his own personal sex doll.

His eyes are so heavy-lidded I can only see a slit of silver gleaming down at me. Then he licks his lips, and a thrill shoots up my spine. I know that look. I *love* that look.

Wes shoves his trousers down. His thick erection slaps my abs. "I want to touch you," I beg.

"No." His tone is commanding. It only intensifies the thrill. "Gotta hold you down so you don't go running off again." He gives me another lingering kiss just to drive the point home. And when he finally releases my wrists, he's off the bed before I can reach for him. "Don't move," he whispers, and I go still, watching in near fascination as he charges across the room to where he dropped his wallet. He opens it, extracts one of his handy packets of travel lube, and returns to the bed.

"Arms over your head."

I obey. He tosses my jeans aside and settles between my legs and grabs hold of my wrists again. With his other hand, he lubes up his dick, then guides it to the place that aches for him.

"Fucking fuck me," I beg.

Humor dances in his eyes. "I'm not going to fuck you."

Now I'm groaning again. Goddamn it. If he plans on torturing me again, I really will lose my mind—

"I'm going to make love to you," he finishes.

My breath hitches.

Smiling, Wes drops his mouth to mine. Our lips lock at the same moment he slowly slides inside me. The burn of pleasure makes me gasp but he swallows the sound with a soft, sweet kiss that matches the soft, sweet strokes of his cock. He fills me. Completes me. My dick is an iron spike against my belly, and I struggle against the tight band of his fingers around my wrists.

"I need to touch myself," I plead.

Wes lightly bites my bottom lip. "That's my job, remember?" And then he wraps his fist around me and gives a fast stroke as he plunges deeper inside me.

The orgasm catches me by surprise. I thought I'd last longer, at least a dozen strokes, but nope, I'm coming and it's glorious and my entire world is reduced to *him*. My best friend. My lover. My...fiancé...oh wow, never thought that word would be such a turn-on, but it totally is. My dick throbs harder, another jet spurting onto my belly at the thought of spending the rest of my life with this man.

Wes continues to make love to me, slow and languid, as if he's savoring every second of this. When he finally comes, it's not in a hard explosion of bliss, but the gentle rocking of his hips and a soft moan of contentment. Then he collapses on top of me, his lips teasing mine in tender kiss after tender kiss, his hands caressing my pecs and shoulders before stroking through my hair.

Eventually he stops petting me and we lie pressed against each other, Wes curled around me, each of us drifting on our own thoughts. I happen to glance at the clock, which reads 1:37. "You must be tired," I whisper. He played a game a few hours ago. "When does the bus leave the hotel?" His itinerary had listed a flight tomorrow morning.

"Eh. Seven-thirty?"

"We should sleep," I say although I'm wired.

"Or you could tell me about the thing at work."

I groan. "I will, I swear. But does it have to be now? Can't I stay in my happy place?"

He chuckles into the back of my neck. "Wasn't I just *in* your happy place?"

"You're quite the literalist this evening." I get up and make a trip into the biggest hotel bathroom I've ever seen. I clean up a little and then bring Wes a damp washcloth, sliding back into bed with him.

"Seriously," he says, wiping his remarkable abs. "What could you possibly have done that's so awful?"

"I slammed Danton up against a wall."

"Hallelujah!"

"No. I *shouldn't* have. I've got better self-control than that. We're trying to teach these kids how to have sportsmanship, right? So why do I ignore all my boss's advice on how exactly to deal with Danton and then I get physical with him? Dumbest thing I've ever done."

Wes is quiet for a moment. "That's the thing, though. You *are* smarter than that. There's no reason to think you'd ever do it again. Blame it on the drugs. Say it's a fluke and hold your head up high and turn in that complaint that Bill keeps asking you for."

"So I can save my job or my conscience, but not both."

He kisses the back of my neck. "Save your job, babe, then give your conscience a break. You seriously think those kids are better off if that asshole wins?"

And here is where I realize for the hundredth time in twenty-four hours how much I love Wes. Lying here pancaked to his naked body, hashing out my career disaster—it's the best therapy ever. There's a reason I trust him. We may not always look at problems the same way, but he's pretty damn smart.

"I'm going to go in there Monday and eat crow," I decide. "I want that job. I deserve it, too."

His big hand rubs my hip. "Of course you do."

We go silent again, and after a while I decide that Wes is asleep. But then he surprises me by speaking again. "Can we talk about your other favorite topic?"

"Your shitty housekeeping?"

He laughs. "Okay, your *other* other one."

"Which is…?"

"Money."

"God, why?"

"Because when the season is over, we're going to throw a wedding and then go on a *spectacular* vacation. I want to plan it without you worrying about the cost. There's still some grueling weeks ahead of us, right? It will be easier every time I look at the screensaver I've downloaded for whatever beach we're going to."

I don't know what to say. "It doesn't have to be expensive."

Wes chews on my neck for a moment before answering. "Privacy costs money. And I have money." He tugs on my shoulder, so I have to turn around and face him. "You know how I got rich?"

I shake my head.

"By waking up one morning to find that my grandfather had died, leaving me a pile of cash. My asshole father can't touch my trust, either. The old man knew Dad was a greedy bastard." He grins. "It's all just the luck of the draw, okay? And even if I'd earned every penny digging ditches, there isn't *anything* I have that I don't want to give you. Not one thing."

He leans in and kisses me while I try to take that in. I get a second kiss, and then a third. I thought I was done figuring shit out already, but there's more you can learn at 1:45 in the morning as your boyfriend slowly eases his way into your mouth, stroking your tongue with his.

I've spent too many weeks worrying about accepting help from Wes, because I didn't want to appear weak. And the whole time he's only been desperate to show how much he loves me.

The realization brings a groan from the depths of my chest.

"What?" he asks, nuzzling my cheek.

"I love you."

"But…?" He chuckles.

"But I'm an idiot. Having your dick in my ass has never insulted my manhood. But letting you pay for my hospital bill made me feel crazy."

Wes laughs and then chews on my ear. "If I set it up so that our whole rent check comes automatically out of my trust fund, will you lose your shit? That's what I want to do. Because then when you buy the groceries I won't have to ask you to save the receipts. What if we just stopped keeping track? Isn't that what married people do?"

"I guess?" All the implications of marrying Wes are threatening to make my head explode.

He must sense it, too, because he goes back to kissing me. Eventually we fall asleep like that—face to face, tangled up together.

WHEN WES'S alarm goes off at six-thirty, we both groan. He hits snooze and I bury my face in the pillow. We lie there half-asleep for a while, clumsily stroking each other's warm skin. Sex sounds like a nice idea, but we're both a little too tired to make it happen. And when his alarm goes off for the third time, he grumbles and gets up.

I don't, though. My flight doesn't leave for another four hours. So I doze while listening to Wes shower and pack up. Eventually there comes a beefy knock on the door. "Dudes! I have vitamin C!"

Wes actually opens the door to Blake, damn him. And the room is now filled with Blake-chatter. Vitamin C is coffee, though, and the scent of it begins to stir me into consciousness.

"Aw, who's a sleepyhead?" Blake crows, flopping onto Wes's empty side of the bed. "Caffeine, J-Bomb! I brought you a cappuccino."

"You make it difficult to hate you," I mumble into the pillow.

"That's what everyone says." He grabs my bare shoulder with one of his big mitts and shakes me.

"Stop." I yank the covers higher. "Or I won't invite you to the wedding."

"To the...? OH MY GOD!"

I've obviously made an enormous tactical error, because now Blake Riley—all two-hundred-odd, suit-wearing pounds of him—gets to his feet and begins *jumping* on the bed. I open my mouth to yell at him, but it's difficult to pronounce words when he's yelling, "Fuck yeah!" and I'm being shaken like a pair of shoes in a dryer.

"Kn...Knock...it...OFF!" I manage to yodel.

And Wes is no help because he's on the hotel phone for some reason. He hangs up just as I hear an awful crack, like wood breaking in two. The bed lists awkwardly and Blake goes bouncing to the floor.

"Don't worry! I'm unhurt!" he yells from somewhere down there on the expensive carpeting.

Wes and I lock eyes, our expressions a matching mix of humor and horror. "Blake, you broke the bed," Wes says with a sigh. "That's going on your bill, not mine."

"Won't be the first time," he says, picking himself up from the floor and straightening his tie.

"At least you broke furniture and not my fiancé. We've had enough of hospitals."

"I'm just so happy for you guys." He grabs Wes and lifts him off the ground to hug him.

Wes looks over Blake's shoulder at me and rolls his eyes. When his feet touch the floor again, he shoos Blake toward the hallway. "Grab the elevator, would you? We should go."

Blake gives us both a big grin. "Kiss 'im goodbye for now, but not for long!" He grabs his own coffee cup and then dances out of the room.

"Whew," Wes says, glancing around. It's like the aftermath of a tornado. Sudden silence and some wreckage. I'm still in the bed but it slopes uncomfortably. My boyfriend walks around to perch very carefully on the edge beside me. "I have to go."

I smile up at his handsome face. "I know. I'll see you tonight. The cheapest ticket had a layover in Chicago. So I'll be a while."

He puts a hand on my hair and runs his fingers through it. "Don't miss your connection. I'll be waiting." He gives me a sexy smile.

My dick perks up at the sound of that. "Don't worry." I tug him down for a kiss. He tastes like toothpaste.

"Mmh," he says when we finally break apart. "Listen,

room service is coming in an hour. My dead grandfather wants you to have a good breakfast before your flight."

I smile while he kisses me a second time. "Tell him thank you for me."

Wes sighs and traces my cheek with his thumb. "Later."

"Indeed."

When the door clicks shut behind him, I'm still smiling.

I drop my suitcase in the hall, lock the front door, and stagger into the living room feeling like a man who's spent a whole year abroad instead of one measly week on the west coast. But damn, it's good to be home. And the apartment smells fantastic, like Wes's aftershave and...pine cleaner? Did someone clean the place while I was away?

Holy crap, someone *did*. The floors are gleaming, the kitchen counters are spotless and there isn't a speck of dust on any surface. I suddenly feel like one of the three bears that got played by Goldilocks—"Someone's been cleaning my house..."

"Wes?" I call out warily.

"Bedroom," comes my boyfriend's muffled response.

No, not my boyfriend. My...fiancé? Wow. Still feels surreal to think it.

He appears a moment later, wearing sweatpants that ride deliciously low on his hips. I admire his bare chest, his multitude of tattoos, his sleek, golden skin. He's gorgeous. And he looks like he's gained some of the weight back. I hadn't noticed last night because I was too busy mauling him, but his pecs and biceps are noticeably more sculpted than they'd been a few months ago.

"How was the flight?" He shrugs into a T-shirt, covering his spectacular chest, then walks over to give me a kiss.

I reach up to rub the nape of my neck. "Boring. And I fell asleep in a weird position, so now my neck is killing me."

Wes tugs my coat off and tosses it on one of the kitchen stools. For once I don't bug him about using the coat tree in the hall. I'm too happy to see him. "Go take a hot shower," he orders. "I'll fix you something to eat, and then I'll rub your neck…" He winks. "Among other things."

"That…" I say, yanking him close, "sounds—" I brush my lips over his, and we both shiver. "—awesome."

Grinning, he smacks my ass and nudges me toward the hall. I walk to our bedroom and strip, then duck into the shower to wash away the stale coffee smell that's lingered with me since I left the airport. I wonder what Wes is making to eat. I love that man, I really do, but cooking is not his forte. He can't even fry up an egg without burning it.

Sure enough, an acrid odor assaults my nose when I walk out ten minutes later. A sheepish Wes greets me at the stove.

"Tried to make grilled cheese," he mutters.

I stare at the mangled, blackened carcass of bread and cheese congealing in my best cast-iron pan. Then I burst out laughing. "It's fine, babe. I'm not hungry, anyway. Let's just skip to the neck rubbing part." I kiss his cheek and turn off the stove burner. "But you get an E for effort."

He brightens. "Nice. And did you see I cleaned? Spent all day sprucing up the place for you."

"Seriously?"

He gives me a smartass grin. "Okay, no. I spent two and a

half hours watching tape with the team. But that's why I hired a nice woman named Evenka to show up once a week and do the cleaning and laundry. Blake swears she has magic cleaning powers." He grabs my shoulder. "Can we keep her? Please?" He asks the same way as a boy who's brought home a puppy.

I have the usual urge to say no based on the expense. So I picture his dead grandfather and take a deep breath. "Sure."

"Yesss." He takes my hand and drags me to the couch. "*Banshee*?" he suggests.

"Heck yeah."

Wes grabs the remote, which he tosses at me. Then he runs to the kitchen for two sodas, probably because I'm not supposed to have alcohol yet. But I don't even complain, because I'm just so happy to be here.

When he sits down, we come together like two magnets realigning. His head on my chest, my arm slung around him, our legs tangled. I'm just about to start the episode when Wes laughs. "Would you believe I got an email from the travel department about a bill for the broken bed?"

"*Already?*"

"It gets better. Below that is an email from the PR department with a link to a gossip blog. Not only do they have a shot of us kissing in the lobby. They have a shot of the broken bed."

"What?" I yelp.

He grabs my hand and kisses it. "Yeah. They must have paid off a hotel staffer for that little nugget. But it's just a picture of furniture, Canning. I care more that they want to charge me eight hundred bucks. So I wrote an email to both travel *and* PR telling them to bill Blake because his fat ass broke it. And you'll never guess what they said." He snickers. "The clubhouse will pay for it because they don't want the hotel to have a record of a *third* dude in that room. You and I are fine by the PR department. But gossip of a threesome is more than they can handle."

"Oh my fucking God," I say as Wes laughs. "You're tempted, right? I can hear your gears turning. You want to recruit Blake to make fake incriminating pictures."

"You know me too well. And why stop at three? I'll get Eriksson and Forsberg lit on scotch and stage an orgy. I'm thinking...naked pillow fight."

I give his ass a pinch. "Meanwhile I'm trying to keep my job *working with children*. But no big."

"Aw." He leans back and kisses my chin. "I'm just teasing."

"Uh-huh." I push Play on our show, but I'm still smiling. Life with Wes is never dull. Even when we're old and gray with saggy asses, he'll still be funny and he'll still be mine.

We drink our sodas and watch our show. It's seven o'clock, and there are probably a dozen things we should be catching up on—calls, emails, bills. But we ignore all of it because we're home alone, and we're together, and that's the only thing either of us care about right now.

Wes smells so good. Like citrus shampoo and home. He runs his fingers through my hair, and when he laughs at the screen, the sound vibrates inside my own chest. Flattening my hand, I run a palm down his neck and onto the broad muscle of his shoulder. He feels so good I have to give it a squeeze. I trace the ink climbing out of his T-shirt sleeve. Then I reach around and tug his shirt up to his pecs so I can lay a hand on the taut skin of his belly.

The show keeps on playing, but I've lost track. He feels alive and so solid against me that I have to lean forward and kiss the back of his neck. "Mmm," I say. It's great to be home.

As I continue to nibble on his neck, Wes sighs and goes

boneless against me. "I'm supposed to be giving *you* a neck rub," he reminds me.

"I'm all better." I move my ministrations to the side, sucking gently on the skin under his ear.

"Fuck," he rumbles. "Feels good." He rolls over all at once, and one second later we're lip-locked. The warm huff of his breath on my face is everything I need. I slant my face to make our connection more perfect, and he opens for me. Our tongues tangle, and he presses closer, forcing a knee between mine.

And everything is right with the world.

Wes's hand wanders down my side, then under my shirt. His palm slides over my ribs, and I wish I weren't wearing a shirt at all because I want his skin on mine. But I don't want to stop kissing him, so that's just gonna have to wait.

"Love you so much," he pants between kisses.

I make an unintelligible growl of agreement, then take a breath and manage to string together some actual words. "Let's take it into the bedroom."

He groans in response, and presses his hips against mine. And, schwing! We both want the same thing. But now our kisses grow even deeper. I'm too busy climbing into Wes's mouth to get up and do anything about the happy ache in my balls.

So we're just lying there, pawing each other and making out when the intercom beeps.

Wes groans, but we carry on.

But it beeps again. And Wes pulls back reluctantly. We both know that whoever has buzzed for us is probably on the way upstairs now. "Think Blake lost his key?" I ask, my voice husky.

He snorts. "Probably."

"If he comes in here, we're never getting rid of him."

Wes sighs and rearranges himself in his sweatpants. "Maybe it's just a delivery or something?" He says it with hope in his voice, but of course we didn't order anything.

I recline on the sofa and take a swig of my drink while he answers the buzzer.

"Okay, thanks," Wes says. "Send 'er up."

"Who's her?" I ask in alarm.

"Katie Hewitt. My teammate's wife. Apparently she's bringing us a lasagna."

"A...really?"

"That's what the doorman said. He's like, 'This smells really good, Mr. Wesley'."

"But why?"

Wes shrugs. "I guess we're about to find out?"

I run my hands through what is probably sex hair.

Someone raps on the door, and Wes yanks it open. "Hey, wow. Evening Katie. Hey, Hewitt. Thought you two would be enjoying the night off."

Wes is marched backward by a woman with thick, glossy hair and a big lasagna pan. "Happy engagement!" she yells, then whirls around at her husband with a look of betrayal. "Ben! You were supposed to shout it with me!"

"Forgot," Hewitt mumbles.

I swallow a laugh, but it slips out when Katie sidesteps Wes and trots into our kitchen like she owns it. I hear the sound of my oven door opening and closing.

I stand up to greet our guests, and Katie runs over and takes my face in two hands. Her nails are very red and shiny. Like shellacked talons. "Congratulations on the engagement! I'm *so* happy for you guys! I know you were away for a week, so I figured you two didn't have time to stock up on groceries, so my first engagement present to you is food." She beams, then gives me a hug.

God, this woman has a scary amount of energy. "Thank you," I say, genuinely touched. "We really appreciate—wait, your *first* present?" How many gifts does this chick plan on getting us?

Hewitt must have read my mind, because he sighs and says, "Dude, you'll be getting weekly deliveries up until the wedding. Deal with it."

Wes laughs. "Aw, that's not necessary," he tells Katie, who waves it off with a manicured hand.

"I like shopping," she says firmly.

"She likes shopping," her husband confirms.

Katie grabs my hand and pulls me onto the sofa, then flings herself beside me. "Tell me how you're doing. Are you fully recovered now? Are you still having nightmares about being in the hospital? When I had my bust lift, the nurses were sooooo mean to me!"

"Uh." Suddenly it's really hard not to check out her boobs. When she says she had 'em lifted, I'm picturing, like, boob cranes. "I've stayed better places, sure. But my mom and my sister were there almost the whole time. And I feel great. The cough hasn't totally gone away, but I'm much better."

Katie grabs my hand and gives it a squeeze. "I'm so glad!"

"Thanks." I look around to see that at the other end of the room Wes and Hewitt are leaning against the kitchen counter drinking beers. "Dude, where's mine?"

Wes raises an eyebrow, the one with the barbell through it. It's hot as fuck when he does that, but I don't like it when the sexy eyebrow lift is denying me a beer.

"That's just some bullshit right there," I argue. "It's like cell phones and airline navigation systems. One thing does not interfere with the other."

Katie laughs, and she's still laughing when the intercom beeps. I'm only halfway to my feet by the time that Katie has sprinted for the thing herself. "Just send 'em up," she says to our doorman.

A minute later, three more people have walked into our apartment. I meet the veteran Lukoczik and his wife, Estrella, who's got a large roasting pan full of barbecue chicken legs. "Congratulations on the engagement! We'll just heat these up for you!" Estrella crows, heading for the kitchen.

Eriksson trails in after them, and he's got a gallon of freshly squeezed orange juice and a sheepish expression. "Hey," he says, offering me his hand. "Katie said to bring food, but I don't do casseroles."

"Uh, that's really okay," I manage as we shake. Then I watch his gaze dart around our apartment. His curiosity tickles me, because I'd love to know what he was expecting. If a gay apartment is supposed to look a certain way, nobody passed us the playbook. "Want a beer?" Maybe I should offer him a cosmopolitan as a joke. Note to self—buy some cranberry juice to freak out Wes's teammates.

"Sure. Love one."

I make my way into what is now a crowded kitchen. Wes is just parked against the countertop, in my way. So I give him a friendly shove on the backside to get him moving. When I touch him, the women grin like I've just done something cute.

Weird.

I find Eriksson a beer, passing it across the counter to him. Then I open a couple more for Estrella and her husband. I haven't been in my kitchen for a week, and Katie is right—our fridge is empty. Wes, of course, decided to go on a beer run today instead of buying groceries, but I can't even bring myself to be annoyed, because I'm just so happy to feel like myself again.

It only takes a few minutes to assemble plates and silverware. Even so, Katie comes clucking over to help me with this simple task. "We didn't want you to *work*," she complains. "That was the whole point of bringing you dinner! Go and celebrate!"

I'm beyond touched. It's incredibly thoughtful of Wes's teammates to come over and congratulate us, to *feed* us, and we're both a little stunned. I sneak a peek at Wes, and find him sneaking a peek at me. We both grin, then look away. I still can't wait to get him alone later. Not only do I want to finish what we started on the couch, but I want to hear what he thinks about this unexpected invasion.

Estrella makes me a cup of herbal tea, the kind my mother left behind after her visit. I'm not a tea drinker, but I take it anyway because she's so desperate to be helpful. By some miracle she's put it in my favorite mug, too. The one my mother made us. "So you're from California?" she asks, pushing it into my hand. "Sorry—I read it in the newspaper."

That's trippy. "Yeah. Sure miss the weather there."

"I bet. I'm from Madrid. Luko and I met when I spent a year working in New York."

"Ah." Luko started his career with the Rangers.

"I thought New York was cold. Then we moved *here*."

"Right." Sometimes I forget how transient this life is. These women have to just pack up and move when hubby gets traded.

That's me too now, maybe. I take a second to test the idea. Does it rankle? I sneak another look at Wes, and he's tipped his head back to laugh at something Hewitt said. I need that laugh and that man. So wherever he goes, I'm going to want to be there, too. He's worth it.

"You come to the games?" she asks me. "I haven't seen you up in the box."

I chuckle. "Well, Wesley has a pair of seats. But I'm the only one in 'em."

Her face softens as she does the math on why that is. Then she grips my wrist. "Next game you come upstairs with us! Us WAGS have to stick together, right?"

I inwardly cringe. I've heard the term before--WAGS. Wives and girlfriends. But...I've got a dick, damn it!

I think she reads my mind—or maybe she sees my horrified expression—because she frowns. "Drat. I think we need to add a 'B' in there somewhere, for boyfriend."

"And 'H'," I correct with a grin. "For husband. But WABGHs just isn't very catchy."

"I mean it, though," she urges. "Sit upstairs with us at the next game. We drink Mai Tais and run up the guys' credit cards ordering appetizers."

I laugh, but she's serious. "Sounds like fun." The food in the oven smells really good now, which means it must be fully hot. I grab two towels and tug open the door, lifting both dishes onto the stove for safekeeping. But the motion triggers the last traces of my cough. So I toss the towel over the dishes' blazing hot handles and quickly exit the kitchen area, coughing into the crook of my elbow.

At the sound of my respiratory distress, Wes sets down his beer and comes close. I warn him off with a stern look, even if I can't exactly speak. *Pat me like a toddler and die*, I say with my eyes.

He restrains himself—smart man—and heads over to the food, fishing two spatulas out of our drawer. The first one he sets into the pan of chicken. But then I see him poke the second one into the lasagna, as if to cut it up to serve.

I'm just clearing my throat desperately to say, *careful, that's hot*, when I see his hand go for the pan's handle…

And I can't move fast enough. His hand grips the burning hot edge.

"Fuck!" he yelps, leaping back.

I flick the tap onto cold and grab him by the elbow, towing him toward the sink. I take his burned hand and—after checking the temperature—I thrust it under the cold water. "Babe, *seriously*. Again? When there's a dish towel draped over the handle, it's not, like, a decoration, it's…"

"A *flag*. I know," he says through clenched teeth. "I forgot."

"How bad is it?" I glance up to see five people watching us in fascination.

"Uh," he says, noticing the same thing. He shakes me off and stares at his hand. It's red, and there's a white blister forming on the lower part of his thumb.

I grab his hand and stick it under the water again. "At least it's not your shooting hand."

There is a nervous ripple of laughter, and Wes sighs.

The only sound is water crashing into the sink. And some kind of stubbornness keeps me glued to Wes's side. I want to shout, *"Look, sometimes men touch each other!"* We've never been out as a couple before. This is going to take some getting used to.

The door flies open again. This time it's Blake, and he's used his key. "Dudes!" he yells. "I smell Katie's lasagna!" His gaze travels to Wes and me. "Cheezus. You burn yourself again, rookie?"

My boyfriend growls under his breath, and Katie and

Estrella leap into action, cutting lasagna without torching their own skin, and handing plates around.

There aren't enough places to sit. I feel bad taking up a spot on the sofa, but Estrella parks me there with a plate and my mug of tea. She and Katie chat me up some more. They're really nice, but I feel a little like I'm being recruited into a club.

"Hewitt!" Blake shouts from his perch by the counter. "Did you hear? I'm planning the wedding."

I twist around to seek out Wes, and my alarmed gaze collides with his. "Not a chance," he tells his teammate. "Only thing you need to plan is how to keep that big trap shut during the ceremony."

Blake scowls. "I'd be good at it! I know flowers!"

"Name five flowers you'd put in the centerpieces," Wes orders, while I choke back a laugh. If Wes can name five flowers I'll eat my helmet.

"Um. Roses. Tulips. Daffodilias—"

"Daffodilias?" Katie exclaims. "Keep him away from your wedding, Ryan. I'll give you the number for the wedding planner Ben and I used."

"He can't have the job anyway," I say. "My sister Jess has decided to become a party planner. She's definitely getting this gig."

Something goes a little wrong with Blake's face when I say Jess's name. That's weird. They must have really annoyed the heck out of each other when they were babysitting me.

After everyone eats, they take all the plates and wash them in the kitchen. And they don't let me help. I end up on the sofa beside Hewitt and Eriksson, and the three of us try to beat each other's best diving-in-front-of-the-puck stories. As a goalie, blocking shots was technically the main part of my job, but their stories are pretty entertaining.

"No lie—I blocked the damn shot with my ass," Hewitt is telling me. "I had a bruise the size of a grapefruit for weeks."

Eriksson snickers. "Hey, you're a d-man. It's your duty to sacrifice any part of your body for the cause."

"Okay, I can totally beat that," I say. "I was sixteen and it was the final scrimmage at hockey camp. Third period, my team was up by one and scrambling to keep the lead. The opposing left wing snaps a wrister at me. I stop it, but one of my d-men gets pushed into me and suddenly we're tangled together on the crease, and the puck is loose. Somehow I've lost my stick—*and* my glove. But I see that puck flying toward me again, and I don't even stop to think—I just slap that motherfucker away with my bare forearm."

Eriksson and Hewitt look impressed. "Dude, that's insane. Did you break your arm?"

I sigh. "In two places."

"That is hardcore," Eriksson says, whistling softly.

Wes pipes up from behind the couch, not as impressed. "Are you telling them about the time you broke your arm trying to be Superman?"

"Yup," I call back.

"I'm marrying a crazy person," Wes informs his teammates.

I snort. "Ha! Says the guy who snuck out at four a.m. to go skinnydipping and then cut his foot open. And let's not forget the tetanus shots from falling off the fences you tried to climb, and that rusty nail you stepped on while hiking barefoot—because you were drunk. And the guy who—"

"Okay, okay, you win," Wes says, holding his hands up in surrender. "We're *both* insane." He turns back to Blake, who starts blabbering on about his own past skinnydipping adventures, while I'm drawn into more hockey talk with Hewitt and Eriksson.

By the time Katie announces that it's time to go, I'm feeling a bit shell-shocked. But I can't deny I had a blast getting to know Wes's teammates and their WAGS.

"Uh, thanks for everything," I say to Katie and Estrella as I walk them to the door.

One at a time they hug me like we're long-lost friends.

"Take care, Jamie."

"Text me before the Sharks game! We'll save you a drink!"

I say a quick goodnight to Wes's teammates, and when the door finally closes behind them—even Blake takes the hint and leaves—I turn to face Wes. "That was…" I trail off.

He hesitates, gauging my expression. "They mean well," he says lightly.

"I know. It's…cool." A smile tugs at my lips. "It's overdue, you know?" Wes and I had always looked forward to the day when we didn't have to hide. But I never gave any thought to how we'd fit into the clubhouse. I'm still not sure, but neither of us can deny that tonight was a screaming success.

"Yeah." He smiles, too. "It was nice. For the first time since the season started, I finally feel like I…" He scrunches his face as if searching for the right word.

"Belong," I supply, my voice gentle.

His head jerks in a nod. "Yeah. That."

My heart gives a squeeze as I place both hands on his cheeks, stroking the dark stubble on his face. "You do," I tell him. "You belong on this team. You belong with these people. You belong with me."

His silvery eyes suddenly look damp. "I love you, Canning."

"Love you too, Wesley."

But in the back of my mind, I'm wondering where *I* belong. Or rather, where I'll end up. Wes is my home. He's my heart. But he can't be my everything. The uncertainties surrounding my job gnaw at my insides. Tomorrow I'll have to go in and meet with Bill, maybe face Danton, see the kids who've been playing so well without me.

I have no idea what tomorrow will bring. But tonight... I meet Wes's gorgeous eyes, a smile forming on my lips despite my uneasiness over my job. Tonight I'm with the man I love, and that's all that matters.

THIRTY-ONE

JAMIE

On Monday I walk into the rink at nine a.m. sharp. The familiar smell of ice and sweat hits me immediately, and I feel it right in my gut. This job means a lot to me. If I lose it, I know I'll get over the disappointment. It won't ruin me.

But it will really suck.

On the subway I rehearsed my eating-crow speech, and I'm ready to face the music. So I march right over to Bill Braddock's messy office and tap on the doorframe.

When he glances up from his desk, he first looks surprised, and then he smiles.

The tightness in my chest eases just a millimeter or two. "Got a second?"

"For you? Of course. Shut the door, Coach."

My brain is working overtime to decode those short sentences. He's still calling me "Coach," so that's good. But as the door clicks shut I wonder if I'll still have that title when I open it again.

"You look better," he says when I sit down in the visitor's chair.

"I feel better," I say immediately. "Finally got all the drugs out of my system. Got some exercise. Things are looking up." This is all true, but I probably sound like I'm overselling it.

"Have you been to the doctor for a medical release yet?"

I shake my head. "Just flew in last night and coming to see you was at the top of my list. But I'll take the first appointment they can give me."

"Good." He picks up a puck—the only kind of paperweight a coach ever has on his desk—and twirls it in his fingers. "I apologize again for not listening when you told me your co-coach used hurtful language."

My first impulse is to say, "No big deal, sir." But I've given this some more thought, and now I'm kind of pissed at myself for letting it go before.

"I'm ready to file that report," I say instead. "I'd like to make my complaint official." Even though I don't feel personally targeted by Danton's language, it's my *job* to stop another coach from saying "faggot" every third word. Even if pointing a finger makes me uncomfortable. "We're trying to raise admirable young men, and they shouldn't hear an authority figure making slurs."

Braddock nods vigorously. "That is absolutely true. I have to print out a new form for you, though. Instead of filing a complaint, you may choose to file a letter in support of another complaint."

I search my mind, trying to recollect what he might be talking about, but I come up empty. The only complaint I know about is the one against *me*. "What do you mean?"

He grins. "Someone already filed a complaint against Danton's language, and it's going to the disciplinary committee on the same day as the complaint against you."

My spine tingles. "Who filed it?"

"Your team. Every last player. They got wind of Danton's complaint—you know this place, it's a gossip mill—and they got all riled up. They stormed my office after practice and demanded to argue on your behalf. So I acquainted them with our disciplinary system and they channeled their displeasure into a proper complaint."

For the first time in ten days I actually feel a little light-headed. "Seriously?"

He raises his right hand. "God's honest truth. Their complaint is eight pages long, detailing instance after instance of inappropriate, homophobic language. And a few racial slurs, too. I drank a very large glass of scotch after reading it. I had no idea things were so bad."

I had to lock my jaw together to avoid saying "I told you so."

"So…" He clears his throat. "Please submit an accounting of your own experience, and it will be added to the file. The committee takes all complaints seriously."

"Including the one against me," I add.

"Right. But I'm sure the committee will acknowledge your spotless employment record with us and with your former position at the Elites camp. And then there's the matter of the complaints against Danton, and your temporary ill health. They may be inclined to give you a warning only. They can do that on a first offense."

The words "first offense" make me feel squirrelly inside. Those words aren't supposed to apply to me. Ever.

Bill makes a pup-tent out of his hands and studies me. "I had something I wanted to run by you. A suggestion I might make to the committee when they consider how to resolve the complaint against you."

"What is it?" If he knows a magic trick for getting me out of trouble, I'm all ears.

"We've never done any diversity training with our staff, and I want to start. In exchange for closing out the complaint against you with merely a letter in your file, what would you think about speaking to the staff about your experiences?"

"My...experiences?"

"With homophobia. You could talk to the staff about what it's like to be a gay man in sports. Tell them your story. The cure to fighting prejudice is finding common ground, right? I want my staff to understand your unique perspective, because it's probably not as unique as they think. You could do some good just by sharing your experience with the subject."

My head fills immediately with objections. *I'm not technically a gay man. I'm bisexual. I don't have a lifelong experience of homophobia. I've been out of the closet for a few weeks, total. I'm not an expert.*

And, even if I was, I hate sharing personal shit at work.

But I'm here to save my job. A job I love. So I do what I promised myself I'd do. "I'd be happy to speak to the staff," I tell Bill.

He smiles. "Wonderful. So I'll circle back on this after the disciplinary meeting next week. In the meantime, please get that doctor's note. Your team needs you, especially since we've suspended Mr. Danton pending his disciplinary action."

I sit up straighter in my chair. "Who's coaching the team?"

"Gilles is a little busy covering both his and your teams with Frazier's help. But don't panic. They need you, but they can stay afloat another week until this passes."

He shakes my hand, and I'm out the door before I realize how confident he sounded about my reinstatement. That warms me. As I tread down the slushy sidewalk, it's only nine-thirty. Wes is probably at his rink, but not on the ice yet. So I try his cell phone.

"Hey!" he says, answering on the first ring. "How'd it go?"

"Not bad. I think I might squeak by." I tell him about the report my players filed.

"Jesus. That's incredible!"

"Right? Love those kids. There's one hitch, though. Bill wants me to volunteer to talk to the staff about my experiences with homophobia. You know—because I'm such an expert." I laugh just picturing it. "It's going to be the shortest meeting ever."

"You want help?"

I almost say no out of sheer habit. There's that h-word again. But I stop myself just in time. "What do you mean?" I ask instead.

"I could talk to them about what it was like being a gay hockey player when nobody knew. I spent my freshman year of college shitting bricks over what they might do to me if they knew. If it helps you and your boss, I'd show up and tell that story."

My pace falters and I stop walking. "Really?" I picture Wes walking into that conference room and the looks on all their faces when Toronto's most successful rookie in a decade steps through the doorway.

"Sure. Why not? Frank Donovan is gonna make me give that speech to the club at some point. This can be my warm-up."

"Wow. Okay. *Yeah.* I'll make you dinner every night for a week if you get me off this hook."

"Canning," he says, his voice going deep and slow. "How about I pick my own reward?"

"That, uh, works for me, too."

He laughs. "Love you. I gotta hit the ice now. Late lunch later?" He has to play the Sharks tonight—a home game. And apparently I'm drinking umbrella drinks with the WAGS in a box somewhere.

But first, lunch with my man. "Absolutely. See you at home."

After we hang up I walk to the subway feeling so much relief and wondering which of Wes's favorites I should make for lunch.

A week later, the jury finds me not guilty.

Fine, I'm being melodramatic. There was no jury, only a committee. And no verdict, just an "official decision" that stated my actions toward Danton may have been both provoked and exacerbated by the medication I'd been taking. My personnel file now includes a warning, but no other disciplinary action was taken, much to my relief. Even though Wes spent this whole week telling me not to worry, I was still imagining all the worst-case scenarios, and I'm glad I can finally breathe again.

There's a spring to my step as I enter the arena on Monday afternoon, inhaling the crisp air and feeling the welcoming chill on my face. The kids are already on the ice doing their warm-up skate. Danton is nowhere in sight. When I checked in with Bill this morning, he told me that Danton is still on leave until his complaint is settled. I didn't ask why my "case" was resolved first. I'm just grateful it was.

The players catch sight of me as I approach the boards. Several of the boys wave, a few call out, "Welcome back,

Coach Canning!" but only one whizzes in my direction. It's Dunlop, who shoves his helmet off as he skates to a stop.

"Coach!" His cheeks are red from exertion. Or maybe joy. I like to think it's the latter.

"Dunlop." I greet him with a big smile and a clap on the shoulder. Then I let go of him immediately. I'm probably going to pay a little too much attention to the way the team interacts with me for a while. Wes says there's one in every crowd who can't get past his sexuality, and that's just the way it is. "I missed you guys," I tell Dunlop.

"Missed you, too." He sounds awkward, and his face goes redder. "Are you feeling okay?"

"Like a million bucks," I assure him. "But here's a tip for you—never get pneumonia."

He snickers. "I'll try to remember that."

I hop over the wall and skate around in a few quick circles. Fuck, it's so good to be back on the ice. I cock my head for Dunlop to follow me, and we glide toward the net. My goalie sets his helmet on top of it, still grinning a goofy grin.

"Did you see our record?" he asks me.

"Damn—" I hastily correct myself. "*Darn* right I did. A four-game winning streak, huh? You guys are rocking it. *You're* rocking it."

He averts his gaze, but not before I see the flash of pleasure in his eyes. "Two shut-outs," he says shyly. "And I only let in one goal at the last game."

"I know. I'm proud of you." Despite my genuine happiness that the team is back on track, I can't fight that niggle of insecurity. I mean, you didn't see them winning four consecutive games when *I* was around. "It looks like Coach Gilles showed you some new tricks," I say lightly.

Dunlop wrinkles his forehead. "He did?"

"I watched a few of the games. Your confidence has skyrocketed since I left." Now *I'm* feeling awkward. Damn it, why am I laying my own insecurities at this poor kid's feet?

He gives me another funny look. "You think I'm doing better because you left? That's nuts, Coach. You know what happened when you got sick?"

It's my turn to wrinkle my forehead.

"We were all really worried," he mumbles, staring down at his skates. "And I was like, crap, I gotta get my shit together because Coach Canning does *not* need one more thing to worry about. You know, us losing all the time." He flushes again. "I thought if we were winning, maybe you'd get better faster."

I have a hard time keeping my jaw closed. This kid stepped up his game because he didn't want me to worry that the team was *losing*? I'm embarrassed to feel my eyes stinging, so I give a manly cough and say, "Well, whatever it is you're doing, keep at it. You're playing like a champ."

A whistle blows. Gilles is at the blue line, barking instructions at some of our forwards. When he catches my eye, he smiles and nods for me to join him.

I skate over, and the kids he was working with all go silent.

Shit. Is this going to be weird? Dunlop welcomed me back easily, but what if the others don't?

I cough to clear the gravel from my throat, then call the rest of the team over. Everyone is staring at me. Waiting expectantly. I clap my hands together. Then I hesitate.

"So," I start awkwardly. "You have another tournament coming up, so we have to put in some work. But before we get started, does anyone, uh, have any questions for me?"

There's a long silence.

Finally, Barrie raises his hand, and I hold my breath as I wait for his question.

"Will Ryan Wesley come to one of our games?"

I blink in surprise. Okay. Well, I wasn't expecting *that*. And when I scan the kids' faces, I don't see horror or disgust. Only curiosity. I can work with that. Except I wonder…if I was marrying some random dude off the street, would they have more trouble with this? Maybe I'm not supposed to worry about that. In fact, I'll take their support any way I can get it.

"I'm not sure," I answer. "I'll look at our game schedule and his game schedule and see if it works out. But I know Wes would be happy to come if his schedule allows it."

All of their faces light up.

"Anything else?" I prompt. When no one speaks up, I clap my hands again. "All right, then let's get to work." And just like that, their expressions turn serious, fixed on me as they wait for me to start the practice.

Damn, it's good to be back.

PRACTICE LETS OUT AT SIX-THIRTY. As I head into the locker room to change, I text Wes to find out if he's already outside. He's picking me up this evening because we're having dinner with his teammates, which is why I brought an extra set of clothes to the rink today. Instead of the jeans and hoodie I walked in with, I put on a blue button-down, a navy blazer and khakis.

My getup draws the attention of Gilles, who's changing into—what else?—a plaid shirt. "You going to a country club or something?" he cracks.

"Dinner with my—" I stop abruptly. I'd been about to say "my roommate", but I guess that's a habit I need to break, huh? Wes and I are no longer hiding. "With my boyfriend," I finish.

I suppose I could've said fiancé, but I haven't told my coworkers about the engagement yet, and it's not really a bomb I want to drop on my first day back.

Gilles takes on a rueful expression. "You must have thought we were idiots taking you to that bar. Flirting with those girls..." He sighs, looking so embarrassed that I can't help but grin.

"Hey, you didn't know that I live with a guy."

That gets me the arch of an eyebrow. "No, we didn't know. Someone didn't tell us."

"It wasn't something I was able to advertise," I admit. "Wes...his career...we needed to keep the relationship under wraps."

Gilles nods. "I get that. But I still felt like an ass."

Hell. That was never my intention. "I'm sorry about that. It was kind of a shitty situation. But it's out now. We're out." I shift my weight awkwardly. "And I know there are some people who can't accept, or understand, my relationship with—"

"I'm not one of them," he interrupts.

I falter. "No?"

"Naw. My sister has a girlfriend."

"Oh."

"Yeah. My parents are in PFLAG and everything."

"Cool," I say, although I'm not exactly sure what that means. I'm, like, the worst queer dude ever. Somebody pass me the manual. "Well, thanks for telling me. The thing is, I'd like to go out to the bar again with you guys. I didn't really like saying no so much, but it's been a weird year."

"Fine." He grins. "But only if you play darts on my team, 'cause Frazier isn't as good as he thinks."

I shake my head. "I was really focused on the bullseye that night because it kept that chick's hands off my ass."

He laughs. "We saw your, uh... We saw Ryan Wesley at the bar, right? I didn't invent that 'cause I was drunk?"

The memory makes me flinch.

"He was there. That was plenty awkward."

"Right. Well, next time, we'll just invite him."

"Good idea."

My phone buzzes in my hand.

I'm in the parking lot, Wes texts.

Be right out, I text back.

Another message pops up. It says:

My dick is so hard right now.

I smother a snicker, and the choked sound makes Gilles chuckle. "Have fun at dinner," he calls before leaving the locker room.

I type back, *How hard is it?*

Will I get arrested if I take a dick pic in the car right now?

My laughter spills over. *Absolutely,* I reply. *You can't go to jail tonight. We've got dinner plans.*

I slip my feet into a pair of dress shoes, shove my other clothes in my locker, and head outside to the parking lot, where Wes's SUV waits for me. The ground is a bit slushy, so I'm careful not to slosh around and ruin my shoes, but I'm happy to see that the snow is finally starting to melt. Apparently it's bad luck to celebrate, though. Last night Blake had warned me that there's always a blizzard or two in March. Sometimes even in April and May. Blake calls it "winter's fuck you."

Wes greets me with a sexy smile as I slide into the passenger seat. I lean in to kiss him, then glance at his crotch. "Liar," I chide. "You don't even have a semi."

He rubs his groin and licks his lips. "I can change that. Give me a second."

I snort. "Where are we headed, anyway?"

He pulls away from the curb, and I enjoy the view of his strong hands on the steering wheel. I wonder if he knows I have a fetish for his hands?

"Some Michelin-rated place Forsberg likes. I'm sure it'll be awesome. And they won't let us pay, so you kind of *have* to order the most expensive thing on the menu. That's what these chuckleheads do."

"Good to know."

The team is taking us out for dinner for Wes's birthday. They usually do the birthday thing on the road, but this time the whole team took an evening away from their families just so I could go, too.

When Wes pulls up in front of the restaurant, a uniformed valet takes the keys and calls him "sir".

Indeed, when we walk inside I see it's easily one of the swankiest places I've been in Toronto. The hostess walks us through an elegant bar and down a set of stairs. We're in an honest-to-god wine cellar, with row upon row of triangular "shelves" built across the stone-clad walls to hold wine bottles. In the center of the cellar there's a glassed-in private room with a table set for two dozen men I don't really know. And most of them are already there, sipping the first cocktail of the evening.

"Heyyy!" several voices shout at once as we approach. It occurs to me that whoever picked this spot is a (wealthy) genius. A hockey team meal can be pretty loud. So why not hold it in a sound-proof chamber in the nicest basement in Toronto?

I'm in the lead, so I enter the room first, but then pause to let Wes catch up. He's right behind me, his hand on my shoulder blade. "Evening, ladies," he says to the room. "Where do you want us?"

"Put 'er there!" Blake yells, pointing at two seats together in the middle of the long table. "Let the games begin."

We sit down, and a waiter in a suit that's nicer than any of mine sweeps in to take our drink orders. I consider ordering something fruity just to fuck with people, but then I'd actually have to drink it. So I order a Griffon Ale instead.

"I'll have a Manhattan. Make it on the dry side. No fruit."

"Really?" Wes never orders a mixed drink.

My fiancé shrugs. "It's my dad's drink, and when I walk into a place like this, I always think of him." Wes leans back in his chair and sniffs the air. "You smell that? Old leather and money."

Eriksson chuckles. "Have I met your father?"

"Nope." Wes shakes out his napkin. "And you never will. I only heard from him three or four times a year *before* my Big Gay Interview. Now he's out of my hair for good."

There's a slightly shocked silence.

"And your mom?" Blake asks.

"She wouldn't dare step out of line. Her loss." He claps his hands together. "What's good here?"

We order vast quantities of rich food. I choose a steak, along with more than half the table. Blake orders the rack of lamb, and I can't help but be surprised. "You know that's a sheep, right?"

He looks at me like I have an IQ of fifty. "Dude. The best defense is a great offense."

Right.

A slew of appetizers arrive. Someone ordered three of everything for the table. We talk about how the playoffs are shaping up while devouring a mountain of shrimp cocktail, an ocean's worth of oysters on the half shell and a whole lot of tuna tartare.

It's good living. It really is.

***

WES

The alcohol has just begun to do its work on me when Hewitt gets up and tosses his napkin on his chair. "Excuse me for a moment, boys." He leaves the room. The men's must be upstairs. They can't possibly have one down here.

I forget he's gone until he returns a few minutes later. And I do a giant double-take.

He's wearing *my* shirt—the bright green checked one that I bought in Vancouver.

"That's…where'd you get that?" I sputter. I actually look down at my chest just to double-check that I've still got mine.

Hewitt shrugs. "I told you my wife liked to shop. She musta seen yours and liked it."

Now, I could swear he wasn't wearing that earlier. But the whole team is here, so maybe I just didn't notice. I take another sip of my Manhattan and feel the burn as the alcohol goes down my throat. My gaze travels around the room, taking in the players' faces lit up by candlelight and the excellent food and drink. The thing is, my dad would love this dinner. He really would. And if he weren't such an asshole, he could probably be here right now.

His loss, as I said before. And it really is.

The sommelier enters with four different bottles of red under his arm. "Nobody chose a white, is that right?" he asks.

"Fuck no," I say too loudly. But it's my party. "Even your local homosexual needs a hearty red with his steak."

The wine guy looks taken aback, but my teammates all laugh like they're going to piss themselves.

Eriksson raises his hand. "But I ordered the fish."

"That's your own fault," someone says, and then Eriksson is pelted with wadded-up cocktail napkins.

Just another night with Toronto's finest.

Eriksson stands up. "I'll go order something from the bar, then." He strides out of the room.

Jamie is talking defensive strategy with Lemming, and I sure don't want to interrupt the conversation. Maybe Lemming can get over his discomfort with the gay thing so long as he's speaking to another D-man. So I take the empty beer bottle out of Jamie's hand and trade it for a glass of red.

"Okay, I'll get a husband too if they put drinks in your hand," Forsberg quips.

"And that's exactly why he's marrying me," I say with an obnoxious wink.

Midsentence, Jamie reaches over to give my head a playful shove and then finishes his thought about the neutral zone trap.

"So," Hewitt asks, looking smashing in my shirt. "How do two dudes get married, anyway? Like…who walks down the aisle?"

Jamie and I exchange a freaked-out glance. Because we haven't had this conversation. This will all be left to Jess. "Uh," I say. "Canning? Thoughts?"

He gives a shrug. "Who needs an aisle? I think we'll just have a judge or something, and do this on my parents' deck. And then we're going to eat a whole lot of ribs. My mom is a genius with the smoker."

Hewitt's eyes open slightly wider. I can almost see the

lightbulb go off over his head. "So, if it's men getting married, the food is better than at an ordinary wedding."

"And the beer," someone adds.

"There still has to be cake," Blake argues. "I think it's not legal without cake. I read that somewhere."

That's when Eriksson returns to the room. Without a drink. But he's wearing—wait for it—the shirt. The bright green "gay" shirt.

"Fuuuuuuuuuck," I say slowly. I poke Jamie to get his attention. "Babe, do you *see* this shit? I'm being pranked."

He turns his handsome face. Eriksson is standing at the end of the table flexing like a bodybuilder directing traffic.

"Oh my fucking God!" Jamie cackles. "I need a picture." He pulls out his phone. "Get over there. All three of you."

Jamie gets his picture. But a few minutes later Blake slips out of the room and returns wearing the shirt in size twenty or whatever that beast wears. And it dawns on me that my team-mates dropped a couple hundred plus express shipping—each —to pull this off. Is it stupid that I'm really touched by this madness?

Hell. I'm turning into a sap.

"Blake," I croak. "How the hell did you pull this off?"

He takes a slug of wine. "Used my key. Searched your apartment so I could figure out who makes the damn thing. Took me a half hour to find it because I had to dig. Dude—you should learn to unpack your suitcase."

Jamie punches me on the biceps. "See?"

"...got the brand and started Googling. Piece of cake, really."

Forsberg stands up. "I'm next. Gotta take a leak, anyway." He bolts out of the room, returning a few minutes later wearing green.

And Christ—when you get a bunch of these shirts together in one small room? It's a little loud, this color. But only under this restaurant lighting.

One by one, even after the main courses arrive, every single player leaves the room, returning in The Shirt. I keep drinking, getting happier and sloppier with every sip of wine.

They even got one for Jamie. He's the last to leave and return wearing citrusy green and a big smile. "*Now* we need the picture," he says. "I've asked the waiter to take it."

And that's how Canning and I came to have a big framed photo on our living room wall featuring the entire Toronto team dressed in very loud gingham. I swear the color rendered a little bolder in print than it looks in real life, because this photo is kind of blinding. But Jamie snickers whenever I suggest that.

But there we are, two dozen grins stained red from the wine, waving at the camera like idiots. Blake is in the back row, his napkin tied around his head like a bandana. I have a hand on Jamie's shoulder right in the center of the shot. His smile is just as relaxed and genuine as the day I met him.

And I look…centered. It's not a word I've ever used to describe myself before. But everything I ever wanted is in that photo—the man of my dreams, and my teammates. I've left my smug smile behind in favor of one that's so shiny I hardly recognize myself.

But it's me up there for sure. It's *us*. And it's perfect.

T h e
E n d

Thank you for reading US! We hope you enjoyed it.

**Good news! The next book from Sarina & Elle begins at
Wes & Jamie's wedding!
Get your copy of GOOD BOY.**

Turn the page for a description!

GOOD BOY BY SARINA BOWEN & ELLE KENNEDY

There's more from the HIM & US gang! The WAGs series has all your favorite characters, and then some.

GOOD BOY (WAGs #1)

Hosting her brother's wedding for an MVP guest list is the challenge of Jess Canning's life. Already the family screw-up, she can't afford to fail. And nobody (nobody!) can learn of the colossal mistake she made with the best man during a weak moment last spring. It was wrong, and there will not be a repeat. Absolutely not. Even if he is the sexiest thing on two legs.

Blake Riley sees the wedding as fate's gift to him. Jess is the maid of honor and he's the best man? Let the games begin. So what if he's facing a little (fine, a lot) of resistance? He just needs to convince the stubborn blonde that he's really a good boy with a bad rap. Luckily, every professional hockey player knows that you've got to make an effort if you want to score.

But Jess has more pressing issues to deal with than sexy-times with a giant man-child. Such as: Will the ceremony start on time, even though someone got grandma drunk? Does glitter ever belong at a wedding? And is it wrong to murder the best man?

ACKNOWLEDGMENTS

Writing *Him* and *Us* has been such a blast. We went into this project knowing it would be fun, but we didn't know it would also be successful! Thank you to everyone who has helped make *Him* and *Us* bestsellers!

We would like to take a moment to specifically thank a few people who have tirelessly championed these books. We're looking at you: Mollie Glick, Emily Brown, Jess Regel and the Foundry team. And at Colleen Hoover, Lauren Blakely, Lorelei James, Nina Bocci, Rachel Blaufeld, Shannon Lumetta, Edie Danford, a million awesome bloggers and the entire Locker Room crew!